DARK
AND
DANGEROUS

Celeste Anwar
Angelica Hart
Marie Harte
Goldie McBride

Erotic Paranormal Romance

New Concepts   Georgia

Dark and Dangerous is an original publication of NCP. This work has never before appeared in book form. This work is a novel. Any similarity to actual persons or events is purely coincidental.

New Concepts Publishing
5202 Humphreys Rd.
Lake Park, GA 31636

ISBN 1-58608-679-0

NCP books are available at special quantity discounts for bulk purchases for sales promotions, premiums, fund raising, or educational use. For details, write, email, or phone New Concepts Publishing, 5202Humphreys Rd., Lake Park, GA 31636, ncp@newconceptspublishing.com, Ph. 229-257-0367, Fax 229-219-1097.

First NCP Paperback Printing: 2004

Printed in the United States of America

Visit our webpage at:
www.newconceptspublishing.com

TABLE OF CONTENTS

BEAUTY RAVISHED

Celeste Anwar

Chapter One

There was more beautiful male flesh on the estate lawn than you could see in a month of Fridays in any club in Atlanta. Cherry Roman had heart palpitations just looking at their bodies glistening in the dwindling sunlight on a white sandy beach. Sheri would weep when she found out what she'd passed up.

The horizon was beautifully striped in gaudy colors in every hue. The setting sun perched above the golden sea like a ball of fire, clouds rippling out from its center domination of the sky in bold streaks of scarlet. A breeze carrying the scent of salt and sand swept across her damp skin, offering some relief from the nearly unrelenting humid heat of a Southern summer. Though she was nearer to the equator here than in her apartment in North Georgia, the air coming off the water made the weather seem cooler than it actually was.

Her skin itched slightly from sea salt and drying perspiration, making her long for a shower. She could forget her discomfort though, gazing upon the scene before her.

She hefted her overnight bag on her shoulder, leaving the dock and retreating ferry behind as she strolled up the pathway to the hotel that looked more like an enormous private beach house than a commercial property. There wouldn't be another ferry until Monday--no going back now, not that she particularly wanted to. She thought perhaps Sheri was right in passing off her own invitation to Cherry--a weekend at this retreat would certainly put the hideous outcome of her life into perspective. Or, at the very least, there was plenty of eye candy to distract herself from her problems. She didn't have to worry about work. She'd been laid off from her job indefinitely due to severe cut backs, but at least she had enough severance for this little vacation.

Cherry tried not to think about how dumb it was to spend any of it. She shrugged the disturbing thoughts off, determined to enjoy herself while she could.

She lost sight of the glittering beach and half naked men as she progressed up the hill to the lodge. The trees stooped and curled over the path like tired, noble sentinels, twisted from the heavy caress of ocean air. Traversing the lane, she could see a pine forest lay beyond the hill, and could make out the edges of a concrete patio and pool spread at the back clearing around the building. There, a buffet of undeniably male forms lounged, as well, soaking in the dying rays of sunlight. She frowned and quickened her step, cresting the rise to the hotel's entrance, eager to check in and get started relaxing.

A large screened in porch, decked with padded, wrought iron chairs faced the view of the ocean. Ferns ascending the stairs in urns rustled in the shifting breeze, touching her leg as she passed too close. A porch swing hanging at one end creaked and slowly moved on its chains, as if recently vacated, but she saw no one enjoying the picture perfect view from the top.

Strangely enough, she hadn't noticed any women on the island. Then again, she hadn't come across any of the guests, just from afar. Of course, she and Sheri had assumed this invitation was to one of those parties where they tried to sell you expensive condos, so it could be the women were off touring while the men lazed about. Who knew?

Wide, glass paneled doors marked the entrance, and Cherry pulled them open and strode into the lobby. The large open area was filled with coral and sea foam brocaded chairs and couches arranged in small groups for private conversations. Muted bulbs lit the space, giving it a soft, welcoming glow. Along one wall stood a marble-top counter and luggage station, but she saw no concierge or bell hops.

Puzzled by the absence of hotel staff, Cherry headed for it anyway. She hadn't taken but a few steps toward the empty counter when a soft, accusing voice spoke behind her, "What are you doin'? You don' belong here."

The deep, accented baritone slid a frisson of alarm up her spine, unnerving her. Cherry turned slowly around, trying to appear as if she did belong. Maybe it *was* just supposed to be men here and they'd thought Sheri a man somehow?

Her heart seized as her gaze landed on the owner's voice. He was standing at the foot of the stairs, leaning against the baluster. She'd read clichés in books her entire life about meeting the man of your dreams, the epitome of how a man should look and move--and they were so true, down to the smallest reaction. She could barely breathe, barely comprehend anything around her--her entire focus was directed on the stranger. Even his accusation was lost as her mind stumbled around, taking in his every feature.

He looked like he'd just come from the beach, and she thought she could even detect the scent of salt water in the air, but surely it was her imagination. His skin was a dark olive, richly tanned and captivating against the open-necked white shirt he wore. He looked as though he'd just shrugged it on, for only half the buttons had been fastened, and even at the distance, she caught a glimpse of toned chest. His black hair was wet, finger combed back off his forehead, but a few random locks had escaped and fell across his brow in rakish disarray.

He sent her a narrow-eyed glare across the room. When she made no answer--or move to leave--he strode across the floor space and stopped directly in front of her, invading her space until she was forced a step back just to look up at him.   Up close, he was fiercer than she'd imagined possible, potent, like the bars of a cage had just been raised.

"Excuse me?" she managed in spite of her suddenly dry mouth. *Oh god.* Green, intense eyes looked down at her beneath straight, angry brows. His was the kind of look that sent women in one of two directions--either straight to his bed or home to her own to huddle beneath the covers. She was torn. On the one hand, her galloping heart was commanding her feet to do the same and flee before she was devoured.   On the other, the moment the word 'devoured' entered her mind, her pussy went into melt down and her knees turned to jelly.

She wasn't sure why her reaction was so extreme, but she sensed that this man was dangerous in ways she couldn't even imagine.   Despite the trappings of civilization he seemed ... savage, his manner inherently untamed.

He crossed his arms over his chest, making his shirt gape. The movement drew her gaze like the needle on a compass. Her belly clenched as she stared at his pecs, sculpted to perfection, covered with a sprinkling of hair. "Why are you here?"

"I received an invitation--"

"No, you didn't," he said impatiently, cutting her off.

"I did. How would you know that I didn't? I have it right here," she said, rooting through her purse.

"'Cause I'm the host, Nigel Francoeur."

Cherry stopped her search and looked up at him, feeling her face redden under his scrutiny. She would've rather had her teeth pulled than to have to admit that she'd crashed such an exclusive party, but there was no hope for it.   That being the case, she summoned the 'helpless female'. "I'm sorry. I admit, I wasn't originally invited, my friend was." She held out her hand, which he ignored. "I'm Cherry--Cherry Roman.   Anyway," she added, dropping her hand once more, "--she couldn't come, so she passed it on to me. There's no harm in that, is there? And, I'm here now."

He was silent a long moment. A muscle in his jaw ticked.

"You have to leave. Now."

The man didn't have one sympathetic bone in his body. She'd spent much of her severance traveling here. Now she'd have to go back without even some pleasant memories to sustain her.

All of a sudden, everything that had happened beset her like a wall of dominos she'd carefully stacked to the ceiling. She'd done her best to look on the bright, keep her chin up, stave off the temptation to just fall on the floor and kick her heels and wallow in her misery. This trip had been her panacea, however. It was going to cure her ills. She was going to have a good time and relax and she'd figure out what to do when she'd had just a little breather from the battle she'd just lost.

Except now she wasn't going to get it. Now, she was going to have to face the fact that she'd blown money she couldn't afford to on a vacation she wasn't going to get. It took a supreme effort of will to ignore the sting of tears in her eyes and nose. "I can't," she said, her chin wobbling. She swallowed, forcing herself to calm down. "The last ferry is gone. I … I barely made it here as it is."

He closed his eyes as if searching for patience. When he opened his eyes again, he stared past her at the setting sun. His face tightened. He gave her a hard look. "It's just as well. Come, I'll show you to your room."

"Really?" She felt instantly better, even though he didn't look like he was very happy about the fact that she couldn't leave.

He glanced toward the glass doors again. "It's gettin dark. It's too late. You can't leave tonight anyway."

He had his hand on the back of her waist, riding her hip, all the way up the stairs and down the hallway to the room he took her to. If it had been a cattle prod, it couldn't have been any more galvanizing. It seemed to burn a hole right through her clothes, right through her flesh and forked outward to spear her erogenous zones electrifyingly. She didn't know if it was that that made it so difficult to catch her breath, or the fact that she traversed the entire distance trying to outrun that hand.

The room was beautiful, far more elegant than anything she'd ever experienced in her life--it looked like the sort of room only the filthy rich could afford, from the elegant furniture, to the carpet that was so thick she felt like she was walking through water, to the king sized bed filled with pillows.

As chaotic as her emotions were after what she'd already experienced, she was still awed enough that it penetrated her emotional roller coaster ride, striking her deaf, dumb and blind.

"You will stay here. Is that understood?"

Cher turned around and gaped at him. "This is my room?"

He frowned. After a moment's hesitation, he left the door and strode toward her. Cher blinked, too surprised even to think about retreating from the purposeful set of his face. He caught her jaw, forcing her to look at him--though why, she wasn't certain. She'd looked up instinctively the moment he came to tower over her so threateningly.

"I must have your word that you'll make no attempt to leave this room this night, chere."

Cher blinked at him, wondering idly whether he meant chere--as in, he was Creole, or Cajun, which would probably explain his devastating dark good looks--or if he'd somehow figured out she was called Cher--maybe she'd mentioned that?

She must have nodded. He seemed satisfied. After a moment, he released her and strode from the room. She was still staring at the vibrating door when she heard the distinctive click of a key turning in a lock.

That tiny little sound acted on Cher's tumultuous emotions like a healthy dose of Metamucil on a clogged pipe line. She went stone cold sober on the instant.

She stared at the door disbelievingly. He'd locked her in! That dirty, low down, rotten, son-of-a-bitch had locked her in! He'd let her think she could stay after all and enjoy her vacation and then he'd escorted her to a prison cell!

She didn't give a fuck how elegant the prison cell was!

Stalking toward the door, she grabbed the knob and

twisted it a couple of times. It *was* locked.

She started beating on the door. "Let me out, you son-of-a-bitch!"

She pressed her ear to the door, but she couldn't hear anything.

Small wonder considering the carpet in this place!

"Hey! You can't do this! I had a perfect right to use that damn invitation!"

Sighing gustily, she gave up beating on the door. It hurt her hands, and it was obvious he had no intention of coming back.

"Some fucking vacation," she muttered, turning to survey the room. She was going to be stuck here all weekend-- because the damn ferry wasn't coming back before Monday!

Furious, she searched the room for a phone. Not surprisingly, she didn't find one. Finally, she dropped her backpack on the bed, dragging everything out of it and eventually unearthed her cell phone. "Ha!" she said, dialing 911.

She got a recording saying her service had been disconnected.

"Shit!" She strangled the phone and then pitched it across the room. It hit the wall with a satisfying thunk, but it didn't damage the phone. Walking over to it, she smashed the thing with her heel until it was no more than fragments and then left it and went to sit on the bed to sulk.

Her stomach growled.

She was going to give that gorgeous asshole hunk a piece of her mind when he came to bring her supper.

If he came to bring her supper.

She realized after a little while that she was tired of sulking, and she was bored. Sighing, she decided to check out the bath. That'd be entertaining for at least ten or fifteen minutes.

There was a TV and a DVD player. She doubted, considering where they were, that the TV would pick up anything. Like she couldn't watch frigging DVDs at home!

The bath was really luxurious. Despite her determination to feel abused, she felt her mood lighten a little when she saw it had a whirlpool . Adjusting the water, she left the tub filling and went back into the bedroom to rifle through the clothing she'd brought. She was irritated all over again when she saw the sexy undergarments she'd brought--just in case she ran into anyone interesting.

As *if* she was going to run into anyone locked in her room!

A twenty minute session in the whirlpool did wonders for her mood. By the time she finally crawled out, her muscles were like putty--not a tense one in her entire body. When she'd dried off, she pulled the under things on.

The under things consisted of a barely there thong and a nearly transparent bra.

She liked feeling 'bad'.

Unfortunately, at the moment she felt more drained than like a femme fatale. Trudging back into the bedroom, she sprawled out on the bed and winked out like an extinguished light bulb.

She wasn't certain what woke her. One moment she was dead to the world, the next she was conscious. Yawning, she rolled over and stretched, smiling faintly at the decadent feel of the thick, silk coverlet beneath her. Finally, reluctantly, she opened her eyes.

Nigel Francoeur was standing over her, a dainty tray with a dainty sandwich, obviously forgotten, in his hand.

The expression on his face sent a shock wave of heat through her. Her mouth went dry. Her nipples got hard.

His gaze moved to them as if he could see the transformation.

It was at that precise moment that it finally dawned on Cher that he *could* see the transformation. She was wearing her all-but-naked underwear and nothing else.

She jackknifed upright, glancing around for her clothes.

As if her sudden movement had finally broken the spell that had bound him, he set the tray down with a thud on the bedside table, turned on his heel and strode toward the door.

Cher stared after him with her jaw at half cock.

"Wait!" she managed to get out as he jerked the door open and started through.

He paused, looked back at her, his gaze brooding and dangerous.

Cher gulped. "Why did you lock me in?"

Something flickered in his eyes. A predatory smile curled his lips. "To keep the big bad wolf away, chere."

Chapter Two

He'd vanished, locking the door behind him before Cher recovered sufficiently to think of anything else to say. "Damn it!" she said, pounding her fist on the mattress angrily.

So much for giving him a piece of her mind!

She turned and glared at the sandwich. She *was* hungry. On the other hand, she hated wasting a good appetite on a cold sandwich when she knew damn good and well the guests were probably dining on … escargot or something like that.

Sighing, she picked up the sandwich and wandered to the window, looking down at the darkened landscape. A wedge of light filtered across the lawn from the back of the building--where she'd seen the pool. Dimly, she heard the sounds of a party.

After a moment, she set the sandwich down untouched and opened the window. Sure enough, she could hear loud music and loud voices. The alcohol must be flowing freely. They couldn't have been at it long and already it sounded like they were having a wild time of it.

Disappointment flooded her. She should be out there. She deserved a vacation if anybody did!

Sighing, she stared down at the lawn speculatively, wondering if there was anyway to escape her elegant prison.

That was when she spied the trellis.

A smile curled her lips. Excitement began thrumming in her veins.

Abandoning her viewpoint abruptly, she searched through her bag until she found the slinky black dress she'd brought for partying. Was it too dressy, though? It looked like night club attire--which it was. And she *was* going to have to climb down the trellis to get to the party. Not that climbing down in a dress worried her, because it wasn't like there was anybody around to see. The party was in the back.

The roses climbing the trellis might present a problem, though, and she really didn't want to get her favorite black dress snagged. Reluctantly, she dropped it and dug out a pair of cut off jeans and a halter top.

Dashing into the bathroom, she did a quick make up job, combed her hair and checked out her reflection. Deciding she looked as well as could be expected on such short notice, she left the bathroom, grabbed up her sandals and studied them critically. Wear them? Go barefoot?

She didn't relish the idea of climbing down a rose covered trellis barefoot. She wasn't at all certain she could negotiate it in shoes, however. Finally, she decided she was just going to have to do battle with the rose canes if she wanted to party.

Nigel fucking Francoeur sure as hell wasn't planning on letting her have any fun!

Moving to the window once more, she struggled with the screen and finally managed to get it off. Unfortunately, she dropped it. "Shit!" she exclaimed, leaning out the window to look down at the screen on the ground below.

Sighing irritably, she tossed her sandals out. She didn't know how she was going to get the damn screen back up, but she decided she'd worry about that later.

Hoisting a leg over the sill, she felt around with her toe until she found a V in the trellis. Slowly, she eased her weight down on it, listening for a telltale crack that would mean disaster. It seemed to be holding, however, and after a moment, she leaned her weight on the window sill and worked her other leg out, clinging to the molding while she felt around for another foothold.

Her heart was in her throat by that time, threatening to suffocate her. She swallowed with an effort. "Whoo hoo!" she muttered weakly. "Par-ty!"

Her legs felt like cooked spaghetti. Ignoring the sensation, she allowed herself to slip slowly over the sill while she searched for another foothold below the one she had. It took her almost fifteen minutes to work herself loose from the window sill. Finally, she focused on her fingers and uncurled them from the molding and placed one hand on the trellis, and then the other, closing her eyes.

When the trellis didn't immediately utter an ominous crack and separate from the wall, she began working her way downwards.

She knew how a Chihuahua felt. Every muscle in her body seemed to be trembling, with both strain and abject terror.

She was nearly halfway down the trellis before she encountered the rose bush.

She yelped, but the noise of the party had grown to such proportions, she seriously doubted anyone heard anything. Nudging the thorny cane out of the way, she managed to negotiate her way down another few feet before she realized the bush was so thick there was no way in hell she was going to be able to climb over it without looking like she'd just been through a meat grinder.

Turning her head, she stared down at the ground, trying to decide just how far it was. It still looked like a long way down, but she thought she probably wasn't that high. Rose bushes didn't really grow that tall--she didn't think.

She almost lost her grip and fell off when she looked up to see how far she was from the window. It scared her so badly, all she could do was cling to the trellis for several minutes and quake like a Chihuahua on cocaine.

Finally, she took several calming breaths and slowly turned. She wasn't about to jump backwards!

She couldn't turn completely around either.

Deciding that the longer she delayed the more likely she

was to completely lose her nerve, she closed her eyes, counted to ten and leapt. Miraculously, she landed on her feet. Unfortunately, the impact shot pain through her feet as if she'd landed on a bed of nails. Yelping, she surged upward, pin wheeled, and landed on her ass--right in the middle of the window screen.

"Shit!"

A dark shadow fell over her.

She looked up guiltily--right into the unsmiling face of Nigel Francoeur.

Nigel glared at the woman, infuriated by her recklessness. Surging forward, he grabbed her beneath the arms, hauling her to her feet and shoving her against the wall just past the thick rose bush.

"Hey!" she gasped as he stood her up. He blocked her with one arm when she tried to move past him. She turned in the other direction and he brought his other arm up, locking her in place.

She sank back against the wall, glaring at him, but her eyes widened when he leaned forward. "You can't begin to imagine how far out of your depth you are here, petite. I've neither the time nor the patience to play games with you, but I will tell you this--you put yourself in danger to defy me."

It was actually probably the stupidest thing that she'd ever done in her life, next to coming in the first place--and the only time she'd ever been stupid enough to do anything like that. Somehow, however, the invasion of her personal space and the threat in his stance, his voice, and his words made her react instinctively to the threat, rather than rationally. She slapped him.

She was horrified the moment she did.

She was more horrified when she saw the heat that blazed in his eyes.

Before she could do more than gasp in an instinctual gulp of air to scream, he enveloped her mouth with his own in an assault of such savage hunger her heart felt as if it was going to beat itself to death against her rib cage. She managed a whimper of distress before his tongue invaded her mouth and assaulted her senses with his taste, with the essence that was him--primal, savage, wild--and her brain simply overheated and shut down. She felt as if she had stepped off unwarily into a vortex of fiery, carnal need that was sucking her down into an abyss of blackness.

When he withdrew, he was gasping hoarsely, his eyes glittering with raw need, his body shaking with the effort to hold it in check.

Cher found that she was trembling with weakness, so dizzy and disoriented she was certain if she hadn't been braced against the wall she would have wilted to the ground like a deflating rubber doll the moment he released her.

Before she could gather her wits about her, he grasped her and tossed her over his shoulder. The impact of his broad shoulder on her belly knocked the breath from her, effectively rousing her from her stupor. "Hey! What the hell do you think you're doing?" she demanded, trying to lever herself upright.

Instead of answering, he gave her a resounding slap on the ass.

That stunned her with outrage long enough that he'd hooked a foot on the trellis before she realized what his intention was. The gasp, begun in outrage, ended in a squeak of sheer terror as he scaled the trellis with stunning agility and the ground dropped away from her bulging eyes.

Her reentry through the window was far more terrifying than her exit had been. Even worse, he stepped through the window behind her.

She stared at him warily for several moments. He still looked incredibly dangerous, and--her feeble mind informed her--sexy. Or maybe it was only that she could still feel his mouth? Taste him?

It pissed her off almost as much as the fact that he'd scared the living shit out of her. "You can not keep me a prisoner in this damned room!" she snarled at him.

His eyes narrowed. His face hardened. "Have you listened to nothing that I have said?"

She glared back at him. "What? The 'Stay! Sit! Down!' commands you've been issuing? I'm getting mixed signals here," she said sarcastically.

He took a step toward her. She stepped back without even thinking about it. "Look! Why don't we just call a truce, huh? I mean, I can see I probably shouldn't have come, but, honestly, I didn't see that there'd be a problem-- anyway, I'm here now and I can't go back until the ferry comes, so...." She broke off when she bumped into the door. She didn't have to look around. The door knob hit her in the middle of the back.

She stepped to one side. He matched her side step, placing a palm against the door and blocking her retreat. Before she could try to side step in the other direction, his heat enveloped as he leaned toward her, crowding her.

She pressed her back against the door, but she had no where to go. Before she quite knew what was happening, she felt the pressure of his body against her entire length. His cock felt like a burning log against her belly--huge and hot. It took an effort to catch her breath as he undulated his body against hers--tipping his hips up and forward so that that rock hard length of mind blowing flesh bumped her mound, sending sparks of heat through her--brushing his chest across hers so that her nipples were trying to drill holes in his hard pecs. Wet heat instantly saturated her labia, as if her body sensed that he would pound into her at any moment.

Just the though of enveloping that thickness inside her made her inner muscles spasm with pleasure.

He dipped his head and she thought she might actually pass out as the heat of his breath fanned across her face. Her lips tingled, as if she could already feel the pressure of his mouth. Her mouth watered as she remembered the feel and taste and texture of his tongue. She swallowed convulsively.

"You're asking for something, chere, that you may not want," he murmured huskily, his lips almost, but not quite, brushing against hers, his heated gaze making promises that had her pussy quaking in anticipation.

Abruptly, he stepped back. She gazed at him in surprise and disappointment.

Something flickered in his eyes. He frowned, looking away. "I'll be putting you on the first ferry Monday morning," he said, his voice sounding harsh with disuse. "Until then, sit tight."

Cher blinked at him as he fished a key out of his pocket. Stepping out of the way as he reached for the lock, she simply stared at him while he unlocked it and stepped through the opening, closing the door behind him and locking it once more.

She was still staring at the door in bemusement when the sound of his retreating footsteps faded away. He had kissed her into mindless oblivion--rubbed that delicious body all over her until she was melting, wallowing in his scent like a cat high on catnip--and then he'd just stopped. Cool as you please! "Asshole!" she said angrily.

And she was back in the room again! A prisoner, again! She paced the room furiously for several minutes and finally moved to the window again, wondering if she quite dared make another try for it.

He *thought* he'd cowed her with all that macho, male chauvinistic bullshit.

Actually, he had cowed her. The thought of climbing down the trellis and meeting up with him again was almost as terrifying as it was tempting.

The door opened while she was staring down at the yard below, enacting a mental scenario of meeting up with him and being thrown to the ground and fucked senseless. Her head snapped around. Her eyes widened guiltily when she saw it was Nigel.

He had a hammer in his hand and she scurried away from the window, hovering in the corner while she watched him warily to see what he had in mind. Ignoring her, he strode to the window, dug a handful of nails from his pocket and proceeded to nail the window shut.

She gaped at him in disbelief.

"You're *nailing* the window shut!" she gasped.

He sent her a look and finished what he was doing.

Without a word, he turned and strode from the room again.

Cher shivered. What the hell was going on? Locking her in? Nailing the window shut? This went just a *lit-tle* bit beyond what she figured she might expect for gate crashing.

She frowned. Ok, well, obviously this wasn't one of those little real-estate jaunts like she'd expected, but it couldn't be a private party either since her friend had gotten the invitation and she hadn't known the guy.

She was almost ready to cross the guy off as totally whack-o, but, despite the things he'd done, he didn't strike her as a mental case. Something was going on and he thought she needed protecting. He was the host. Whatever the something was, he would certainly know.

A drug free for all? They were going to do ecstasy and have a wild sex orgy?

Because it sure as hell sounded like a regular old party going on down there to her. Well, a little wilder than a regular party, she supposed.

Still, she hadn't seen a thing that might suggest there was anything sinister about this place. It had looked like a really posh vacation getaway, but when all was said and done, *just* a vacation getaway.

Maybe Nigel knew *of* Sheri? Didn't actually know her personally, but did know about her through some of her friends? And he'd freaked when she'd shown up because he didn't know her at all and thought she might be a narc or something?

That actually made a little more sense than she liked. The way they were partying down there seemed a little excessive for regular old alcohol induced freedom from inhibition. They were baying now, for chrissake!

Frowning, she moved to the window once more, wondering if maybe the reason she could hear them better was because the party had spilled around the side of the house.

The full moon had risen above the trees when she reached the window and peered out. The lawn below was bathed in its light. Sure enough, the party *had* moved around within plain view of her window now, and she could see dozens of men milling about.

Nigel stood in the center of the group. Almost as if he sensed her watching, he looked up at that moment and, despite the distance, she felt as if his gaze locked with hers for several heartbeats.

Unnervingly, about a dozen or so other men also looked up toward her.

Cher wasn't exactly certain why it was, but the moment she realized she'd attracted the interest of at least a dozen of the men milling about on the lawn below, the hair on the nape of her neck stood on end.

It might have had something to do with the fact that, after staring at her for several frantic heart palpitations, they whirled upon Nigel and their body language was definitely both hostile and challenging.

Chapter Three

"What's this?" Rocco demanded, his voice low and threatening.

"Looks to me like our host has got a female tucked away all for himself," Zeke growled.

Brandis snarled. "You know the rules, Nigel. You've got no right to withhold one from the hunt."

Nigel dragged his gaze from the woman's pale face with an effort. The little fool, he thought angrily. He couldn't protect her now that they'd seen her. The pack would tear him apart if he tried and take her anyway. Their beasts were already upon them. They wouldn't care that she wasn't one of them, that she didn't belong in the hunt. He forced a feral smile. "Mes amis! You misjudge me. It was never my intention to withhold her, only to present her when the time was right. But, since you are all so impatient, I will go and get her now."

He strode briskly toward the house, aware even as he did

that a number of the pack, no doubt distrustful of his motives, detached themselves from the others and moved around the perimeter of the house to watch the exits. Several followed him, as well.

Ignoring them, he walked briskly through the house and up the stairs, surreptitiously fishing the key from his pocket as he walked. He had a slight lead on them by the time he reached the door to her room, but not much.

Unlocking the door, he strode quickly across the room. She was staring at him, wide eyed with fear, as if she had sensed, finally, that she was in grave danger. He grasped her upper arms, leaning close and spoke quickly in a low voice. "Don't ask any questions. Do exactly as I say. When you're told to run you must go to the old storm shelter and stay there. Take the path through the woods toward the rising moon. When you reach the fork in the path you will see an oak about six feet in diameter. Swing to your right, away from the fork and go into the woods twenty paces. The door is in the ground, covered with leaves. Go inside and lock yourself in and whatever happens, *do not unlock the door*. Understand?"

Cher nodded shakily. "The storm shelter in the woods."

He flashed her a brief smile. "Good girl."

He turned as he heard the two men who'd followed him come into the room, holding her tightly by one arm. "As you see."

The two men looked her over almost … hungrily. Cher shivered, glancing at Nigel.

Without another word, he escorted her from the room, down the stairs and out into the night.

An eerie quiet had fallen over the group gathered in the yard. It wasn't a calm sort of silence, however, but rather it seemed to shiver with tension, as if everyone who stood on the lawn were only waiting for a signal to launch into action.

To Cher's surprise, Nigel escorted her to the center of the group, then released her and stepped away. Nervous, she looked around. A wide circle had been cleared at the center of the group. In the circle with her stood four other women. Beyond the opening, several dozen men crowded shoulder to shoulder, their faces taut, their eyes gleaming.

Cher swallowed with a gulp and glanced at the women, wondering if they were as unnerved as she was. She saw that they were studying her almost as intently as the men were, though their faces were filled with suspicion and maybe even a little hostility.

They looked like--gymnasts--lean, taut.

She suddenly felt like a marshmallow--soft and squishy in all the wrong places, although she wasn't entirely certain why. She kept in shape. She had a good figure, by damn. Maybe she wasn't as taut as these snotty females, but she wasn't a blob either.

"Most of you who have come for the gathering have been before and know the rules. For those of you who do not, they are simple:

The females will be given a fifteen minute head start.

The male who catches her can only claim her for his mate if he is strong enough, and determined enough to face any who challenge him for the woman.

Once a male has marked his female, however, she is his by Lycan law and no one may challenge him for his mate."

Cher stared at him blankly. He might as well have been speaking Swahili for all the sense she could make of it. He couldn't, surely, mean that she–they--were supposed to try to outrun this pack of men? She glanced around at the other women and saw that they looked as stunned and horrified as she felt--obviously they hadn't known they were on the menu either.

Outrun them to where? For how long? They were on a fucking island for chrissake!

She glanced nervously at the men and saw that a good half dozen had begun to inch forward into the circle--they almost seemed to be--sniffing her, like they were trying to get her scent.

Exactly what the hell was a Lycan, anyway?

"Get back!" Nigel roared, making her jump and turn to stare at him.

"Shewolves," he ground out, staring straight at Cher.

"Run!"

Cher froze. Stunned as the four women ranged beside her tore off toward the woods as if their life depended upon getting as far away as they possibly could as fast as they could.

"Now!" Nigel growled.

Cher jumped about a foot, whirled around toward the trees and sprawled out on her belly in the dirt so hard she grunted as the air left her lungs. Terror had her firmly in its grip now, however. Without hesitation, she scrambled to her feet and headed for the trees. "Path, path, path," she muttered looking around frantically as she reached the tree line and began running back and forth along the edge of the trees, too mindless with terror to form a coherent thought. "The moon," she thought suddenly and glanced around.

She saw a patch of moonlight and realized it had spotlighted the entrance of the path. "One Mississippi, two Mississippi--Jesus fucking Christ! Where the hell was I supposed to go?" she panted out as she swung onto the path at last and spared a look back.

The sight that greeted her put an extra spring in her step. She bounded along the path like a white tailed deer, her mind focused on trying to figure out just how many minutes had passed. Five? Ten?

She heard baying behind her. Her hair stood on end.

She ran right past the oak. Unable to put on brakes fast enough, she skidded like a baseball player sliding into home plate. Clawing at the ground, she gained her feet again and ran back to the oak tree, huffing for breath as she looked around, frantically trying to remember what Nigel had said. The tree. The fork. Left of the tree? Right of the fucking tree?

Right! That was it, swing right. The tore off the trail, ran a couple of yards and remembered she'd been facing the opposite direction. It was her other right.

Swinging around, she charged across the path again, this time away from the fork, like he'd said.

Twenty paces. Her paces? His paces?

She counted twenty long strides and got down on her

hands and knees, feeling along the ground frantically. The baying was growing louder and she had a real bad feeling it wasn't dogs.

She couldn't feel anything that felt like wood.

Had he been fucking with her?

She widened the circle of her search. Suddenly, as she brushed away a handful of leaves, her hand slipped along something rough, and definitely wooden. Thrusting the leaves aside she searched desperately, blindly for a handle, a catch. She found the hinges and felt along the opposite side until she found what she'd been searching for. Almost weeping with relief, she heaved upward.

The door was heavy. She felt like she'd ruptured something important before she managed to lever it open far enough to squeeze inside. She screamed as she fell, landing in a stunned heap at the bottom of the hole. "Shit!"

It was as profoundly dark as a black hole--a complete and total absence of light that felt suffocatingly thick.

A totally new terror seized her. Blindly, waving her arms in front of her, she searched for steps, a ladder--there had to be some way into the damn thing besides just falling in!

She found the ladder with her nose. She had absolutely no clue of how she could've been waving her arms in front of her and still managed to walk right into the thing, but she did mange it. She was stunned for about two seconds, then she was searching for hand and footholds and scaling the ladder right back to the top.

She's already stared heaving at the door, trying to get out, when she heard the wolves. She stopped, trying to listen over her heart, which was pounding in her ears like Indian war drums.

It sounded like wolves.

She decided she didn't want to find out.

Easing the door down, she felt around and finally found the bolt Nigel had told her about and shoved it in place. She slipped off a rung as she started back down and landed in a heap on the floor again.

She stayed where she was, curling into a tight ball and trying not to think what might be in the hole with her.

That wasn't as difficult as it might have been.

Insulated as she was, she could still hear the baying and hassling of the wolves.

They had to be close.

She heard something scratching at the door and her hair stood on end again. Covering her mouth with her hand, she stared upward, wondering if there was any possibility they could actually get that heavy wooden door open.

Surely not? Surely to god all she had to do was just sit tight, wait, and they'd go away.

They didn't go away, however. They could smell her. They began clawing at the door, rattling it. Cher began chewing on her nails, her eyes glued to the point where she could hear the rattling growing louder and louder, as if they were heaving back and forth against it.

She jumped all over when she heard the sudden crack of wood. Abruptly, the door was heaved open. A square of dim light appeared above her but disappeared almost immediately as something big and dark leapt through it.

Cher screamed, whirling mindlessly to flee even as a great weight slammed into her, driving her toward the ground. She struggled, kicking, biting, scratching at the man who'd grabbed her--because it was a man, not a wolf, and she was no less terrified.

Another dark shape appeared. The two began pulling at her. Within a few moments, she was dragged up the ladder and through the opening. She screamed again when she saw that others waited there, in the darkness. Dozens of hands grabbed at her, dragging her first one way and then another.

They fell upon one another, snarling, biting, rending at each other with their claws. One managed to fight the others off and started dragging her toward the path. Abruptly, another dark shape flew from the trees, this one notably larger than the others. Within moments, he'd waded through three of the men. Two had fallen to the ground and did not get back up. A third fled.

He watched the man who fled for a moment and turned, leaping toward the two men and the woman that struggled a few yards away. Knocking both men to the ground, he caught one around the neck and tore at his throat. When he'd defeated his opponent, he looked around once more, only to discover that they last man had scrambled up while he was occupied, grabbed the woman and was struggling to drag her deeper into the woods while she fought and clawed at him.

He caught up to them in four bounds, landing squarely in the man's back. The woman rolled free and began scrambling away as he and his foe faced off, flew at each other, rending each other's flesh with their teeth and claws. It took him longer to dispatch the man than he'd expected.

He rose shakily to his feet when he'd killed him, looking around for her, testing the air for her scent. It was difficult to pick it up, however, when the others had dragged her all over the clearing. "Cher?"

He lifted his head, listening.

"Nigel?"

As he turned toward the sound of her voice, she flew from the woods, slamming against him so hard, he took a step back. Her scent engulfed him instantly in a red haze of lust. He wrapped his arms around her. "My beast is upon me, chere," he growled warningly.

Instead of moving away, she hugged herself more tightly to him, as if she would crawl inside of him.

She did crawl inside of him, seeping into his pores, arousing his beast until he had to struggle to keep it at bay.

Chapter Four

Nigel growled fiercely and took her to the ground, sending up a spray of leaves as they hit it. She gasped in surprise, too stunned to struggle. He was beyond holding himself back.

He crushed his mouth down upon hers, thrusting his tongue inside to rub against her own. The urge to taste, to dominate was too great. She went stiff with shock, and he tasted fear before tremulous desire took hold.

He didn't have the time for finesse, and he damn sure didn't want to be caught in the open before he had a chance to mark her. She would not be safe until he had.

Tension throbbed in his gut, tightening his chest and groin until he thought he would explode. He tore his mouth from hers, dragging his lips and tongue over her jaw and down her neck.

She tasted of salt and woman, sweet and soft to the touch. He couldn't feel enough of her to satisfy himself.

Her hands moved along his shoulders, a shy touch that had him gritting his teeth for control. He didn't know her, but she evoked a powerful response in him he was hard pressed to ignore.

He dragged his mouth down her chest, roughly pushing aside her halter top to latch on to one small, firm breast. Her nipple was hard before he reached it with his lips to tug on the tip. She gasped harshly, arching as he took it into his mouth and suckled her with a furious hunger. He moved, scraping her with his teeth, nuzzling her skin with his nose as if he could inhale her and appease the ravenous beast from taking hold.

Lust rioted off her body, potent, making his head swim with the faint scent of her arousal. Nigel's mouth watered with the desire to taste the cream of her flesh, to bury his tongue deep in her pussy until he slaked this insatiable thirst. His cock surged to attention, straining against his pants. With a rough hand, he freed it and ground himself between her thighs, nearly coming with the molten feel of her trapped cleft. He groaned in frustration, to be so near his goal but so far away.

Even through her shorts, he could feel her damp heat, and the knowledge that she was as aroused as he was sent lust spiraling through his body.

He slid his lips over hers again, kissing her, allowing her to know just how desperately he wanted her.

Cher sucked his tongue, too aroused to care where they were, what had happened … what he'd done. He'd saved her from god only knew what, and she was so damned attracted to him, if he'd wanted to screw her in the middle of her parent's house, she'd be tempted.

She arched as he ground against her mound again, heightening the desperate need to feel him deep within her. With frantic hands, she plunged them between them, trying to peel her shorts off.

Breaking from her mouth, he lifted his hips and she pushed her shorts off her hips and down her legs with his help. In seconds, he was back against her, rocking, as if he couldn't bear to leave her touch for so long.

His hands roamed over her body, pinching her nipples, massaging her breasts before moving lover, down to her panties. He hadn't given her the chance to take them off, but as if realizing there was still the barrier to their joining, he snapped the flimsy sides and ripped them away.

Cher didn't care. All she knew was that if he didn't ease this incredible ache soon, she'd throw him on his back and ride him until he couldn't move anymore.

Nigel pulled back and hauled her legs up, throwing her ankles onto his shoulders. Her calves pressed against his chest, aching at the unfamiliar touch of hard muscles and crisp hair. The position left her completely vulnerable to him, her lips taut and exposed like a tight smile. He leaned forward, pressing her down.

A molten tip of flesh prodded her bare slit, making her belly jerk in response. She felt her juices gather, felt them slither down her cunt to her anus. She'd never been so wet in all her life.

His cock lodged at the entrance of her vagina, preparing to invade. He shuddered, as if trying to control himself, and then he pushed. Pushed that incredibly thick thing inside her, past the delicate edges of her hole.

Cher hissed in pain and pleasure, unable to believe how large he was. She could barely hold him, and couldn't keep from clenching as he worked his way inside. Her muscles spasmed with his advance, quivering with a sensation not unlike fear.

Desperation clawed at her loins. She planted her palms

on the ground, giving herself the leverage she needed to move. She tightened her legs against him, muscles screaming from the position.

He groaned and jerked, then drove so deep inside, she screamed. He sank to the root of himself, holding still a moment within her, allowing the burning of her passage to ease and accept him. Her cream seemed to have sizzled away, leaving her bereft of moisture, and her body overreacted, forcing her to gush as he retreated and thrust inside her again.

"You're mine now," he growled softly, so quietly she almost couldn't hear him past the roar of blood hammering in her ears.

As if possessed by some violent need, he moved, thrusting in and out of her with a rhythm that had her muscles cramping to resist the ecstasy that hovered so close. She wanted the feeling to last, for hours, forever.

Cher clawed the ground, tossing her head from side to side, whimpering with need. The piston movement of his cock drove her mad, a tight slipping that had her nerves skyrocketing out of control. She could feel every veined ridge stroking in and out of her. Her flesh seemed to devour him with each pounding thrust. She couldn't seem to weep enough moisture to keep from burning alive.

His hips ground against the backs of her thighs, the friction of his hair making them tingle with sensation. His scrotum slapped against her anus. The lips of her cleft seemed to swell as he connected with them, again and again, drilling into her hole faster and harder, pumping shorter as the tremors of orgasm took hold of her.

Her pussy clutched him like fist, desperately trying to climb to that peak that stood at the root of his shaft. He bent forward even more, pressing her knees down until they brushed her tight, aching nipples, squashing her breasts between her body and his.

Cher closed her eyes, welcoming the tightening of her nerves, the quivers of sensation that sizzled through her veins. She couldn't quite reach orgasm, and the feeling, like an unscratched itch was driving her crazy.

As if sensing her need, he shortened his strokes, locking a hand down to massage her clit to awakening. The touch was like a brand. The bud plumped to instant, roaring life. It tingled with the pressure of his fingers.

Cher gasped as he flicked her clit and the rapid move of his fingers sent her orgasm crashing over her. She screamed, clenching him and going tense as if she was dying. He removed his fingers, pumping into her with abandon once more, riding the clenching and unclenching of her muscles to his own orgasm.

Her body seemed to melt beneath him, shatter like glass. Every nerve burned, tingled with pressure that threatened to make her explode. She was gasping, panting for breath. Her throat ached, and she couldn't seem to breathe enough air to satisfy her lungs.

His semen erupted inside her quaking pussy, prolonging the orgasm that trembled through her. The climax was unlike any she'd ever known--so powerful, it drowned out all other senses, leaving her deaf, dumb, and blind. Her body convulsed on his rod as it went soft, soaking up wave after wave of utter bliss, until stars sparked behind her eyelids and her head rushed with dizzy sensation.

He stayed above her, inside her, breathing raggedly, holding still as the sweat of their bodies cooled in the night air and their hearts returned to a normal rhythm. Finally, he pulled his flaccid length from her grasping muscles with the soft sound of breaking suction, and he rolled off of her onto the ground, seeming as exhausted as she felt.

Cher caught her breath, unbelievably weak. "I can't believe we just did that," she whispered.

He propped on an elbow, looking at her in the dark. The moonlight made his eyes look even hungrier than they had before.

If she was herself and not so sated, she might've been worried.

Chapter Five

Cher felt the next thing to catatonic as Nigel lifted her in his arms and carried her through the woods. It wasn't until he emerged from the trees that she realized he was carrying her back to the house. Fear instantly reared its head and she began to struggle to be put down.

"It's all right, Cher. No one will challenge us," Nigel said soothingly, as if he knew exactly what was running through her mind.

She shivered. "How can you be sure?"

"Because I made you mine," he said simply.

Cher stared up at him, feeling a strange mixture of emotions at his words. She was a modern woman. She shouldn't have felt such a strange flicker of excitement at that Neanderthal type, male domination–but she did. At the same time, she felt a good deal of uneasiness.

Somehow, however, she didn't doubt his assessment of the situation, and she relaxed against him, content to enjoy being carried, thrilled that he seemed to do so so effortlessly.

Aside from the sense of security she felt being held close to him, she wasn't completely certain she could have made it back to the house under her own steam. She ached and hurt all over from her race through the woods, and from trying to fight off those crazed maniacs.

They must have been high on something, she decided, shivering all over again.

He surprised her when they had climbed the stairs. Instead of taking her to the room he'd imprisoned her in before, he continued to the room at the end of the hallway.

She knew the moment they entered that he'd taken her to his room.

And without so much as a 'by your leave'.

Not that she minded. She really didn't want to be alone after what she'd been through.

Instead of carrying her to the bed, he turned and headed toward the door she knew must lead to the master bath. If possible, it was even more luxurious than the bath that adjoined the bedroom she'd occupied.

Setting her on her feet at last, he adjusted the water and began to peel his clothing off. Cher watched him, interested despite everything that had happened.

His eyes gleamed, a faint smile curling his lips.

When he'd finished undressing, he moved toward her and began peeling her clothing off as he had his--well, her halter top and bra. Everything else had been left behind. Pulling her into the shower, he bathed the ache from her with the hot water and a soapy cloth, instilling an ache of a very different kind.

Almost as though he were reluctant to hurt her, his hands moved gently over her skin. She was achy all over, but not bruised, and unbelievably, her sex burned to feel him inside her again despite the dull pain throbbing there.

Shivering with the steam tickling her skin, she wrapped her arms around him and rubbed herself sensually against his body. He stiffened in surprise a brief moment, and then his hands locked around her, going straight to her ass to cup it. He curled his hands against her cheeks. His cock hardened, digging into her belly, leaving her feeling as weak and womanly as she had before.

She kissed his shoulder, nibbling up his neck, enjoying the tension of his muscles as they reacted to her touch. He groaned sharply and picked her up, forcing her through the stream of water to the back wall as he trapped her against it and hauled her up until his cock found the opening of her body.

He nudged her opening as she sucked at the corner of his jaw, her hands gripping his shoulders with desperation. Shifting until he'd centered her, he pushed through the seeping moisture of her body straight into her core, impaling her on his cock.

Cher cried out, arching her head back. She dug her nails into his shoulders, biting her lip at the fierce mingle of pain and pleasure.

He grit his teeth and buried his face at her temple, fingers digging into her buttocks as he hauled her tighter to him, rocking his hips until he could pump fast and hard inside her.

Cher's back rode against the tiled wall, her breasts rubbing sensually against his chest, her clit massaged by his pubic bone as he ground into her.

Their rutting was hard and fast, but unbelievably enticing. Her pussy clutched him, her previous orgasm making her come so much the faster this time, and within minutes, they were both crying out as they climaxed.

She thought he was finished with her. Instead, he withdrew, washed his semen from her body, and carried her out of the bathroom into the bedroom, where he dried her off before drying himself.

Almost as soon as he was done, he was on her again, wrapping her in his arms, kissing her with a fervor that she was nearly dismayed to realize rose inside her again. She couldn't believe how *hungry* he was, and how much her own hunger matched his.

She sucked his tongue, kissing him as if she was dying of thirst, and she was surprised when he broke away to take them tumbling down on the bed.

"I've wanted to taste you from the moment I laid eyes upon you, chere," he said with a husky growl, his eyes devouring her like his words implied.

Pleasurable shivers coursed down her body, making her pussy cream with renewed need.

"So what are you waiting for?" she said tauntingly, lying back on her elbows. Something about him made her incredibly bold, like she'd fed off him and absorbed some of his essence inside her.

With intense eyes, he held her gaze as he moved down and settled between her thighs, pushing them wide apart. He cupped her mound, dipping his fingers inside her cunt and withdrawing them. She could see her frothy lubrication glistening on his fingers as he brought them to his lips and tasted her. His eyes darkened just before he closed them and groaned softly, as if he'd just tasted ambrosia.

He withdrew them and looked at her. The hunger was there again, so darkly sensual, it aroused her need to fevered heights. "I've never tasted anything so good in all my life, Cher. I could devour you and never appease this hunger."

"Oh god, Nigel, I want you to eat me. Please!" she said desperately, quaking with frantic need as he continued to stare at her, tormenting her with his nearness. She shouldn't feel like this, not after having so much pleasure, but she did. "Eat me until this fire goes out. I'm burning up."

"As you wish," he said hoarsely.

Raw heat fired her loins. Her breathing quickened as he planted his hands on her thighs and spread them further apart as he lowered his head. She nearly screamed when his fingers pulled her lips apart and his hot breath fanned over her damp flesh just as his tongue swiped a heated trail up her slit. Her clit throbbed with his nearness, begging as his rumble of pleasure vibrated through her slickness.

"Please, please lick it. Suck my clit. I can't stand it anymore," she said on a hoarse gasp, her throat aching with the need. "Lick me. Eat me," she begged.

Her thigh muscles jerked in response as he moved upward. She whimpered, choking on a cry as his lips at last locked over her clit.

She did scream then, her hips jerking upwards, grinding herself against his open mouth. He held her still, forcing her to accept his slow, sensual invasion. He tugged the swollen bud, swiping it with his tongue in a flickering, erratic move that had her cunt spasming with near orgasm. Her clit throbbed against his tongue, her sex swarmed with her rapid pulse and the beat of desire.

He tortured the bud, toying with it, his tongue rough, wringing whimpering cries from her throat. He moved one hand to plunge two fingers into her, setting her body into the awakening that occurred when completion was near.

Her muscles clutches his thrusting, curling fingers, tightening. Lightning seemed to sizzle along her nerve endings as he finger fucked her, driving her toward orgasm.

It leapt to life, whirling through her system in a torrent of feeling. She gasped, her muscles tensing, her fingers digging into the mattress like claws as he continued to lap at her clit and drive his fingers in and out.

Pleasure spiraled out of control, making her mindless with it, enveloping every sense until she was in tune and anticipating each lick, each suck and thrust. She rode the climax, trembling, and still he continued, pushing her past it into another, more intense. So intense she blacked out as it burst through her body. And finally, his thirst slaked, he stopped and moved up beside her, pulling her against his chest to stroke her back as she rode the high down to nothingness.

Warm, relaxed and more thoroughly sated than she could ever recall being in her life, Cher lay against him limply, half drowsing.

Nigel rolled back, propping his head in his hand as he studied her. "You've no notion of what any of this is about, do you, chere?"

Cher roused enough to lift her eyelids. "You're damn right I haven't got a clue. The sex I understand. But what was that little ritual thing in the yard? And what in the world is a Lycan?"

"Wolf folk."

Cher was wide awake now. "Wolf folk?" She frowned. "You called us shewolves," she remembered suddenly.

"The others were."

"The others were what?"

"Shewolves--Lycan--as I am. As is everyone else you saw when you came. You stumbled upon our mating rites, chere."

Cher sat up. "Wait a minute. I saw the look on their faces. They looked as scared as I was. Now you're trying to tell me they knew?"

He shrugged. "Some of them probably didn't even know they were Lycan--but no, they did not. I find them, bring them here, and the males vie for mates."

There was that aggressive male arrogance again. She glared at him. "What, exactly, are wolf folk?"

His eyes narrowed, gleaming predatorily. "Werewolves."

"You think you're a werewolf?" she asked uneasily.

He studied her a long moment. "You think those were mere mortal men out there?"

She shivered. "They were strung out on something, that's for sure."

"When the moon is full, the beast comes upon us-- whether we shift or not, the beast is barely within our control--and sometimes not at all."

She studied him skeptically. "So…. You're saying I'm a shewolf now? A werewolf?"

He shook his head. "You are human. That's why I tried to send you away. That's why I tried to protect you. I knew your chances for survival were not good if any lost control of their beast and bit you. Females--human females--rarely survive the transformation, which is why females are so sought after. This is why we have the hunts."

Cher frowned at him. "Ok--just so we're straight on this-- I'm not a shewolf, but you're a werewolf--so we're not mated."

"Almost correct," he murmured. "I'm Lycan. You're human. But we most definitely and thoroughly mated."

The End

DREAM SHADOWS

Angelica Hart

Chapter One

The dream closed around Violet with familiar warmth. It started a year ago and had increased as the nuptial auction drew near. She knew that it was only a dream, and that no one would save her from being coupled with a conjurer, a being whose power came from darkness and intensified in shadows.   She was a creature of the sun, yet they kidnapped her to train her as a proper spouse.

Violet twisted beneath the coverlets as the truth emerged. She hadn't been taken, simply sold, for despite the purity of her intent and soul, she had a rebellious streak that her family couldn't abide once her father had passed.   He wouldn't allow her to be sold. She remembered his words before he died. "My daughter, you have a light within that none will quench. In that light, your soul will speak. In that light, your spirit will thrive. In that light, you will learn control and the true nature of being of the sun caste."

When he died, her relatives thought only discipline and training mentors were strong enough to turn her into a docile and proper mate. Violet showed an unusual talent for magic and that instantly propelled her into training for the arts. She fit well and outmatched her peers, but she never fully became the compliant lady that everyone expected. Oh, she faked it well enough. Even with her stubborn nature, she could only take so much torture before submitting. They never broke her spirit, and she hoped that spirit would one day set her free of the Seraglio.

But not tonight, tonight she wanted only to slip into the ecstasy of the dream. Everything around her turned to wispy threads of fog except for the brass bed, strung with gauzy drapery. It wasn't the sensible iron bed of her cubicle. It belonged to the fantasy, where a sun mage claimed her in a world where the Seraglio didn't exist. Since childhood, the mage invaded her dreams. She welcomed the specter first as a friend and mentor, and then as a lover. As always, he appeared within seconds. She couldn't make out his features, but she sensed power and confidence; experienced warmth.

She held out her arms, and he drifted into them. She still didn't know who he was, nor could she see anything that would define him. He existed in mist, and her loins burned for him. When his arms closed around her, she felt his hard flesh rippling over his long muscular frame. Felt his breath as it stirred the tendrils of her hair. Felt his hands as they moved over the feminine length of her curves.

Closing her eyes, Violet melted against him, lips parting, accepting the bold invasion of his tongue and offering her own exploration as she had done so many times before. He ravished her mouth with sensual expertise, and she surrendered her will, for here she could, here no one would know, here she was free to experience and capitulate without consequence. They tasted each other for long minutes, her body molding itself to his. She couldn't get enough of this mage and found her lips at his throat, marking him with succulent kisses.

His hoarse moan spurred her confidence. She wrenched open the billowy shirt, popping buttons as her tongue trailed downward, tasting hard nubs, then lower to swirl about his belly button, then even lower. Would she dare this in reality? Would she be so bold? She who barely knew the look of a man and had never held a masculine hand? Violet didn't know. Perhaps she'd fight or run. It wasn't what they were taught. The talented beauties of both sun and shadow castes had been pooled together as treasures for the gifted of the realm. The girls were taught sensuous, compliant positions and submissive stances, taught to be at their husband's disposal in every way whether sexual, an assistant, a hostess, or a breeder. They were to be perfect in speech and manner and outlook, a reflection of their future husband. Violet could only be herself, and in her dreams she gave as she willed and the mage took all she offered. His breeches slipped down about his ankles as she found the male swell of him. She licked and teased and filled herself with his hardness, moving her head slowly back and forth, sucking as if she could devour the throbbing manhood of him.

He gasped, and then pulled her away, taking back control before she could utter any protest. Catching her up in his strong arms, he laid her across the bed, ripping away her nightdress as if it were no more substantial than the fog about them. He cupped her breasts, fondling them as his mouth once again found her lips. He wasn't in any hurry. It was as if she was a banquet and he intended to savor every morsel. And, oh how Violet yearned to be savored and taken with slow procrastination even as her body demanded instant release.

He took even more than she relinquished. He captured her wrists, holding them above her head as he spread her thighs with his knees. His mouth toyed with swollen nipples and his free hand played with the enflamed nub throbbing between folds of nether flesh. She arched to better feel his taunting. She begged for more with tiny whimpers and soft moans.

He obliged. His ravishment became rougher, more demanding. He squeezed her breasts with wild abandon. "More," she begged. "Please, more."

He didn't disappoint her. He forced her knees to her breasts until she was totally exposed to him, totally vulnerable to his cravings and her needs. He positioned himself at her opening, the hard, vivacious tip of him ripping into her in one deep long thrust. She caught her breath for she had forgotten the size of him and how pain mingled with pleasure at that first invasion.

Suddenly, though, the sweet eroticism of the dream evaporated. Rough hands pulled her to wakefulness and tossed her across the tidy, sparse chamber as if she were lighter than parchment. She smacked into the wall and knew bruises would soon mar her pale flesh. She was going to remind Sir Venore, the lead eunuch, that it wasn't wise to mark a lass so close to the nuptials, but seeing the extent of his fury, she thought better of it. Besides, they had balms that healed damages quickly.

"What is this?" Venore screamed as he held up a colorful rope that had taken her months to weave. Fibers *borrowed*, as she preferred to call it, from discarded rags and worn clothes to misplaced scarves and lost mittens. Well, at least her chamber sisters thought they lost a mitten or two.

Violet didn't even blink. Instead, she gathered herself up stiffly and kept her gaze on Venore's rather large feet strapped in leather sandals. She said, "It's a rope, sir."

She stole an upward glance and noticed the vein throbbing under his monk-like cap of graying hair. A green cassock with a scarlet-lined hood covered his bullish form while a medallion with the house crest identified his rank. The eunuchs weren't a religious order, but they were honored for their devotion to the training arts. Many saw it as a spiritual vocation. Violet doubted that any of the trainers chose to have his manhood eliminated. Their families had sold them, too. It always spurred a measure of compassion for them no matter how tough they had been on her.

"I know it's a rope," he spat, spraying her with frustrated spittle. "I want to know what you intend to do with it."

"That isn't what you asked," she responded with aplomb. Her sisters would have been in a pool of trembling tears by now. Violet refused to give him the satisfaction. She should have, though. Her continuous impertinence only enraged him more. "Considering the amount of times I've attempted escape, one would think you'd already know the answer."

Large, blunt fingers knotted a fistful of long, unruly blond hair and yanked her up off her feet. She expected something quite like this, yet couldn't hold back a small yelp. It wasn't enough to satisfy his rage, and he carried her by the roots of her hair through stone halls lit by torches whose walls dripped with condensation. There was a time when she would have kicked and screamed, hands ripping at his fingers to free herself, but it never did any good. At six-feet, five inches, and three hundred pounds of muscle and fury, she wasn't even close to a match for his strength. All she could do was to press stiff palms against her scalp to lessen the pain.

Violet, so named for her unusual dark, purple eyes looked as delicate and fragile as her name suggested. At five foot, three inches, her full breasts contrasted nicely against a waist tiny enough to accommodate a man's hand span. Slender hips tapered into tight thighs and calves. Her nose was a tender thrust of perfection while pink-tinged lips appeared just lush enough to demand a thorough kissing. Hair, twisted in an unrelenting mass of spiral curls, fell past her tiny, curved buttocks. It was those extraordinary eyes, though, dominating the heart-shaped countenance that could mesmerize any normal man. Those of the arts, though, weren't of the norm.

"I do not know why we put up with you!" Venore exploded as he carried her without effort.

"Because I'll fetch a fortune," she spat back through tears and whimpers, instantly regretting her remark as he shook her by the roots of her hair. Maybe her hair wouldn't hold. Maybe he'd pull every strand of it out and toss her into the forest, bald and empty-handed. Somehow the thought wasn't all that disconcerting. After all, at least she'd be free.

He froze, twisted her until she faced him, and with renewed rage, bypassed the instruction chamber where she had expected to be taken. Instead, he carried her up a flight of stairs until they reached the balcony outside the turret.

Night hovered over the valley like a stalking creature. Not even the moon creeping in and out of clouds dispelled the ominous shadows, nor did it illuminate the nocturnal crawlers that kept the villagers snug around hearths and under well-lit lanterns. Being born in a sun clan, shadows and darkness unnerved her. She preferred the sky littered with bright stars. Now, though, it wasn't just the unrelenting night that provoked a sensation of sand ants crawling under her skin ready to devour their prey from the inside. It was the chilled wind throttling her body. It was the emptiness beneath her feet. It was the moat far below riddled with carnivores.

Even more, it was Venore's fury-induced words. "Perhaps you are not worth the profit after all, Violet Haze."

* * * *

The blindfolded naked lass trembled, drool spilling from one corner of her mouth, but she did not cry out as the flogger marred her once smooth, pale breasts. She no longer had the strength for anything but whimpers. Her entire body, stretched like an X and anchored by chains to the floor and ceiling, resembled a patchwork of purple-black bruises and raw, crimson lines.

Lord Darth surveyed his work critically and watched the eyes of his caste, analyzing their desires. What would thrill them more, her instant death, additional punishment, or a show of raw lust? Those of the shadow caste craved perversion in all its fathomable depth, and this show of brutality and the promised lust-fest afterward fed his caste like ambrosia. Darth was once again bored.

He had gutted the spirit of many stolen from their homes and terrorized into submission. Their fear nurtured his dark soul, but it wasn't enough. He longed to devour a fighting spirit, a spirit who refused his dark advances, who would spit in his face with her dying breath knowing in the end she would be totally his no matter her protests. It was the battle that honed the evil within.

There was only one that honored him with that sort of courage, one that nearly brought him to his knees with her unrelenting fortitude and he had inadvertently killed her. He had bartered his soul to the Dark Master to secure the woman's heart, and despite all her fight, he had her love. She couldn't help it. The spell came from the fiend itself. The Dark Master, though, betrayed the bargain. Darth won the woman, but her mind shattered under his hellish torment. In turn, her death haunted him and enraged him simultaneously. Part of him wanted revenge. The rest of him wished another chance to draw the pain out slowly. He doubted he'd have that chance with any other. There was only one like her, and he had searched well.

He used to attend the nuptials every year and had purchased many girls. Few survived more than a couple of weeks, some only days. The peasants his minions confiscated barely made it a full night. This last girl was nearly gone and he hadn't even spent his seed. He doubted she'd outlive the dalliance now. At this point the thought of plunging into her near-lifeless body repulsed him. Dropping the whip, he cued the servants to allow his guests to feast on her spirit.

There was a time even her small soul would have tasted sweet. Now the submission was barely worth the effort. Little was worth the effort anymore, not even acquiring souls for the fiend. No one noticed the lord's melancholy. At six feet, nine inches tall and two hundred and fifty pounds of lean, raw muscle, Darth was the definition of evil. His onyx gaze, rimmed by kohl and devoid of light, could be changed to any shade with a willful blink. White-blond hair and death-pale flesh could equally be altered. Only his features remained the same, sharp and angular ones that boasted dark fascination. Many a lass surrendered to his haunting countenance. And all but one submitted more than her life.

Long blunt strides took Darth through the twists and turns of Shadow Manor, a fortress set high upon Spider-Wolf Mountain, so named for the amount of dens riddling the dense timberland that unraveled up the steep slopes. Spider-wolves didn't look much different than any other canine breed, except their teeth were larger and like a spider they had the ability to create webs. Enormous webs that trapped victims for days, allowing the beasts to slowly absorb their blood.

From outside the manor, there appeared to be no entrance or drawbridge to span the surrounding abyss. From within, a huge archway opened to the outside world. Many a guest walked right into the invisible barrier. It used to amuse Darth, but that no longer prompted even a smidgen of elation.

The lord paused at the waist-high circular Well of Misery. It was the origin of shadows and a place of vaporous death. Set opposite the entrance of the great hall, it squatted beneath a wall etching of Darth baring sharp teeth as he tormented an innocent soul. Leaning over the well, he braced large palms upon the stone ledge surrounding the well as he stared into its fathomless depths. The layers of darkness mesmerized him and the unthinkable entered his mind. If he tumbled in would he find Hell? Or would there be nothing but endless darkness, endless emptiness? The latter wouldn't be much worse than his current existence. Nothing amused him any longer. Nothing provided challenge. Not even the struggle to unleash shadows and claim the light. Everything remained status quo--an endless battle where each side lost and gained an equal measure of territory.

Few others could resist the luring whispers of the well, but Darth was immune to it and walked away with ease. He wasn't ready to have his questions answered. Surely, this banal existence possessed some thrills. Surely, there was more.

"If only…." he whispered and deliberately entered the salon on his right to view the single adornment in the room, a painting of daunting beauty, a nearly life-like image of the woman he loved. "Aye," he said to the vision. "I did love you, despite the torment I inflicted, despite the rage I vented. I loved you as I could never love again." That distant love was the only light Darth had ever encountered and it tasted like cool, honey-water.

With a thought, he willed the drapery of webs that covered the painting like a curtain to part. The vivid illusion drew a person much like the Well of Misery did. Darth had woven a spell into the painting, and men from commoners to nobility had lost their sanity to the woman in it. She would become real to the victims and they'd instantly become lovesick. Men could not pull themselves away, and those who did, wouldn't eat, wouldn't drink, and wouldn't move. He'd live out the remaining few days in a dream, a dream that ended in a nightmarish death. The same type of death that Darth felt every moment since the lass had lain shattered within his embrace.

"Milord, by your will, a moment?"

Darth turned, glaring at the youth who dared to interrupt his contemplation. A new member of the caste, he barely emitted a shadow, let alone comprehended his own talent. A more mature conjurer would have known to fetch a servant rather then risk his own hide for such a direct approach. Not that long ago, Darth would have smote the fool just for his audacity.

The idiot wasn't worth the exertion. With a flick of his hand, the web-curtain closed, and Darth moved out of the salon with Slith on his heels. "What is it you will of me?"

"A tremendous favor," Slith said, his hiss-like tone reflective of the snake symbols he wore. "I depart for the nuptials in the morn and was wondering if you could help with my purchase. It is said you can see any girl's soul and I wish to feed slowly and long on the one to be my mate, one that might even bear my line." Bowing his chin nearly to his chest, his voice became low, sketchy. "And it is known I lack experience in the art and as a lord. I would forever be in your debt if you could guide my choice."

"That you are in the caste and that I allow you to draw your next breath makes you obliged to me. However, I might cast a crumb your way if I still attended the nuptials. As of late, I find them exceedingly droll and devoid of worthy merchandise."

"Oh but my Lord, it is said the Seraglio has outdone itself. They have trained only the brightest and most lovely of the clans. Some are said to actually possess talent, and others have pure, untainted spirits. This will be a selection beyond all its predecessors. Even if you don't guide me, it would be a shame to miss such a showing."

Darth had enough of this talk and would have left the lord in mid-sentence if the man hadn't reached into his robe and snapped open the invitation. Within the parchment folds, an access arch evolved. Seraglio never spared the coin in its advertisements, but this time they outdid themselves with such a costly charm. Although it lacked voice, a quick showing of all the merchandise unfolded. Young women from every part of the kingdom appeared and disappeared in a continuous array of sparkling eyes, tempting forms and enticing smiles. None of them excited Darth. He was beyond the physical hook that prompted both men and lords to act like slobbering fools.

Darth was about to walk away for the second time when an angelic vision caught his gaze. Grabbing the invitation from Slith, he ordered a halt. It paused on the wrong lass. "Back one," he barked.

The charm obeyed. He stared for an endless moment, his pulse racing in a way it hadn't in years. "Be gone!" he said to Slith.

Slith reached for the charm, but Darth clutched it within a white-knuckled grip and vanished in a spiral of smoke.

* * * *

"Venore!"

Kanith, regulator of the instruction chamber, spat the eunuch's name as if it were a threat. "The hierarchy will have you gutted if you destroy a prime lass just before nuptials!"

With a slew of curses that would make a ruffian blush, Venore yanked Violet roughly back onto solid footing, and then still holding her by the hair, he dragged her until they reached the instruction chamber.

The regulator eyed her with an elaborate sigh. "You will never learn, will you?"

Violet whimpered and hated herself for showing such weakness.

This wasn't her first time in the chamber, and it probably wouldn't be the last even this close to the nuptials.

Although she doubted she'd have any company. In fact, it had been a month since any lass other than Violet had graced its dour walls.

Venore dropped the rope at Kanith's feet at the same instant that he released Violet. "This was found outside the lass's window. She actually cut away a stone, hid it in the open nook and replaced the stone. If we hadn't had a tremor this last day, she might have actually kept it hidden. Instead, it fell free along with the stone which nearly bopped Sir Dankask on the noggin!"

Violet winced, but only because she liked Sir Dankask. It would have been awful if he had gotten hurt because of her actions.

"What do you have to say for yourself, lass?" Venore demanded.

Violet massaged her scalp and mewed softly. The one good thing about pain was that it always felt so wonderful when it stopped. "I'm sorry?"

Venore sighed. "It is useless. It might just be worth the gutting to have the pleasure of silencing her."

"Aye, but look at her. What she lacks in sense and obedience she makes up for in beauty and light. You know how the dark caste are drawn to those of the light."

"Aye," Venore returned. "But once they look at her record, they will throw her to the wolves."

Violet suppressed a smile. She had been in the forest enough times to know she could survive the wolves, even the spider-wolves. In fact, she had learned their ways and could safely nestle herself in a den without harm. She actually used to play with the beasts until the Seraglio realized how easily she escaped and adapted to the wilds. Since then, they had kept her imprisoned.

It was the dark conjurers that terrified her, and that is what the Seraglio had planned for her. They had honed her to be the wife of a dark lord. Not that it meant a lord of light might not claim her, but she didn't want to be married to just anyone who had the coin. She wanted to be free, free to choose, free to love, free to find the one that invaded her dreams. He probably didn't exist. He was nothing more than mist and wish, and she was a fool to think it could be anything more. Still, she'd rather have the dream than her reality. Somehow she had to escape-- she couldn't allow herself to be purchased like chattel.

"The nuptials are only days away. Do not mark her," Venore said, ripping away her flimsy garment with a single motion.

Kanith shook his head at the fresh slew of bruises decorating her back. "Looks like you already took care of that."

Venore winced, then stared directly into Violet's eyes. "There is not one, not a solitary one, who has ever enraged me so thoroughly this close to the nuptials."

A toothy grin spread across Kanith's face. "Then you have a short memory, Venore. There was one, don't you remember?"

Rolling his eyes, Venore's fists clenched and unclenched. "I try not to remember."

"Must be the color of the eyes. She had the same eyes."

"Of course she did. It's a family trait."

"My family has blue and gray eyes," Violet interjected, feeling as if something dark had invaded the chamber. "My coloring is just a fluke that can't be explained."

"You don't know, do you?" Venore said with a satisfied edge to his tone.

"Know what?"

"You have your mother's eyes."

"Nay, she had blue eyes like my father."

"That is what your clan told you."

"It is the truth."

"Have you ever seen a painting of her, or a window charm?"

"I was conceived upon the nuptial night and she died at my birth. There hadn't been time to contract a painter or mage to construct a window."

"They had window charms. After all, your father was a renowned mage in his time. He created our charm windows. That is when he first saw her, and amassed a small fortune so he could purchase her. They didn't tell you her eye color, for if you mentioned it once, all would know of her and relate the tale. Since your family intended to send you here, they didn't want you to seek out the truth while in training. Your family didn't wish you to be even more disruptive than you are. After all, they had had been shamed enough by your mother's betrayal."

"What betrayal?"

"She deserted your father for a shadow lord."

Chapter Two

Daniore paced before the throne, his haunted gaze defying the King's glare. "You may be King of the Illumi, but you no longer have authority over your son."

"He joined the caste to make certain of it, but mage or not, he still owes the kingdom and I *will* have an heir."

Daniore paused and turned, feet braced apart, one hand on the hilt of a sword, the other upon a stiletto. "Myith has produced numerous heirs."

King Pathros sprang upright and mirrored Daniore's stance. "Myith is a twit who has married a twit. I will not pass the kingdom on to a brood of twits."

If the situation weren't so grave Daniore would have smiled. He couldn't fault the King's logic. Myith was indeed a twit, a sweet, muddled, brainless twit that you couldn't help adore, but equally couldn't depend upon. It wouldn't have been so horrid if she had married a somber wise man. Instead, she chose the court jester, literally!

"Those children have lineage, Sire. I am certain one will prove wise enough to--"

"Silence!" the King commanded, his voice even more authoritative than his looks.

Despite his simple attire of leather jerkins and tunic, a corded belt, and a hand-honed sword, King Pathros reeked of royalty from the wealth of dark locks to jade-green eyes. No one would ever mistake him for anything but the monarch. In contrast, Daniore wore court fancy with a long burgundy waistcoat, pale leggings, a striped ascot, and a cocked hat. The attire drew unwanted attention to his bulky frame while the delicate purple hat, perched on his wheat colored hair made him look like a buffoon. The mage had told him this was the proper dress for the encounter. He now knew that he had been played a fool, and would get his own back. It was a game between friends, but he never expected it during such a serious assignment.

"You will tell my son I command him to attend the nuptials to purchase a spouse and produce an heir. At a suitable age, the first born male will take his place here and learn the ways of leadership like my son should have done."

Daniore lifted a well-formed brow, not at all perturbed by the King's show of authority. "He had no choice but to follow his calling," Daniore casually returned. "The talent was too obvious to hide."

Pathros sunk back into the throne and sighed. "Aye, he had no choice, but if there had been any way at all, I would have kept him by my side. It is not easy keeping the balance, but we cannot allow the darkness to encroach on any of our territory. If only the legend was true. If only there was, indeed, one to be born who'd sweep the darkness into the bowels of Hell from whence it came. Then there would be no need for this constant vigilance."

The weariness in Pathros gaze, the deep worry lines bracketing his mouth, softened Daniore's heart. Would it be so horrible for his friend to purchase a mate? True, the mage already had someone he preferred, but that someone was totally unattainable. And he never made time for any other sort of dalliance. Alas, he didn't even make the time for this interview and asked Daniore to go in his place.

Daniore's large hand clenched into a fist and he slammed it against his heart as his heels clicked. "As you will, Milord. I will convey your wishes and make certain they are followed fully."

Pathros nodded and waved Daniore away. Another salute followed but Daniore's heavy steps betrayed his misgivings. He should never have put himself in the middle of father and son. There were only two outcomes, and Daniore would end up infuriating either his king or his friend.

* * * *

Eyes the color of coal, skin bronzed from the sun, small, delicate body molded to perfection, and features refined as if by an artisan, Amlet was the most valuable product that the Seraglio had to offer. It wasn't just her looks. It was the sweet submissive quality that drew coin. She would bend her will to any man be he of the light or of the shadows. She'd break herself for his longings and forfeit her life for his needs. In total opposition to Violet's obstinacy, she was a tonic to Venore's frayed nerves. "Fetch me an ale," he ordered the girl.

A sweet smile tilted apricot-tinted lips. "Of course, Milord, it is an honor to serve you."

Vernore sighed. Aye, this was exactly what he needed. Next he'd have her massage his tired muscles with warm oil. He could just see commanding such of Violet. She'd probably pour the ale over his head and use boiling oil as an ointment.

"It pains me to see you so troubled, sir," Amlet said in her gentle tone as she handed him cool ale in his favorite horn. "If there is any way at all that I can soothe your worries, please let me know."

Indeed the girl was a treasure. He truly hated putting her on the plank, but he kept her as long as he dared and it was time to reap the profit of such careful training. "A massage, sweet."

She undressed him with such precise, expert movements that it was nearly as if the clothes vanished. Her hands pressed just enough, eliciting moans of pleasure as she released each knot of tension in turn. If he was not a eunuch, this was the mate he would have chosen for life. Only death would have separated them. Of course, it was the only way to divorce oneself of a wife and it kept the women docile, compliant, and even eager to serve, for there was no casting off or separation. A purchased wife's only escape was through death. Violet wouldn't last very long as a wife. It saddened him somehow.

Violet had a kind heart, always helping her Seraglio sisters, always ready to take their punishment to save them the pain, always honest to a fault. The right man could turn her stubbornness into spirit, but he doubted any would have the patience for such things. She would have been better off as an Amazon but she had not been bred of that land and the female warriors had no need for nuptials.

Amlet's delicate fingers held surprising strength as she worked his calf muscles. "Is it Violet that troubles you so?"

"Aye, she is in the instruction chamber even now."

"Oh, how sad. I hope Sir Kanith doesn't mark her. She will already be so hard to sell."

"You are wrong, sweet. What she lacks in attitude she makes up for in beauty and spirit. There is not one among your sisters who outshines her." Face down on the lounge Venore didn't notice Amlet's lips tightening. "There are those who would happily pay a high price to rape a spirited virgin just for the joy of beating her into submission."

Amlet moved her hands up and down the backs of his thighs, adding more warm oil and digging her thumb into any resistant flesh. "She does not seem the type who'd submit no matter what they do to her. After all, she is still a trial to you and the punishments here are…." She paused, her voice catching. "So intense."

"We have boundaries, sweet. After all, we cannot sell damaged merchandise. A husband has no such compunction, and she will either submit or break. I'd wager my job that the latter will occur very swiftly."

"Such a waste."

"Aye, but soon it will be out of my hands."

Amlet finished the massage at his feet, and then automatically went to fill the surround, knowing a bath normally followed a massage.

"Wait," he said, pulling himself up into a sitting position. "Fetch the illusion crystals first. I have need of escape."

"Aye sir," she said and pulled out a tall bottle filled with various colored crystal candies of odd sizes and shapes.

He took it from her and spilled several into his hands. "What should it be tonight?"

As if knowing his thoughts before he did, she knelt between his thighs.

He smiled. She knew his mind so well. He popped a candy into his mouth. Within a moment, his mind would trick him into believing he was still a virile man. He motioned for Amlet to move forward. She obeyed, wrapping her full lips around his limp member and sucking. Nothing happened in reality, but in his mind he swelled and throbbed. After many minutes of pumping, he ejaculated a stream of semen into her willing mouth.

Amlet's gaze lifted, watching the eunuch twitch and moan. She had all she could do not to gag. His mimicry of sexuality repulsed her, but he never suspected. Not one of them had suspected in all the years that she had used this body to achieve the Dark Master's will. Once there had been a lass, docile and sweet as Amlet pretended to be. Cora still existed, existed like a puppet deep inside the body shell, living day by day by Amlet's will when the sorceress' spirit sought another temporary host. She couldn't risk using Amlet's body when she practiced her craft or sought the Dark Master's counsel or when she needed to be her own viperous self. Last week Amlet didn't depart from the body. Everything had to be perfect.

She pulled away from the eunuch and flipped her hand upward. "Sleep!"

Venore fell backward and snored.

Tired of playing submissive to this fool, she planted the suggestion of a perfect evening within his mind. It freed her to seek a sacrifice. After all, only blood could ensure the potency of her power and within just days, her power had to be at its peak.

Leaving the chamber, she put Amlet's body to bed and let her spirit roam. The pub just outside the Seraglio would be bursting with those attending the nuptials. Diving into a tall, vivacious lass with an ample bosom and full hips, she sashayed into the bar. It would be easy to lure one of the drunken patrons into a dalliance. After the fun, she'd drain his spirit and his blood. Just the thought intoxicated her, and she was as close to being pleased as a demon could ever achieve.

Only moments before catching the eye of a swaggering dupe of the shadow caste, her gaze settled on the body of a young girl, hooded and chained to the wall, spread-eagled. Although rules forbade any to penetrate the girl, all were allowed to touch and torment as long as the marks weren't lasting.

A rough looking man with a full beard and eye patch nibbled one of the girl's nipples. Another man played with her other breast, squeezing and slapping it alternately. Yet another used a strap against her splayed open triangle. Every now and then, a man would shove a torturer aside and claim his place. Amlet wondered how receptive they would be to her taking a turn. What a lusty, perverted prelude to her evening that would be. Before she could take a step in that direction, a man with brooding good looks, aquiline nose, firm jaw and jutting cheekbones stepped forward. He had no insignia to mark his caste or clan, but his bearing spoke of nobility. His lean tight muscles covering a medium stature belied the true intensity of his strength. His eyes were a remarkable shade of gold and green while ebony hair, layered almost like a lion's mane, sported a singular swath of silver from right brow to tip, betraying he used the arts well and often. His black leather garments, adorned with an onyx handled sword and matching dagger, could just as easily be of the shadows or of the light, and strangely Amlet couldn't see beyond the obvious to figure out which.

With several swift and precise maneuvers, he tossed each man away from the lass, and then drew his sword. He didn't say a word, but there was something about his stance and bearing that elicited a threat more daunting than if he had ten men standing behind him. Grumbling, the small crowd fell away. Amlet watched as his gaze ravished the girl. He held out a hand as if to touch her, but yanked it away just as quickly.

He turned to the robed man downing ale just a few feet away. Few things shocked Amlet, but she didn't expect to find a eunuch in the pub let alone one of the ranks. Her gaze jerked back to the chained lass. Kanith actually dared to use the ultimate torment on none other than the obstinate Violet.

* * * *

Violet willed herself not to cry, but she couldn't stop shivering and silent screams echoed in her mind. How could Sir Kanith do this to her? It was against the rules to take a lass from behind the Seraglio's walls. Then again, she went entirely against regulations when she slapped him.

But Venore's words had shattered her world. Her family had lied. Violet was a copy of her mother. She, too, had been sold to the Seraglio. She, too, tried to escape but ended up sold to Violet's father, Sol, who grieved her death until his own only a few years earlier.

But it wasn't hearing the truth that infuriated Violet. It was Kanith's cutting remark that Tama was a slut. Violet refused to believe her mother willingly deserted Sol for a shadow lord. Upon Sol's knee, Violet reveled in her father's stories of funny moments and intense love he had shared with his wife. It had to be a spell that her father couldn't rebuke. Only, who would have dared such a thing? Her father's power had been legendary, and beyond what any expected from the son of a warrior.

A man didn't have a choice to the clan he had been born into. That was blood, family. However, upon his twenty-second year he chose to serve either the One or the Dark Master. It didn't matter if he was a merchant, laborer, warrior, or royalty. All had to decide before they chose a profession or a mate. Commoners worked side by side no matter the choice. Warriors, royalty, and those of the castes, light mages and shadow conjurers, stood apart and waged war between good and evil.

Sol said Tama was of the light, pure, unsullied. How could she have been drawn to a conjurer? It had to be beyond her control. Violet couldn't think on that any longer. She had to get past this moment and the feel of filthy hands mauling her.

She willed her mind to retreat. She willed herself not to experience. It took every ounce of magic she possessed but she willed herself to sleep, and with sleep came the dream and the stranger. The stranger who parted the shadows and promised her succor. With small whimpers she spread herself for him, welcomed him into her bed, and pleaded with him to take her away from the torment.

"Shhh," he whispered. "You are with me now. Feel what they are doing, but it is me."

And it happened. The suckling of nipples became his lips wrapped around her taut buds. The massaging fingers became his, stirring wild sensations within her. If pain invaded, it dulled under his endless caresses. She could barely breathe under the hood, but it was now because of his potent kisses, fierce and endless, stealing her breath away.

"Come for me," she pleaded.

"I am coming," he said.

"I'm so scared."

"There is nothing to fear. Give me your heart and I will protect it always."

"Who are you?"

"Soon you'll know. You'll see me in the light."

"Hurry."

"Shh, soon," he whispered, and the dream intensified. He was inside her thrusting, slow gentle thrusts, taking her beyond veracity. Moans bled into the mask. Her pulse raced. Her body burned. She met every plunge with a thrust of her hips. The torment without could no longer touch her, for she was with him. He was real. He would come for her.

Every movement claimed her anew and in a moment she'd shatter, but before she could, the dream dissolved and her body cried out in protest as pain claimed her muscles.

She felt herself freed of the chains, but somehow that made the agony worse. Tears clogged her eyes and blocked her nose. She couldn't breathe. Panic set in and she fought with inefficient blows and kicks.

"It's okay. It's coming off," a masculine voice assured.

The hood fell away and she gulped night air, but she couldn't stop the tears, couldn't stop shaking. Darkness and wind fell on her naked form, but someone wrapped a cloak about her with more gentleness than she had ever experienced. "You're going to be okay," a voice whispered against her ear.

The tears blinded her from her champion's face. Somehow, she managed a thank you, but it was just a hushed whisper. For the first time in her young life, she let go. All the fight left her. For this moment, this solitary moment, they won. Only, it wasn't because of torment. It was through kindness. The stranger who held her, who carried her close to his chest, who whispered soothing words, managed what all the torture could never achieve. She submitted.

* * * *

"Help me take her down," the dark-haired man ordered. "No lass should be used and displayed."

"She needed a lesson, a good one."

The stranger's face tightened. His voice became low, almost a whisper, but Amlet's keen hearing picked up every syllable. "I'd venture to say your superiors would not approve of such a lesson. Now help me take her down or I will claim her here and now as my bride, the Seraglio will make a little less profit, and I will not have to part with my coin."

Kanith blanched. It was well known that if a eunuch did anything to devalue a lass, they would make up for it with his hide. He would be sold as food for the spider-wolves that howled at the city gates.

The stranger carried her gently out the door. Her moans and sobbing tore at his heart. "Get that hood off!"

Kanith obeyed.

"There's a cloak in my saddle bag, there," he said, indicating the steed tethered to a post. "Get it."

Again Kanith immediately responded, retrieved the cloak, and tucked it around Violet.

"Now take me to her room."

"I can't--"

"You will!"

Kanith led the man through the back way into the Seraglio and up several flights of stairs that passed the more luxurious chambers of the eunuchs to that of merchandise. He unlocked Violet's small chamber and stepped aside.

The man gently eased her onto the cot and pushed her hair aside so he could regard her face. "Is she still a virgin or did you take that from her as well?"

"She is still pure. I'm not that stupid."

The man gave him a look that implied the opposite. "What's her name?"

"Violet Haze."

"What did she do that was so wrong?"

"Slapped me."

The man grinned. "Not one of the more docile of the brides, eh?"

"Docile? A crazed spider-wolf is more docile than this lass."

"Why do you keep her?"

"Look at her," was all Kanith said.

"Aye," the man returned. "You should take better care of your merchandise and learn the value of compassion. The sun warms the cloak off a man whereas the cold only makes him clutch it more tightly. Same holds true for a lass."

Violet moaned and scanned his face, seemingly aware of him but not quite. He softly kissed her brow, and then whispered, "You have a light within that none will quench. In that light, your soul will speak. In that light, your spirit will thrive. In that light, you will learn control and the true nature of being of the sun caste."

Violet had heard those words before. At the moment she couldn't place them, and fatigue and pain claimed her so quickly, she couldn't even respond as the stranger took his leave.

Kanith let loose a long, scared breath. He had gone too far taking Violet to the pub, but she just pushed him beyond endurance. He doubted Venore cared what he did to her as long as she could stand on the plank without aid at the nuptials. Even now the urge to torment her nearly overwhelmed him, but she was totally unconscious and he doubted that she would feel it.

Besides, he recognized the stranger. He was lucky to have survived the encounter. He had heard that a man could die at Lord Ash's hand for simply crossing his shadow.

* * * *

Anxiety hovered over the Seraglio like fog on the moors. Even the brides longing for a husband knew a beast could purchase them as easily as a prince. They had to be at their best, to show their beauty and submissiveness, to display their talent but not show off, for both conjurers and mages alike had an ego one should not overshadow.

Violet didn't care one iota about their egos. If she had her way a wife would be equal to her husband. Sun would light the day and stars would brighten the night. They said there had been a time that the kingdom had been different, that women had a say in their lives, and then the shadows crept into existence, bringing about change. The women who rebelled became Amazons who lived in the deep forests and treated men as slaves. That was no better than the way men treated the women of the kingdom. Violet prayed to the One that the legend of old was true, and that one day a mage of sufficient purity and strength would destroy the shadow beings.

Panic emerged at the thought of being sold to a shadow lord. How would she survive? Her craft would be lost in darkness. It would be swallowed up whole and her spirit would dwindle until she was nothing more than a puppet for a dark lord to prey upon. And if she ripened with his seed, how would she raise her children? How did one teach them that dark was right? She'd rather die than live in the shadows, and die she would after her display on the plank. They would have no choice but to free her or slaughter her. For none would dare to buy a lass as brazen as she.

Chapter Three

Mirrored wall sconces lit the Seraglio's central hall on nuptial day. The circular chamber displayed rows of balconies with luxurious chairs and tables. Those of the highest rank claimed the best view of the plank, which occupied central stage. Venore, donned in a crimson gold-edged robe, slipped his finger over the charm viewer positioned at the head of the plank. One poke at a scripted name brought up a lass's three-dimensional image as well as her stats from her birth clan to her disposition and her craft level.

A blunt fingertip jabbed Violet's name. He sighed at the marks against her obedience record, but he knew there were those who craved the spirit she possessed. If only she knew the discipline had been for her protection. Only the most submissive or shrewd women survived in the kingdom. Violet was neither. They'd devour her like a delectable sweet. Venore had done his best, and could only offer a prayer that the One would be merciful and place her with a husband who'd nourish her spirit rather than destroy it.

Venore touched the charm's side and another list appeared. He reviewed the names of the clientele who had arrived. Many attended in disguise, but Venore knew who was in every box seat. Usually, only one box remained empty, but even that lord had arrived. Venore's spirit fell. He now knew who would purchase Violet. He knew that just as Violet had mirrored her mother's rebellion in life, she would mirror it in death. The eunuch could not worry about her now and focused on the auction and clientele.

He had just enough time to make certain the novice eunuchs, dressed in severe black, served refreshments with sufficient respect and elegance. The Seraglio catered to its elite and tried to make each customer feel they were privileged. Indeed they were, for only mages and conjurers, the warriors of Heaven and Hell, were invited to the nuptials. Commoners bargained with family for their wives, and unmarried girls ended up as servants in either their own households or others. Royalty offered their daughters as bargaining chips.

Some women fled to the Amazons, who slaughtered the weak and accepted the strong. Other rebellious souls wandered to the mountains, but all knew that meant death for the land held nothing but endless winter. Survival taught women ways to enchant men, to submit to them. Yet some managed an underhanded way of controlling them as well. A very select few rose to the rank of sorceress, but that meant being in league with the Dark Master.

In the floor above the hall, Amlet stood still and silent. She had chosen that course rather than be subservient to any man. She never regretted her actions, and now was a major player in the battle for control. Today wasn't the first or last step toward eliminating every sun clan, but it was an important one. Over the last few nights she had made blood sacrifices and now possessed undiluted power. She would manipulate the proceedings to her will.

Across the hall, Violet was the only other one who was silent and very still. Some girls paced, others prayed, still others fussed with their attire or hair. Many chatted in hushed tones. All learned to control tears, but hugs were exchanged and promises that they would somehow stay in touch. A few would even manage to keep that vow for they would be sold into the same clan. Most, though, wouldn't. They grew up as sisters, and now most would find themselves in opposing clans or castes.

Amlet might even manipulate Violet's sale. Not to help the lass, but to dispose of her quickly. Fortunately, Violet didn't realize she had the power to become a rival sorceress if she slipped into shadows. Equally as providential, Violet didn't know that mated to the right mage she had the potential to raise a child of light that could destroy Amlet's master. If she had her way, Amlet would have destroyed the girl long ago, but the Dark Master had hopes of drawing her into shadow. Amlet would not allow that. She would have no rival, but she had to be careful that the Master did not know she had a hand in Violet's demise.

A clang sounded. Silence, still and dark as a moonless night, devoured the chamber as the first lass stepped into the cage that was lowered to the plank.

* * * *

Lord Ash, attired in a similar leather outfit from a few nights hence, settled into his box. A fresh charm window could be activated to display the various wares. Ash found the purchase of a wife archaic, despite its expediency. Still, if clan and friends hadn't been so persistent in prodding him toward this endeavor, he would have put it off yet again. Exploring the craft had absorbed every moment of his thoughts and quite a few of his dreams. He didn't have time for a wife or family, but such was the way of the kingdom and he could no longer evade his responsibility.

Besides, there was one out there that claimed his heart, one he didn't really know, but yet felt such an intense connection to, that he knew her to be real. Months had bled into years and he never even came close to finding the lass and had finally given up. Now, he had obligations to fulfill and would stop thinking about the dream. It was time.

Using the charm window he flashed through the merchandise, wincing at what the Seraglio considered attributes. Finally, he came to Violet Haze and couldn't help grinning at her record. The eunuchs certainly earned their coin with this one. She was a handful and obviously didn't want to be a wife. He could purchase her and set her free. Wouldn't that stir the Seraglio and his own clan to a frothy rage? If he had the time to deal with the consequences, he would do so just for the fun of it. He didn't have such leisure and decided to spend his coin on the pretty, submissive Amlet. One who'd just do her duty and remain in the background. The more she bored him, the more dedicated he'd become to the craft, and the more time he'd have for dreaming.

A loud bong claimed his attention as the first lass exited her cage. Her hand-made white satin gown dipped over sun-bronzed shoulders, gathered under small but firm breasts, and then trailed to delicate slipper-covered feet. A touch of face enhancement had been applied and sweet breaths, a tiny white flower, had been braided into her lengthy chestnut colored hair. Each lass made her own garment to prove she could clothe her family if the need ever arose. The bronzed skin and face adornments proved she would always look her best.

A trained voice emerged, announcing her name, talents and submissive rank of ten, the highest level of attainment. A simple dance and a demonstration of her craft followed. She plucked a rose out of the air along with a tiny shower of glitter to dust the pink petals. It was a simple spell, proving she could be a capable assistant yet not powerful enough to surpass her husband. No master of either shadow or sun wanted to battle his own spouse for domination of the craft.

"The bidding begins at one-hundred thousand gold coin," announced Venore, the acoustics of the chamber amplifying his voice to cut through the muted chatter slithering among the patrons.

Several novice mages emerged from their box seats to view the lass closely. A few returned without bidding, but a volley of warring bids emerged in loud, excited voices until the lass sold for triple the amount. The older caste members knew better than to bid on the first batch, for the Seraglio reserved the finest for last. However, novice conjurers and mages didn't have the finances to wait regardless of their caste's wealth. They were only to bring in coin that they themselves had accumulated. Of course, many families helped their offspring earn their coin.

After the tenth lass, similarly attired, performed an almost identical dance and demonstrated the same spell, Ash decided to place a bid on the very next girl and not bother waiting for Amlet. He wanted to be done with it. They were all replicas of each other--different hair color and complexions, slightly different movements, shapes and stances--but so much the same that it didn't matter who he chose.

Only the next lass happened to be Violet. Unlike the others, she didn't wear white, nor did she wear a gown. A silk amethyst colored top hugged her breasts while low-slung pants with transparent, billowing legs matched the sheer fluttering sleeves of her blouse, both pinched at wrists and ankles with golden braids. A satin ribbon caught the wealth of her hair and simple cloth slippers adorned tiny feet. The cascade of hushed whispers halted.

A mischievous smile appeared on the lass's delicately etched countenance. Not a shred of face enhancement had been applied. Her flesh remained free of sun bronzing and there was nothing submissive about her stance.

"I am Violet Haze," her tiny voice proclaimed. "My greatest talent resides in the ability to run like the wind and escape the confines of any imprisonment. My obedience level," a sweet, totally impish laugh emerged, "is a minus one."

A collective gasp filtered through the hall, yet a few chuckles could be heard as well. Lord Ash shook his head and laughed aloud. Venore looked as if someone had just punched the wind out of him.

"Now, I suppose you expect me to dance for your enjoyment? I think not," she proclaimed, her sweet, angelic sounding voice so in opposition to her statement.

Instead of a dance, she performed a feat of warrior patterns, ones that proved she could defend herself well if the need arose. She did everything she could to offend and deter any from wanting her as a wife, but all she managed was to entice those bent on breaking a lass's spirit.

Lord Ash no longer laughed. Fear prompted a cold sweat. The lass couldn't possibly know the element she attracted with her willfulness. Ash couldn't allow her to flounder in her own stupidity. Ignoring stringent rules, he wove a spell to still the girl's obstinate nature. It unraveled and evaporated. To his astonishment, the girl had a spell protector in place.

That wasn't the only surprise. She slipped right into demonstrating her craft. Unlike the single rose most of the other girls produced, an array of various wild flowers rained upon the entire length of the plank. Glitter didn't follow either. Twin rocks thumped to the plank. Her voice became husky. Her pupils widened until they nearly covered the irises. Thunder echoed through the hall, glasses rattled, torchlight dimmed. The rocks blurred and a white vapor appeared. Through the mist, loud roars could be heard. As the fog evaporated, snarling lions emerged, clawing the air.

"Be still," she ordered, and they obeyed. With determined steps she walked down the plank toward the nearest box seat, fingers freeing her locks as she moved. A conjurer jumped up at her approach, and she stilled him with a wave of her hand, freed his dagger from its sheath, and severed the length of her tresses. The remaining locks layered themselves to her shoulders, rendering an even more enticing and mature visage to the lass. Before anyone could react, she returned the dagger and strode back to the lions that prowled the plank like sentinels. Her severed locks twisted in the air as gentle words spilled from lush lips. Braided leashes appeared and attached themselves to the lions' throats. She gathered the ends in her hands and brought the animals to heel.

No one moved. No one spoke. Not a breath could be heard. Everything remained still until Violet released the leashes and clapped her hands. The lions disappeared. The torchlight brightened.

"Not one of you will purchase me now. Your choice is to either kill me or release me. Either way I will be free."

* * * *

From her vantage point Amlet grinned. She didn't have to aid Violet one iota toward her destruction. The girl did a fine job on her own leaving Amlet liberated to contemplate which of the two most valued alliances would be best. She could wed a shadow lord and spawn a demon that would bring a reign of darkness or she could choose the purest sun mage and corrupt him and his caste until only the Dark Master reigned. Either one would be a challenge, starting with manipulating their bids, but she was more than up to it.

As she contemplated her options, she stepped into the cage waiting to be lowered to the plank after Venore slit Violet's throat. After her display, the eunuch had no other option.

Amlet didn't expect the pandemonium that broke out beneath her. She didn't expect the ensuing bidding war. Mostly, she didn't expect Violet to be purchased by one of the two lords she had intended for herself.

"No!" Violet screamed from the plank, attempting to run from the hall. An enormous eunuch snatched her up and tossed her easily back on the plank. She attempted to grab his sword by using levitation, but too many of the craft joined, broke her protection spell, and bound her with astonishing ease. She would have summoned the lions back. Only, they were nothing more than illusion and all knew it. "No," she uttered with such helplessness it touched more hearts than she would have ever suspected.

After dropping the appropriate coin in Venore's open palm Lord Darth knelt beside her his voice soft, coaxing. "Hush, child, it will be all right. I promise."

Violet lifted her gaze to the most mesmerizing eyes she ever saw. Clear and blue, it was as if she could see right through to his soul. A mage had purchased her, not the dark lord the Seraglio had thought she should serve. She had been prepared for death, and now to discover she would once again live in the light was more than she could have ever imagined. Only, she couldn't imagine why he would want such a defiant being as her.

He grinned and responded as if reading her mind. "Talent like yours should be honed, not wasted. Now, if I free you, will you behave?"

She nodded affirmation and found she could move again. Darth helped her up, and then in the tradition of the hall, tossed her fragile weight over his shoulders and strode toward the door. Violet glanced up once and saw a man being held back by two eunuchs.

"She is mine!" he shouted. "I gave the final bid. Darth silenced it! Let me go."

There was something about him that tugged at her, something familiar and warm. Yet, it was obvious he belonged to the dark caste. Unlike the lord who purchased her, donned in shades of ecru, that man wore unrelenting black. Even the hilt of his sword and stiletto were made of obsidian. Oh how very close she came to being his and living a life in darkness, a short life to be sure, knowing what those of that breed did to their wives.

At that moment, his gaze met hers. Such anguish and appeal seeped from them, such magnetism that she felt drawn, as she had never felt drawn to anyone before. It took every ounce of her will to sever his hold. She buried her face against Lord Darth and willed herself not to look back.

"Violet, look at me!" the stranger shouted. "Don't be deceived."

Violet didn't obey. She just clung to her owner, knowing that a single visit to the nuptial chamber would make her his wife.

Darth felt the tension ease out of Violet. Darkness invaded his cool blue gaze, turning it back to ebony as a half-grin twisted his lips.

Chapter Four

"Where are you going?" Daniore asked, a large palm gripping Ash's arm to stop him from mounting a stallion.

"Where in blazes do you think?" he snapped back, ignoring the bustling about him. Lords carried their purchases to ornate carriages while commoners gawked from the other side of guarded barriers and vendors plied all with food and drinks.

"You owe it to your father to get back in there and purchase a wife."

"I owe it to my conscience to get that lass out of Darth's clutches."

"I'll go after her."

"No! She is my responsibility."

Daniore folded his arms across his massive chest and leaned back on his heels. "And just how is that?"

"I should have realized someone like him would play dirty. I should have had protection about me. Even that snip of a girl had protection about her until the dark lords combined strength to break it." Ash squeezed his eyes shut. "I had the last bid."

"None heard it?"

"Darth prevented anyone from hearing it."

"I believe that, but rumor has it she got what she deserved and had been prepared for death."

"Death, aye, not this, not living with the darkest of the shadow lords. Don't you get it? Because of her record, and her talent, they had groomed her for such as him. She knew it, and preferred death. Why else such an outlandish display?"

Daniore cocked a brow. "Was it really that outrageous?"

Ash couldn't help a smile. "Venore looked like he got prodded by a hot poker. I've never seen anything like it, never seen such fire, such spirit, such audacity. Daniore, I wanted her. I never wanted anyone more except…."

He sucked in a breath, and then released it, slowly. "Doesn't matter. I can't wed a fantasy."

"You're still having that dream? Still think you can find the girl?"

"Aye, the dream is a constant. The girl isn't real. I know that now," Ash admitted. "But even if I didn't want Violet, I would have bid on her. Darth won't just torture her--he'll break her and then capture her soul. I can't allow that."

"I--" Daniore began, only to be cut off.

"The other night I could have taken her, deprived the Seraglio of their coin and wed her like any commoner taking a bride. But I didn't act on the impulse. I didn't act on what was right. Instead, all I could think about was my precious craft and becoming a mage beyond any other. It was the only way I could...." He paused, redirected his thoughts. "That emotion is worthy of any dark lord. Those of the sun put people above all else. I didn't and now that innocent child will suffer for it."

"With talent like hers, Ash, she might not be so innocent."

"Again, you don't see. For one of her age to have such talent, she has to be thoroughly pure. Her illusions reeked of it. One of a dark line wouldn't have tamed the beasts, they would have unleashed them."

Daniore nodded and smacked Ash on the back. "What are we waiting for? Let's go and snatch that little one right from under Darth's nose."

* * * *

Amlet smiled her sweetest smile at Lord Slith as he climbed on top of her, plunging in to her moist depths with ravenous hunger. She gave into the lust with as much vigor and intensity as the lord, shocking him with her experience and expertise. In the aftermath of her failed plan, Amlet needed to expend her rage and allowed the dark, inexperienced lord to wed her, knowing neither clan nor caste would miss him. She couldn't believe Violet managed to ensnare both lords! She was more of a hindrance than Amlet ever suspected.

Renewed rage climbed through Amlet and she exhausted it on the naïve lord. Hours later, finally spent, she pushed his dead body off of her. She had used him so well and long, that the young conjurer's heart gave way.

"Well, at least you died in the pursuit of pleasure," she quipped as her spirit fled the host body.

Cora soul, finally free from Amlet's control, collapsed in a comatose heap. The girl would remain thus for the remainder of her life.

Amlet didn't even look back as she sought a fresh body, one with access to Darth and Violet. Soon enough Darth would see the girl's true potential as not just a spirit to feed upon, but as a sorceress in her own right to be nurtured and offered to the Dark Master. Amlet had to prevent that. By all that was unholy, she had to destroy Violet and mate with either Darth or Ash.

Either one would do. It was the only way to bring about the fall of light, and she had to do it soon or the Master would notice her disobedience. If he knew she had spent all her time following her own agenda rather than adhering to his orders to manipulate the nuptials for the dark side's advantage, he'd toss her into the ninth level of Hell. Amlet knew the only way to ensure an eternity of comfort was to prove her worth. Any second rank demon could fiddle with the nuptials. Such sorcery was beneath her skill. The Master was wasting her talent, and she just wouldn't have it!

A plan formed in her depraved mind, and with a gleeful cackle she sought the most appropriate host.

* * * *

Exhausted beyond comprehension, Violet didn't know when they arrived at the inn, or when she had been placed in a tub. She only felt the hushed lap of water, the distant trill of twilight birds, the caress of being sponged free of the day's dirt. She tried to drag herself out of slumber, but something told her it was a spell to keep her still and compliant. She wasn't the first lass to be taken to the closest inn to seal the nuptials as quickly as possible. It was a blessing Darth chose one that provided such luxury. Still, an innate embarrassment at being scrubbed by a stranger crawled through her. Even more, she hated the paralyzing effects of the spell. She struggled within herself, but her body remained limp.

Tired of the struggle, she surrendered to the warmth and comfort. With her will estranged, the dream erupted. She still couldn't make out her lover, but it was the same chamber, the same bed. Only this time, his hands were already on her, tracing fingers along her length with possessive exploration. His kisses held desperation as did her own. Would this be the last time she'd be with him? Would being married chase away the phantom lover? Tears spilled into the kiss. She tasted the saltiness as her hands roamed over sinewy muscles. She knew this body so well. She knew every crevice, dimple and scar.

"Don't leave me," she uttered, tearing at his shirt to plant kisses along his collarbone. She who had never been kissed in reality, who reddened every time the eunuchs stripped her for punishment, found herself eager and bold within the dream. Not an ounce of shame plagued her. How could it? She knew this charmer forever. As a child, he'd filled her dreams with harmless adventures and playtime. As she grew he taught her potions and spells, thoughts of philosophy and truths about the One. When sensual heat erupted, he taught her love, not physical but that of the heart and spirit. Then he claimed her, took her as his wife as surely as if he had attended nuptials and purchased her. He taught her the delight of fingers and lips and tongue. Whispered the delights of her heart. Showed her how spirit and body could cling with a love beyond time.

Spirals of light caressed them as they dove deeper into each other. Tongues met in thrills of sensation, hearts pounded, pulse raced. His mouth deserted hers and trailed downward to suckle turgid nipples. A gasp floated up from depths set free, and with all her might she begged to remain in this ecstasy of escape. Nerve endings rippled as if pinpricked by fire. She arched, said his name, but didn't know that which passed her lips. Who was he? Did she really care?

She could brave all that had been done to her. She could fight battles of dark. She could court death for the sake of freedom. But could she stand to lose her dream? Sobs erupted in the mist of passion and she needed to show her love. Real or not, in this universe, in this world that had no past, no future, she belonged to him and he to her.

Bodies turned leaving her in control, something that had never happened before. Lips rained kisses upon a naked throat. Teeth tormented his nipples. A taut tongue laid patterns of fire over male flesh, down and down the erotic path to the tight, throbbing shaft. Spreading him wide, she licked his underside, again, yet again, around his sacks, within the crease.

His fist clenched. Groans exploded. "Violet … my love," he said her name on a splinter of sound. That, too, never happened. With widening eyes she realized that they were drawing closer. Suddenly she knew he was real. That there was a man out there who dreamed with her, only they would never meet. They only had this.

Her mouth closed around him, swallowing his hardness, filling her with his essence, his spirit, pulling away and gulping once more, again and again. Her tongue slipping over tense flesh, teeth nipping the bulging head as fingers sought his and knotted. He thrust into her mouth, taking back a measure of control and she claimed each thrust, encouraging more until he erupted within her, until she tasted his seed and the words she longed to hear since the moment he claimed her dreams broke through the mist. "I love you, my Violet. I love you."

* * * *

Ash pulled back on the steed's reins and gasped as a waking vision abruptly halted. For the past several miles he had been lost in sensuous oblivion and had ridden automatically as his mind wandered in a familiar fog of sensation and delight.

"By the One," he whispered, comprehension coming to him in waves.

"What? Why are you stopping?" demanded Deniore.

"It's her."

"Who?"

"Violet is the girl from my dreams."

"It can't be."

The wet stickiness drenching his lions spoke of just how real the vision had been. "It is real. Some say the One speaks his will through dreams. Since we were children we've been connected. I am a few years older than she is, but in many ways we grew up together. There was a time I believed she was my destiny."

"I know I've helped you search for her."

"Even though you didn't believe she was real."

"Aye, because we are more like brothers than friends. If it was important to you, it was important to me."

"Aye, you even supported me in going against my father's will. She was the reason I joined the caste. I thought magic would be the key. I honed my skills, kept increasing my potency in the hope that one day I could climb into the dream and either remain there or drag her out into reality. As the years passed, the lure of magic became more important. I no longer sought the girl, only relished the endless dreams that gave me all the sensual stimulation and satisfaction that I needed. I had planned to devote my life to being the consummate mage. After all, what need had I for a wife? I had the dream."

"Until your father demanded an heir."

"I would have ignored him if not for your urgings."

"I adore your sister, Ash, but neither she nor her offspring are fit to rule. I'd like to see light overcome darkness within my own lifetime."

For a moment Ash looked lost. He spurred his horse on, but at trot. "The magic hardened my heart to the point that I didn't recognize my Violet when she was in my arms."

"Whoa," Daniore said, and not just to his steed. "When was that?"

With his mount still moving he explained about finding Violet in the pub being tormented. "I felt something for her, but I ignored it. I'd like to blame the Dark Master for having manipulated events, but this didn't have anything to do with outside influence. My greed for power led to blindness and I accept responsibility for that, but I will not lose my way again. Violet is spiritually mine by the One's will and she will soon be mine in reality, too."

With that, he urged the mount into a gallop and didn't even check to see if Daniore kept up.

* * * *

The stone inn with its turrets and ivy-laced facade had a fairy tale quality about it that extended to the nuptial chamber. Scarlet roses, springing from numerous crystal vases, scented the air. Hand woven carpets rose above polished hardwood floors. Sheer, white silk draped the four-poster bed and crisscrossed windows below arches of stained glass. Candlelight and a crystal chandelier cast golden hues over the entire chamber. Outside, spider-wolves brayed at the emerging moon, night creatures stirred, and the wind scurried through dying leaves.

Violet stood in the center of the chamber, trembling. The dream had shaken her. More than ever, her lover seemed real. What if he truly existed? What if he was her destiny? Then again, what if he was from the Dark and this was a lure to capture her, much as her mother had been captured?

Besides, soon she would be wed to a lord of light. She never even considered such a possibility. And, Lord Darth appeared to be such a good man. He was the epitome of kindness and patience, assuring her that she'd have a good life with him, that he'd further her craft, that he'd awaken her spirits and sensuality to levels she couldn't even imagine. He begged her to give him that chance. How could she refuse? It seemed too noble to be genuine. Or was she just seeing spider-wolves behind every tree?

Pacing, she fiddled with one of the twenty knots binding the nuptial robe together from neck to ankles. Scarlet in color to symbolize that their marriage was a blood bond, it seemed more like a wash of color than an actual garment. Once Lord Darth shed the robe and possessed her body, she'd be his wife until death. If he wasn't all he appeared, death might be a welcome alternative. She had already been prepared for it, but having escaped the blade made her anxious for another chance at life. She glanced at the window, wondering if there was a trestle outside it.

"We are too high off the ground to climb down from the window," Lord Darth said as if reading her thoughts.

She turned to him, hand held against her throat. For once a retort escaped her. "I wasn't…."

"You were," he said with a smile. It was a nice smile, coaxing, but it was his eyes that trapped her, suckled at her will, eased her tension. She smiled back. Somehow it didn't seem of her volition. The room seemed a bit darker, the shadows longer. Something wasn't right, but she couldn't discern the source of her unease.

"Come here," he ordered his voice a trifle stern.

She obeyed. That wasn't like her either.

"I wanted to wait until we arrived at the castle, but without consummation, the marriage is void."

She nodded as if that were consent to proceed, but she didn't want him to proceed, she wanted to crawl back into the dream.

A fist knotted in her hair, yanking her head back. He looked down at her, his breathing raspy. He seemed to absorb her essence. For a split instant, she swore his gaze turned ebony, but a blink assured her it was still clear and blue. Her body tensed as his fingertips slid along the side of one breast.

"Be at ease," he murmured, as shadows swirled beneath their feet.

And she obeyed.

"Let go of your barriers."

Her guard shattered.

"Respond to my touch."

She sucked in a tattered breath as heat crawled through her body.

"That's it," he purred.

Her lips parted and she watched, mesmerized as his mouth claimed hers, a total expert ravishment intended to melt her from the inside out. His tongue found hers, sucking, nipping, and probing. His body pressed into her, his hard maleness against her gentle flesh, his seeking hand massaging her breasts. She had expected to feel as she had in the dream. She didn't and the strangeness of his touch triggered rebellion. She pushed against him, struggled, even as he kept muttering assurances and possibly even spells to break down her resistance.

"Yield," he urged.

"I can't."

"Do it now!"

"No!"

Candles sputtered out. Dark hues deepened. A jumble of words spilled from him, indistinguishable sounds that twirled around her, intensifying the heat that he had

originally stirred. It was as if she were on the outside of
herself, watching her arms go around him, watching her
body surrender, hearing a moan spill from divided lips.
Waves of pleasure swept through her, encouraged her to
spread herself open to him, submit totally, beg for
everything.

The emotion overwhelmed her. The plea became alive,
tangible, poised on her lips, ready to escape. Deep within,
though, it still didn't seem right to give herself to this man
she barely knew even if it were legal. Yet … yet … A
silent prayer rose through the confusion, begging the One
to decide what she couldn't hope to discern.

Darth intensified his invasion and Violet slipped into an
erotic abyss she couldn't fight.

* * * *

At Daniore's insistence, they watered the stallions at a
creek and draped a feedbag off the horses' muscular necks.

Ash stared at his mount as if that could make it eat faster.
"Don't you think they've had enough?"

"If you expect them to tear turf, you must allow them time
for fuel. Don't worry, my friend, we'll get there in time."

"It is already nightfall. For all I know, he could have
taken her in the carriage. Some do that to seal the marriage
before any can interfere."

Daniore looked at his feet, and then up at Ash. "What do
you know of the dark lord?"

"You mean besides being a brutal soul thief who tortures
and kills for pleasure?"

"That description could be applied to many of the dark
lords."

"Aye, but Lord Darth has presented more souls to his
master than a legion of his caste combined."

"Do you know why his appetite is more ravenous than
most?"

A decisive chill rode the wind as it whistled through
pines. Moonlight, spilling through branches and dried
leaves, provided the only illumination. "Nay, and cease
with the questions and be done with your thought."

"He was once a lord of light, and fell in love with a rare beauty who was sold to another lord at the nuptials. Not to be deprived, he contacted the Dark Master and bargained his soul in exchange for the woman's love. The couple fought the spell, but in their arrogance they failed to seek the One's help. Only He could have saved them. In the end, Darth, using the power of shadows, abducted the woman. She died loving and hating Darth simultaneously. Yet, rumor has it that he never recovered from the loss despite having killed her through endless torment."

"How do you know all this?"

"Had an ale with a shadow lord the other night by the name of Slith, young, chatty, and proud of the fact that he got Darth to attend the nuptials."

Although Ash already knew the answer, he couldn't stop himself from asking, "How did he do that?"

"Showed him the invitation. Violet is a replica of her mother."

Face tightening, Ash tore the feedbag off his steed, mounted, and without a word to Daniore, spurred the stallion forward.

* * * *

Fight him!

The words cut through the haze of abandonment. They weren't her words. They came from a distant voice that spoke in her head.

He's not what he seems.

She gasped. The voice was familiar.

You are mine, not his. Fight!

Now that she knew the story of her mother, confusion gushed through her. Was the voice that of a dark lord, seeking to lure her from Darth? Or was it the voice of sanity, urging not to surrender too quickly?

If she surrendered to the sensations, she would never know the answers. Besides, she finally realized this wasn't her will, but Darth's.

"It isn't me," she managed between heated kisses. "You are forcing responses. They aren't mine."

"Don't fight it, lass."

"It's not natural."

Darth growled softly and pushed her away. Violet didn't notice how the room brightened considerably. Stumbling backward, she fished for the edge of the bed trying to land on it rather than the floor. Finding the soft mattress securely underneath her, she sighed and felt chills chase away searing desire.

"Damn you, girl, this is the most natural thing in the world. You are mine and I will have you!"

"With a spell? That is no better than rape."

He froze. Indiscernible emotions fled across his handsome expression. He swallowed several times before responding. "It was only to take away your fear so the joining would be more pleasurable."

"But wouldn't it be better to coax a real reaction from me? Wouldn't that be sweeter, knowing you did it without trickery?"

Again she couldn't read his expression, but his response settled upon her like a warm wash.

"Aye, it would be something to savor. I do not wish to rush you, Violet Haze. I guess I am just anxious to have the nuptials finalized. Now that I found you I don't want to lose you. I saw how that dark lord lusted after you at the auction. Such as he stole your mother from your father soon after you were born."

Her gaze widened. "How did you know?"

He offered a soft, compassionate smile. "Many tales have been fashioned from the reality. It is those tales that have some mages consummating the nuptials right outside the Seraglio in any dark corner they can find."

"They said she loved the conjurer."

"It is rumored, but he would not have gotten to her if her love for your father had been stronger."

Every muscle within Violet tensed. "She loved him more than life."

"Aye, but the conjurer loved her more than his soul. Your mother put her dedication to the One before her love. If both she and your father bargained their souls, they would have remained together."

"In darkness?

"Aye."

"Better to be the least among all in light, than live in the shadows."

He took slow, measured steps to her. Pulled her back to her feet, kissed her softly, eliciting a small shiver. "Enough of this depressive chatter. I will let none take you from me. I will always protect you from darkness, and I will savor every moment of your surrender, every nuance that brings you closer to me, every…."

He stepped away and something flashed in his eyes she didn't like, but it was gone so quickly, she knew she had imagined it.

"I will woo you lass, and will not consummate our marriage until you submit of your own will."

Her voice lowered to a very soft hush. "Thank you."

"Hungry?" he asked.

A true smile appeared and barriers toppled from her gaze. "Aye, ravenous."

* * * *

After a meal of roasted duck, wild greens, stone grilled bread and sweetened berries washed down by honey-water for Violet and ale for Darth, Violet curled into the luxurious nuptial bed alone. She could grow used to Lord Darth's gentleness and patience. It was something she hadn't expected, but she knew it existed. Her father had been that way. The voices in her head had to be from the conjurer. The one she saw at the Seraglio hall fighting off the guards. He wanted her the way the dark lord had wanted her mother. Even now, he was after her. She had to cling to Lord Darth. She had to allow him to consummate the marriage. Even more, she had to learn how to love him.

Only, it could wait until the morrow. For the first time since she was a wee one, Violet had a comfortable mattress beneath her dainty body, a full stomach, and no worries about being wakened in the night by rough hands and beatings.

Violet was only partially right. Just before light spun through stained glass, a strong hand covered her mouth, yanked her from the bed and carried her toward the window.

Chapter Five

"Has the One scrambled your brains? Untie her!" Lord Ash spat, his hands still streaming luminosity beams to vanquish shadows. Without darkness or shadows, Darth's powers would wane and without them, he wouldn't be able to detect either a mage or Violet's abductor.

Daniore leaned back in his typical, haughty stance, staring at the bound and gagged Violet. "And have her run back to Darth?"

"Why would she do that? I'm rescuing her."

With a shrug, Daniore released Violet's gag.

"Let me go, you son of a spider-wolf, you excuse for a lord, you … you…."

Daniore stuffed the gag back into Violet's mouth. "Heard enough?"

Dropping one hand, he stared at the girl struggling against her bindings. "I don't understand."

Huffing a breath, Daniore yanked the girl off the ground and threw her over his saddle. "She thinks Darth's a mage, and you're the conjurer. I discovered that as we were sliding down the rope. Ever try to hold onto a screaming, thrashing feline? It's not easy. By the One, she would have allowed me to drop her rather than comply. If you didn't create a shield for us, Darth would have had me for spider-wolf feed."

Shaking his head, Ash tossed a sleep spell over Violet. Although her body stilled, he could still see the struggle within. The girl had an unquenchable spirit. No wonder Darth had been so determined to acquire her. Still holding up his hand, he mounted Daniore's steed.

Before Daniore could object, Ash said, "I want to keep her close."

Again, Daniore shrugged. "As you wish. Where to?"

"The caves. I can brighten the confined space and shield us from Darth's shadow seekers."

"Shouldn't we go home and beg the King's protection? A regiment of warriors and mages would stand a better chance against Darth than you alone."

"Too far, Darth could catch up to us by then." With a whoosh of one finger, he untied Violet's feet and settled her before him, straddling the steed and leaning against him. Her warmth settled into him and he had to ignore the engorging of his loins. He had felt the attraction from the first moment he saw her, so vulnerable and battered. He felt passion gushing through his veins when he had carried her to her chamber from the pub. He knew she was irresistible, but he had chosen selfishly, and that vice blinded him to her familiarity and the fact he nearly lost the one woman he could truly love.

A few hours later, Ash had Violet resting against a bed of furs, leaves, and plumage cast off by the wind birds that resembled eagles but were five times larger and fed on spider-wolves. It wasn't much of a nuptial bed, but it would have to do.

"It's noon. Darth's powers are at their weakest. Shouldn't we travel a little farther?" Daniore asked even as he piled logs onto the fire Ash had created to consume encroaching shadows.

"No more hiding places between us and home. Besides, you will go on ahead and bring a regiment here. I can keep her safe until then. It should only take half a day to get there, and if they travel through the night you'll be here by morning."

"What if your father won't send the army?"

"He knows what it takes for me to ask for anything. He'll send his finest." Ash cocked his head, and his gaze narrowed just a bit. "You, of all people, should know that."

"Aye, I do. I just feel as if I'm abandoning you both."

"You aren't, friend." A small grin appeared. "Besides, I'd prefer to consummate this marriage in privacy."

Instead of the usual good-natured quip Ash expected from Daniore, the man simply blinked as if dazed then strode away.

Something didn't sit right with Ash at that moment, but a sudden kick directly between his legs, bowed him to his knees.

* * * *

Darth's rage tore through the inn with such abrupt intensity, the sturdy stone structure shook as if being torn from its foundation. In the dining hall, dishes toppled from tables, crystal glasses, decanters and vases crashed into each other and joined the shattered plates. Food and drinks splattered patrons who fell off chairs or plummeted to their buttocks or knees. Candle flames burned draperies and a few garments even as fountains sprayed rugs and hardwood with large sloshes of water. In rooms, sleepers fell out of bed. Dressers slammed into windows. Then, just as quickly as it had begun, the fury ceased.

With a will that had seen him through the conversion from a light lord to a conjurer, he settled his fury. Violet's escape was nothing more than a brief setback. If she hadn't tried, she wouldn't be as much like her mother as he had hoped. It was this sort of defiant spirit that drew him, that invigorated him. The best was that she thought him a mage and actually wanted to be with him. Something held back her total compliance, but the coaxing was so sweet. She had been right to resist the spell, and he had been wrong to use it. He had to slow down his absorption of her. He had to savor every morsel so that when she finally capitulated it would be all the more intoxicating. And in that exact moment when she surrendered herself fully, he'd reveal his true nature. She'd be as trapped as a victim in spider-wolf webbing.

That was when he'd truly start to feed on her spirit. Unlike his younger self, he now knew how to bring one back from the brink of death. He'd do that to her again and again, offering the hope of escape or rescue to keep her going. He could draw this out for years and make certain she bred a child as well, a girl child not from his seed but from a young mage. Maybe the one who was so eager to buy her. He'd place the child in the Seraglio so that by the time Violet's spirit shattered and there was nothing left to absorb, he'd have another waiting for him. Oh, such fun, such adventure awaited him. Only he had to remain calm and take it slow. After all, how far could she have gotten on her own?

Unlike other conjurers, Darth never recruited a lackey, for he had the spider-wolves at his mental command. He summoned several to his chamber. They arrived within minutes, crashing through windows on the main floor just as servants started to help injured patrons and sweep up the shattered remains of valuable crystal and ceramics.

Screams echoed through the inn and Darth smiled, swallowing each morsel of fear that accompanied those screams. With a flip of his hand the double doors to his chamber sprang open and several wolves appeared. They were the ebony-coated ones, known for their venomous bite and vicious attacks. Sometimes, they didn't bother to cocoon a victim. Instead, they ripped them apart and lapped up their blood until sated.

Darth pointed to Violet's garments hanging from pegs in the closet. The wolves sniffed the clothes within moments.

"Find and trap," Darth ordered, "no feeding until you return."

With growls and bared teeth, the wolves rushed away.

About to close the doors with another wave of his hand, he noticed two young lasses stumbling down the hall, fear etched on their pretty faces and fine, elegant garments in disarray. They probably belonged to a sun clan, traveling with their parents. For they were too young to be wed, yet old enough to be bargaining chips. Darth didn't wish to bargain. He simply needed a diversion until the wolves brought back his Violet.

He clasped his hand and uttered a spell, ending with, "Come."

Both girls froze for an instant, and then entered the chamber. A finger flick had the doors slam shut and the lock clicked.

"Strip, slowly," he ordered.

Layers of clothing fell before him. Vacant, dark eyes peered at nothing.

Once they were naked, he moved around them, inspecting the perfection of their skin, the gentle swell of small breasts and the lush, dark fuzz trapped between thighs. He'd use them one at a time, having the other watch so she'd know her fate.

However, he didn't awaken them until he had them securely tied and gagged, their bodies spread before him like a banquet, one on the dining table, the other on the dresser, one facing the ceiling, the other with her head draped over the floor. He took out a flogger, a poker and a sharp thin stiletto, lapping up the fear oozing from them like liquid ambrosia.

"Which one should I start with?" he uttered, his voice raspy.

Their terrified moans were like exquisite music to his ears.

He couldn't decide whether to rape them first or torture them. Perhaps a little of both, he thought with a grin, and began to disrobe.

Hours later, splattered with blood, but still not satiated, Darth contemplated whether or not it was worth feeding off the other girl. She was so catatonic, he couldn't even rouse a whimper, and that was just from her watching what he did to her sister. Besides, the wolves should have been back by now with Violet. Something was wrong. He doubted she had enough talent to cover her trail, but what if--

Before he finished the thought, the double doors banged open.

Darth's deep raspy voice echoed as if in a vast cave. "How dare…."

He didn't finish as the large, muscular man strode in and collapsed. A black, pulsating vapor rose from his body and moved forward, sculpting itself into the form of a naked, voluptuous woman, a very *transparent* woman. "My name is Amlet. I think it's time we met."

* * * *

Long, silver tendrils poured from Ash's palm and wrapped around Violet, yanking her backwards before she could flee. "Oh no you don't," he bit out between groans.

"Release me, lord of vipers, heart of ice, breath of toad!" She screamed, clawing at the streams of light that she could see through but could not break.

The pain eased only enough to straighten from his waist, but not enough for him to stand. "You never complained about my breath when I kissed you."

"Your lips have never touched mine," she spat with indignation and wild struggles.

"Perhaps not in the natural, but in more dreams than can be counted."

Violet froze. The beautiful hues of her eyes flamed. "Nay!"

"Aye." He managed to climb to his feet, releasing the pain through harsh breaths. "Now, if you'll stop fighting me, I'll release you and show you that I shared your dreams."

Staring at him as if he'd turn into a spider-wolf at any moment, she nodded and stood.

He remained in place, sensing any abrupt movement might have her scurrying to the cave entrance again. In an even, velvety tone, Ash recalled the various moments they shared in their dream world. He started with simple things like the day they rode stallions, the day they swam in a stream the color of pale roses. Then he moved to erotic moments, to intimate kisses, to the first time she offered herself, to the last time they reveled in a mutual orgasm and finally to the last dream when her lips folded around his manhood.

He didn't know what reaction he expected, but not for her to flee toward him and knock him flat to the ground, fists pummeling his chest, tears streaming down her beautiful face. All the while her crimson robe split open at the ties from her wild foray until it just hung from her shoulders and arms like a flaming cloak.

"Nay! Nay! It cannot be you!"

"I am not a conjurer, love. I am a mage."

"Nay," she spat. "I will not be fooled. I will not! It is just a trick, just as my mother was tricked."

He allowed her to unleash the worst of her rage, and only when he couldn't take it any more did he capture her thin wrists between his and hold them above her head. Simultaneously, he tossed her onto her back and pinned her beneath him. "Enough!"

To his amazement, she stilled except for her bottom lip. It quivered. Tears blurred the depths of her eyes until they turned a pale lilac.

"I refuse to love a dark lord," she said, the words muted under such sadness it unhinged Ash's emotions.

"Why do you think I am a conjurer?"

"Look at you. You wear black, have a gaze that mesmerizes, lips that torment, and a spirit that has invaded my dreams. Maybe that was how the dark lord fooled my mother. Maybe he stole her heart in her dreams. Just as you have stolen mine."

"You recognize me now?"

"Aye," she whispered, lowering her gaze. "It was you at the pub, too. You rescued me."

"Would a conjurer do that?"

"Aye, if it furthered his plan."

"I will somehow convince you that I have no plan other than to keep you safe and love you just as I always have."

"My mother married a mage, but then fled with a conjurer." Violet searched his gaze. "They say she loved him. I think he ensorcelled her."

"And you think that is what I am doing to you?"

"Aye, I seemed to have mirrored my mother's life thus far, why not further still?"

"Have you been intimate with Darth?"

"Nay, he is honorable. I was not ready and he yielded to my wishes."

Tension filled Ash like taut wire. He didn't know why Darth didn't violate her, but he knew it wasn't because he was a man of honor, and the quicker he dispelled that illusion the better.

"He was once a mage who had abandoned the light, bartering his soul for your mother's love. It is he who killed her. It is he who wants you to follow in her footsteps down to her death. I will not allow it, my Violet. You are mine. And, unlike the kingdom's philosophy dictates, I am also yours."

His words startled Violet to the core, but it was his sudden kiss that toppled her defenses. In some ways, it was as if they were in the dream. Only the fog had lifted. The feel of him was so familiar. His touch was as stimulating as ever. She searched for the spell he had surely woven to keep her so aroused, so compliant, and found none. Was this how her mother felt? Was this why she ran?

Violet knew she had to resist. Only, how could she when every fiber of her being responded? They were in perfect harmony, anticipating moves, mirroring actions even with her wrists still bound above her head. Tongues mated in erotic play. His fingers sought crevices of arousal. Her heat automatically responded to his hardness, pressing against him, swaying, moaning, surrendering even as she urged herself not to. Her mother paid for her slide into darkness, but had the slide been this pleasurable? Had she wanted it with the depth and passion that Violet wanted to join with this lord?

She rained kisses over his face, his throat, the nub of his ear, the stubble of a day's growth of beard. Bound wrists struggled against his hold, but she knew it wasn't to flee.

"I don't even know your name," she said, through the tantalizing sweep of a tongue across his bottom lip.

"Ash," he provided as he licked the curve of her ear. "Lord Ash of the Illumi Kingdom."

"I love you, Lord Ash. I don't know if I believe that you are of the Illumi Kingdom. I don't know if I'll submit to you. All I know is that I love you, and I don't know how to stop."

Releasing her wrists, he braced himself on palms and looked down at her, watching a blush creep over her body. The rosy tinge melted away the golden splash from the log fire. For the first time he saw her without the dream veil.

Yet he knew her by feel. He knew her legs were long, slender, and paler than cream. He knew her slim hips surrendered to a fragile waist and her breasts were just large enough to overflow his hands. Her nipples were pink and perfect to suckle. A pliable mouth beckoned in a way he had never experienced. Yet it was her eyes that held him. Emotions ranging from fear and desperation to undiluted love and unquenchable passion nearly overwhelmed him.

"I love you, too, my Violet," he said, repeating the words from his dream.

Her eyes widened, and he knew she recognized the exact cadence in his tone. A small whimper slipped from somewhere down deep.

He stood. "I wed you in the dream. You surrendered to me then, love. Do you surrender now?"

She shook her head. "Nay."

He lifted and carried her to the bed of furs, feathers, and leaves. Her crimson gown remained parted, exposing every swell and dip to his ravishing gaze. He couldn't stop looking. He couldn't stop anything. It wasn't about keeping her safe from Darth. It wasn't even about sealing what the One had begun when he placed them in each other's dreams. It was about loving a woman with such totality that he no longer knew the difference between right and wrong. If she truly stopped him, would he? He didn't know.

Swallowing hard, he unfastened the leather ties of his tunic. A white, colorless shirt followed. "You know your protest won't stop me. Darth will come for you, and when he does we will need the strength of the nuptials behind us so he cannot take you outright."

"He purchased me."

Leather pants slid down muscle-hard legs. "It means nothing without consummation."

Her gaze followed his every movement. She remembered the feel of hair-matted flesh, but she didn't know it would look so good, or that she'd crave to touch the scars littering his side, his shoulder, and his upper thigh. She didn't understand how the masculine length of his sun-bronzed body would arouse her beyond anything in her dream world. She didn't comprehend how much she could love a man of darkness. How much she wanted him to take her. Even though her mouth protested, her body surrendered.

"To men of honor it does."

"Darth doesn't know honor. He killed your mother through torture."

"A dark lord did that, but not Darth. He is of the light. It is not right what we do."

When Ash was naked, he knelt and parted her thighs. A tawny, nearly invisible patch of hair covered her sex. He slipped a finger up and down the moist slit. She gasped and arched against it.

"We don't have a choice. You don't have a choice. You are my wife in spirit. Now, I claim what is mine."

"Nay," she said, her mouth forming the word as she threw back her head and tossed her arms over her head in such obvious surrender, Ash couldn't help smiling.

"Nay," he repeated and closed a mouth over her turgid nipple, tugging, nipping as his fingers clenched her other breast and massaged. She moaned and thrashed beneath him, lifting her chest off the floor as if to give him better access.

"Nay," she whispered and combed his wild mane with her fingers.

He laughed softly as the flames within grew, as the ancient dance tantalized them to greater rhythm. He switched his mouth to her other breast. Her legs spread, knees bending. Her mouth found his, kissing him with total abandon. It was his turn to moan.

"Ash," she whispered without conscious volition. "My Ash."

Whatever reserve kept him in check, snapped. He knotted his fingers in her hair, yanked her to him, all gentleness gone as his hands slipped over her, testing flesh just moments before his mouth tasted it. Over her eyes, back to her breasts, then down, further to her feet and legs and inner thighs, and finally into the dewy mist of her inner desire. Licking, thrusting with his tongue, bringing her to highs that didn't end.

"Nay!" she screamed as she felt the surrender of flesh, the invitation of her loins, the explosion as her inner walls pulsated and her clitoris throbbed in reaction.

"Oh, nay," he mouthed through every tender bite and succulent kiss. Saying it again, when she pulled him down to him so her hands and mouth could explore in the same way she had in the dream. She sucked him long and hard, but pulled away before he could climax. She teased and tormented, even as she kept denying each moment.

Finally, he pressed his shaft against her opening. "Nay?"

She throbbed and ached. She needed and wanted. More than any of that, she simply loved.

"Aye," she said on the wisp of a whimper.

With a loud groan, he thrust into her.

Pain splintered her senses, but it lasted only an instant as consummate pleasure ensued and she rocked against him, meeting his plunges without restraint. Her nails dug into his shoulders. Her hips kept lifting from the ground. His shaft moved in and out of her, slow at first, then with increasing insistence. He didn't know who was more lost to the moment. The dream joined with reality and it was more glorifying than either. As they reached higher, all barriers collapsed. They were the lovers of the dream. They were the strangers of the night. They were a man and a woman who knew the simplicity and complications of love. Mostly, they were in the moment. This singular moment which would be with them through eternity.

She reached the apex first, crying as it overtook her in throttles of sensation. He followed, emptying himself into the warmth of her, and knowing that she was truly now his, not just a dream, not just a spirit. They shuddered together. His tears mingled with hers and in the moment, Violet couldn't help wondering if all he had said was true.

He collapsed on her, held her tightly. "It is done."

"You are my husband."

"You are my wife."

They repeated the ceremonial words each were taught, but the emotion behind them had nothing to do with ceremony and everything to do with love.

A slow smile lifted pink-tinged lips. One finger slipped through a lock of Ash's tumbling hair. "For good or evil, this has been done. Please, be of the sun."

Rather than answer, Ash slipped into her once again, taking her, possessing her, showing his love in the ancient way.

The day slipped to twilight, and they both dozed between bouts of renewed joining. Now and then, Ash used magic to keep the log fire fresh and glowing. Then exhaustion totally claimed them and they slept solidly until darkness captured the day.

The throaty growl of spider-wolves awakened them to a dim fire and Lord Darth's scowl.

Chapter Six

"Knave!" Darth shouted from the cave's entrance. "How dare you defile my wife!"

Ash covered Violet with his discarded shirt before standing and tugging on his clothes. "By law, she is now mine. You didn't consummate the marriage."

"I will contest this, and in the meantime, she will be with me."

Violet didn't don Ash's shirt, but quickly fastened whatever ties were not torn beyond salvage. "It is too late, Lord Darth. To my shame, I did not protest. I gave in willingly. I am my mother's daughter after all it seems."

"But I am not like your father, lass. I will reclaim what is mine. You are of the light as am I. You must now choose between the One and the Dark Master. It affects your eternity. Do not use your heart as a guide, use wisdom."

Taking a step closer to Ash, she looked up him, her face marred by anguish. "How do I choose? If it were just a matter of choosing between the two of you, I'd be yours for eternity. But the One is in my heart, in my soul. It is the One who saw me through every rough moment in the Seraglio, through every escape venture, through discovering my mother had chosen darkness over light."

"Ah, love, I am of the Illumi. Don't let him deceive you. The One gave us the dreams, that connection. I am not much older than you and the dreams started when we were children. I would not have had the power to seek you out and create such a connection. Think, and know I am of light. The choice is easy. Use wisdom, but do not disregard your heart."

Violet searched Ash's eyes. She felt herself falling into them, felt herself believing. Yet she knew her decision could not be made hastily, and she took a step back, turned toward Darth and examined the depths of his translucent gaze. Despite it being through dreams, she had known Ash for a lifetime and had never felt an iota of evil from him. What did she really know of Darth other than what he claimed?

"Enough of this!" Darth exploded. "You are too enamored to make a rational choice, lass. You must leave it to others who know what is best for you."

Before Violet could react, Darth tossed a binding force around her, much as Ash had done earlier. Only, Darth's felt like biting whips, tightening around her flesh whereas Ash's had held without pain.

Almost instantaneously, Ash spoke a word that severed the binds. Without conscious volition she fled to his arms. He held her close. "It's okay. I won't let him have you."

Holding up a palm, he spoke several more words and rocks cascaded into the cave's opening, sealing them in. "Soon, Daniore will return with my father's mages and warriors. We'll be safe then, and you'll see that…."

Before he could finish the rocks vanished, and Darth stepped into the cave. With a movement, he created another webbing of binding fibers. They tore Violet away from Ash. The same sort of fibers curled around Ash, stilling his movement.

"Violet, use your power.   You can fight this!" Ash prompted, even as he unraveled his own trappings.

Closing her eyes, Violet concentrated and found that she had the power to escape the trap. It was strange that she hadn't even considered using that power against Ash's bindings.   Still, the realization was invigorating and the instant the tendrils dissolved, she promptly added a spell of protection, being bold enough to contain Ash within its field.

Ash smiled. It was obvious that simply by fighting Darth, she had chosen. The mage added his spell of security to hers. Darth couldn't touch the double shielding. "Come here, love. We will simply wait it out."

"It is not as easy as that," Darth supplied and took another step into the cave. The spider-wolves snarled. A crack of lightning creased the sky. Thunder awakened a squall of night creatures into frenzy of sound. The log fire burst into an unexpected blaze at the same moment that Daniore stepped into view.

"You have returned with the legions so soon?" Ash asked in surprise.

"You should have known that your father would not do anything to help you. From the moment you chose to be of the dark caste, he had vowed you were no longer his son."

"What lies are you speaking?" Ash demanded.

"I'm sorry," Daniore said in a tattered tone, his gaze seeking Violet's. "I should never have been part of this, but Ash and I have been friends for so long, I couldn't deny him. My conscience would not allow me to be part of this deception a moment longer. Ash is a dark lord, Violet. If you choose to be with him, you choose to serve the Dark Master."

A scream of pure anguish tore from Violet as she pulled away from her husband and lover. "You serpent from Hell. How could I have been such a fool!"

Ash didn't deny the accusation. Only stared at Daniore. "Why are you doing this? Has Darth cast a spell?"

"You would sense the spell if he had," Daniore explained. "As would Violet. She has the power of discernment."

"Wait!" Ash said. "You haven't had enough time to get to my father's kingdom and back by now. You didn't even go."

Daniore grinned. It wasn't a smile of friendship. "Of course I did."

The obvious lie didn't penetrate Violet's misery. Her frail body collapsed as if she bore a weight too heavy for her slender shoulders. Sobs broke free as she curled into a fetal position. No one had ever broken her spirit before this, but now she felt broken, used and unable to even think coherently.

She didn't see the sudden explosion of force being enacted around her. Darth and Daniore positioned against Ash, binding him with dark tendrils, gagging him with spider-wolf webbing. She didn't see Ash's valiant efforts to defend them both, nor hear his cry of anguish as they stilled his voice and bound his power. She didn't know that Daniore wasn't a mage and didn't possess an ounce of power.

Ash knew, and realizing that Daniore hadn't betrayed him, but was possessed by a dark being was Ash's only speck of relief. That relief, though, evaporated under the certainty that he had failed Violet. He didn't have the skill or force to save himself or the woman he loved. All he had left was regret, and the sudden urge to seek help from the One. Only Ash wasn't certain if he would be heard after a lifetime of leaning only on his own resources.

* * * *

With no further use for Daniore, Amlet deserted his body. He dropped in an unconscious heap right beneath the spider-wolves jaws. They had brought the lass that Darth hadn't yet tortured, and Amlet overtook her body without a peep of protest from the young one, for her spirit had retreated behind layers of terror. Darth might not have tormented the girl as yet, but he had planted his seed and it already begun to ripen. It was Amlet's price for her help. She'd take him to Violet in exchange for his seed. Now, she'd have a child of such darkness that it would eliminate all light from this world.

"My pets will feast on Daniore and we will be done with him as well," Darth offered as he moved from the cave into the starless night.

"And I have your word that you will never teach Violet the ways of darkness," she said, reminding him of the second condition he had agreed to.

Ebony eyes stared at her. Sensuous lips twisted into a feral grin. "As much as any dark lord can give his word. But do not fret, do you really think I'd bring to fruition a power that could destroy our Master?"

Amlet's smile matched his. "It is what I am counting on."

"What are your plans?"

"Same as always, to further the Master's bidding."

"I suspect you haven't been doing his bidding according to his directives."

She shrugged, straightening the quaint garments that belonged to her host. "Nevertheless, he will be pleased by my actions. Our son will terminate all light. It is a given, and it often surprises me that Master hadn't considered such an alliance."

"I think our Master likes the game, the ebb and flow of it, the challenge, and, of course, being a constant hindrance in the One's grand scheme."

"Perhaps, but I do not think he will be displeased by me. After all, it is for his honor alone I exist."

Darth nodded, eager to be done with the spirit and begin his exploitation of Violet. He didn't think he could hold out much longer in this guise of light. Oh what exquisite pleasure he will derive from that moment when she realizes she has been deceived.

"Do not forget," Amlet said as she hefted herself onto Daniore's steed, "if their dalliance has borne fruit, destroy the babe. Just like our child of dark, their child could be the one to destroy shadows."

"I won't forget," Darth lied. The only reason Ash still lived was to make certain Violet already had his seed so that Violet would bear a girl child for Darth to torment after Violet's death. The wee lass would never have a chance to toy with her powers. He'd see to it.

Pleased by the day's events, Darth willed himself to the manor. He vanished in vapor and appeared the same way next to the Well of Misery. With an unusual smile plastered to his lips, he prepared for his guests.

* * * *

Ash woke in a dimly lit chamber, no longer bound by the double spell. Instead, a force had been placed around him, imprisoning him in a chair before a web-covered portrait. The gag, though, was still in place and he couldn't speak out a spell. Even if he could, shadows devoured what little light the room provided. A mage's power came from the light. Without it, he was helpless.

Only, he wasn't alone for long. Lord Darth appeared dressed in layers of ecru, eyes once again a startling, almost transparent blue. He looked the part of a sun lord, but how could Violet be fooled by this manor? Surely, she would see him draw his power from the shadows that crawled and slithered like lucid entities.

"She sees what I allow her to see," Darth said in that uncanny way he had of knowing a person's mind. He couldn't read anyone's thoughts, but always had a feel for what they might be thinking. "Everything is fashioned in the way she remembers her childhood home to be-- sunlight spilling into the rooms during the day, with star- shine and moonbeams at night."

Darth waved his hand and Ash's gag fell free.

He worked his mouth back and forth several times before being able to speak. "How long have I been here?"

"A full day. It is all I needed to convince Violet that you are a dark lord, whereas, she is totally convinced I am of the sun. To insure her trust, I haven't even taken her as yet. I want her secure in her new home. I want her to feel totally safe."

"And then you'll let her see the truth."

Darth offered his lurid smile. "Aye, it will make the moment all the more enjoyable."

"Why?"

He laughed a self-assured laugh of total evil. "Because it is how I serve the Dark Master. It is how I exist. It is my way."

"You were once of the sun."

"Aye, and the One did not hear my prayers. So, I turned to the Master who'd at least fulfill my desires."

Darth placed his hands on either side of Ash's chair and stared into his eyes; his own momentarily flashed ebony, dark, deep, empty. "So, no pleading to let Violet go? No attempts at escape your self? No spells to battle the shadows?"

"I'm sure none of it would do any good. You made certain there wouldn't be enough light to draw power."

"Violet will see it ablaze with candlelight," he said, flaunting his hands to take in their surroundings. "As for the portrait, she will see a beautiful woman she doesn't recognize. That is until I'm ready for her to see her mother."

"And what will you do with me?"

"Once Violet isn't so enthralled by you, I'll leave you to the portrait. It has a strange effect on men. One you will find very interesting."

Almost instantly Darth's demeanor changed, softened. His smile turned warm. "See, I told you I am treating him well," he said, waving Violet into the chamber. "Although, I cannot release him as you wish, my sweet. He might try to take you again, and I will not allow history to repeat itself."

Dressed in a shape-hugging white satin frock embroidered with violets, the lass entered the room seemingly composed. Her hair had been swept up into a fall of perfectly formed ringlets. Her wild mane had been tamed just like her spirit. The battle between good and evil had trampled down what the Seraglio hadn't even touched. A singular beam of light spilled through the open doors, but it wasn't enough to break the power of the shadows.

Ash wanted to beg the lass to see the truth, beg her to know he loved her, beg her to side with him and destroy Darth's evil for good. Darth, though, had every path covered, every path but one. Lowering his eyes, Ash mouthed a prayer to the One.

"Please set him free," she said quietly. "I will not desert you as my mother deserted my father. I will be faithful. All I ask is that you let him go without harm. I will do my duty."

"But you left me once."

"I was abducted. I told you that."

"But you didn't deny him your body," Darth said with a harsh edge to his tone.

"I told you of the dreams."

"You knew him to be a dark lord."

"I wasn't certain, but..." She lowered her head, tears spilled between mink-colored lashes. "I would have given myself to him even if I had been certain."

"You love him that much?"

"Aye," she responded without hesitation.

Hearing the affirmation tugged at Ash's heart.

"Yet, you will deny that love and stay with me."

"I am a child of the sun. I need to serve the One."

"And to raise your child in the light as well," Darth added. "It will be the only way to keep the babe from ever being a conjurer like its father."

"Child?" Ash echoed.

Closing his massive hand around Violet's delicate wrist, he escorted her to Ash. Their eyes met for an instant, and then, for their own reasons looked away. Darth lifted Ash's paralyzed hand and placed it on Violet's womb. Even through the deadening spell, Ash could feel the life within Violet. The knowledge that his child would be in Darth's control spawned a mixture of rage and despair. Only years of training with the best mages allowed him to remain silent as he ravaged his mind for a way out of this, begging the One to come to their aid.

His hand dropped. Violet moved away as if she couldn't stand the proximity. Darth grinned. The spider-veil draped over the portrait began to split. Ash felt compelled to look.

"The time is here, Violet. If you tell him you have made your choice, that you will no longer allow him into your dreams, then I will let him go."

Violet pressed her fingers into her womb. As long as she had Ash's child, she would always have a part of him. Yet, everything within her urged her to defy Lord Darth, to give herself to Ash and damn whether they lived in the sun or the shadows. For she did not know if she could exist without him. He wouldn't even be part of her dreams. No matter what Darth and Daniore said, she didn't really believe that Ash was that far gone into the shadows. She couldn't believe he had fooled her so completely.

"Let me have a moment alone with him."

"Nay!"

"Please. I beg you … please?"

"It is too dangerous," Darth bit out.

She sighed and nodded. Tears refused to heed any control. She knelt before Ash's chair, placed her palms on either side of his lean face. "I love you. I will always love you, but it is best for our child for us both to be part of the sun world. Please, try to understand. Please."

He didn't respond. His gaze lingered on the portrait behind her. It was as if she didn't exist.

She closed her eyes. A small sob escaped her lips. She pressed her lips against his for such long minutes that Darth, finally, had to drag her away.

"This is a good thing you've done, Violet. You made the right choice. Now, let us leave and let the servants show him out."

She looked up into Darth's open gaze. "You are truly letting him go?"

"I don't wish to, but I know it would grieve you too much to imprison him or have him killed." Darth touched her hair, ran a finger over her bottom lip.

"You trust me now?"

"Aye," she whispered.

"Then you are finally mine with no regrets?"

"Aye," she said again, stilling her tears.

A slow, eager grin spread over Darth's countenance. His eyes deepened to a shade as dark and impregnable as obsidian. Even his garments turned from the soft ecru shades to midnight black.

Violet gasped. Horror invaded every crevice of her soul as the brightly-lit chamber filled with shadows, as spider webbing appeared on furniture and walls, as Darth's cruel laugh echoed with unrelenting delight.

"Aye, that is it! That is the look I've waited for, sweet. That is the look I've yearned to see. That is the look I will feed upon for years, just as I will feed upon your soul, your fear, your misery. And you brought it all about yourself. You chose me over Ash. You made the fatal mistake of not listening to your heart. Your mother did and she at least had a few years with the man she loved before I bartered my soul for her love."

Gripping her shoulders with both palms, Darth spun her around to see the portrait of her mother. "Many say I killed her, tormented her until she died. Oh, I did torture her, endlessly, but she didn't die by my hand. She died by her own. Her love for your father broke the spell I cast, and she ended up hating me. No one ever knew that. It was I who began the rumors that said she willingly came to me. It was I who fostered the misconception that she wanted to hate me and couldn't. But I won't let you kill yourself. I will savor you and after you, your child!"

Violet yanked away from him as everything inside her collapsed into a smoldering heap of rage. The rage only made Darth laugh harder. "That's it, give into it, fight me. It will nourish my soul almost as much as watching your lover die under the portrait's spell."

"Nay!" she shouted.

"It is too late, Violet. Your joint powers could have defeated me. You really don't know how powerful you are. You could have been a great sorceress if you had chosen that path."

"But my powers didn't work against you in the cave."

"Mostly because Daniore had been possessed by a sorceress and aided in my spell, partly because you had given up. Now, watch your lover wither away. Give in to your defeat."

She shook her head, trying to summon powers to fight him.

He brushed her meager attempts away as if she weren't anything more than a pesky gnat.

She tried again and again, feeding off the rage, using the paltry amount of light from outside the chamber to assist her.

Darth continued to laugh.

The shadows circled around him.

Ash groaned.

Despair filled the chamber.

Violet's eyes met those of her mother's in the portrait, seeing herself there. Would her face too stamp a canvas and destroy a man's heart and soul? Would her child be forced to submit to Darth as substance for a perverted being? She couldn't allow this. She didn't know how to stop it.

She pressed against her womb, spun away from the horror and suddenly saw the Well of Misery. Having seen it enough times in her studies, she recognized it immediately. Perhaps it was time for her to deprive Darth of his treasure. At the thought, the seed within her stirred and pulsated. A bright light shimmered through her fingers. Suddenly, words from long ago came back to her. The words her father spoke on his deathbed. The words that Ash had said the night he rescued her from the pub.

She spoke them aloud. "You have a light within that none will quench. In that light, your soul will speak. In that light, your spirit will thrive. In that light, you will learn control and the true nature of being of the sun caste."

She repeated one phrase. "The true nature of being of the sun caste."

What was that nature? No one ever told her. It was something they said each had to learn on their own. She hugged her stomach and turned back to the cackling lord and the mesmerized, dying Ash. Oh how she loved him, always had loved him, loved his child, though a seedling, already spiritually strong, glowing from within, telling her … telling her….

A soft, slow smile appeared as she heard the whisper. She saw Darth in a fresh way. She saw him as the tormented being he was, as the wretched man who gave up his soul for the love of a woman who ended up hating him. She knew the totality of his crimes against her, against her mother, against probably countless people throughout his life. She knew if she didn't obey the whispers of her unborn child, Darth's shadows would grow and consume more and more of the light.

With quiet steps she went to him, stood before him.

He sensed something. The laughter stopped.

She lifted up her arms and hugged him gently. "I forgive you, Lord Darth. And, the One, He loves you still."

It was as if she had punctured him with a blazing dagger. His screech ricocheted off the walls. He stumbled backwards, holding his head. Light began to pour out of his eyes, out of his fingers, out of his heart. He screamed again and again, each step taking him further from her. His body began to crackle, light streamed from those cracks. It seemed to go on endlessly.

Candles and torches sprang to life. Shadows began to retreat. Spider-wolves poured out of nooks and crevices, chambers and dungeons, howling like crazed beasts as they jumped into the Well. Darth continued to shriek. Pieces of his body dropped and disintegrated. Until finally, with a last wail, what remained of him leapt into the Well.

The portrait of Violet's mother burst into flames, and Ash fell from the chair. Violet went to him, cradled him, cooed softly. "It's over, my love."

* * * *

Months later, Violet's laughter chimed through the hall just outside the dining room as she studied Ash's frills and velvet attire. "Ash, what *are* you wearing?"

He pointed to Daniore, who managed to escape the spider-wolves, but still suffered a limp from the ordeal. "I made him dress like this for an interview with my father.

He told me if I dressed like this for at least one meal, he won't tell anyone I cheated the Seraglio out of their coin."

Violet wrapped her arm around Ash's waist. "You look adorable. I think it will be all the new rage."

"My father will think I've gone court happy."

"Well, we have lived here since…." She paused, wet her lip and swallowed. Every now and then, her mind drifted, evidence that the ordeal with Darth still haunted her. "We have lived here a while now, so I guess he would be right."

"You okay, love?"

"Aye," she whispered, and then more forcefully, "your father might not be after I finish my discourse on destroying the Seraglio and coming up with a more honorable way of uniting people in marriage."

"Oh, another discourse," Daniore said and took a step backward. "I don't think I'm that hungry, after all. I mean the last one about girls not being sold to the Seraglio gave the King a choking fit."

"He survived," Violet said calmly.

"Aye, it was the rest of us that had to hear his outbursts for the next month on how I chose the only untrained lass the Seraglio every produced."

"And aren't you just proud of that fact?" Violet asked, smiling.

"So proud, love, I'm going to the pub with Daniore for a nice roasted--"

"Oh no you don't." Violet said, pushing them both ahead of her. "The father of the future Queen should not dawdle in pubs. Neither should the child's sun-father."

"But," they both said in unison, and then in complete shock, "Queen?"

"Aye, it is a girl I carry and didn't your father recently sign that contract saying your firstborn shall rule?"

"Um, aye."

"Well, it didn't mention the gender, you know."

Again, Violet's laugh pealed out as she watched horror give way to grins on the faces of her two favorite men.

"Just promise me, love, that I'm not around when you tell the king about the firstborn's gender."

"I want in on that promise," piped Daniore.

Brushing past the two of them, she rolled her eyes heavenwards and muttered. "Chickens, both of you."

With a fresh bout of laughter rolling through the air, she composed herself and entered the dining room, rubbing the slight swell that contained her child.

Miles away, deep in the darkest shadows of a dismal manor, Amlet rubbed her own unborn's nest.

The End

BLACKTHORNE'S LIGHT

Marie Harte

Prologue

With a husky groan the shadowed figure continued to feed, his mouth moving hungrily over the smooth white neck of the limp woman he held tightly in his arms, his body primally thrusting into hers, hungry and ecstatic to feed on both her blood and her sexual essence.

He groaned as he sucked at her neck, his teeth keeping her veins open as his tongue laved her lifesblood like cream. His hard body drew moans and gasps of delight from her, even though she surely knew she would not survive this night. Her red hair swung like a bloodied scarf from her wan features, her eyes half-closed in ecstasy, her lips pale and trembling under the constant pleasure-pain of his touch.

And as he climaxed, drenching her womb with his fiery passion, he drained the last drop of bright red blood from her body as she found her own fulfillment. He released her and watched as the sated woman cried out for more, needing his body in hers like a starved addict. But he could only watch as her body suddenly lost its golden glow of life and faded under the inky blackness of her dark soul.

Like a flickering light, he watched as she passed into the

world beyond, where those better than he would judge her. His eyes darkened in pain but not regret. He knew his course in this world, and only prayed he would gain enough redemption to save himself such misery in the next life.

Chapter One

"Ms. Vansant? This is what you wanted, right?" the young woman asked in a husky voice as she cracked her gum. She handed Adara a leaflet showcasing the hottest club in town.

Adara glanced at the page and smiled, then handed the desperate young woman a twenty and left the small porn shop where she'd been doing some of her research. Now won't this make a fantastic article, she thought to herself as she narrowly avoided tripping over a homeless man lying on the sidewalk.

She tossed a bill out of her pocket to him with a small shake of her head and quickly moved out of this section of town. She didn't exactly scorn the nightlife, but anyone stupid enough to foray around this area of Rathan after dark was begging for trouble.

She glanced up at the glimmering moon, taken with the dark blue blanket of sky fading to black, the indigo clouds racing with the wind in the chill October air. Shaken out of her contemplation of the night sky by a few lewd propositions, Adara quickly hopped into her car and drove towards her home. She had enough material to start this new journalistic endeavor and felt a strange excitement. She had a feeling that this story would definitely cap all the others.

As Adara passed several better neighborhoods, she sighed at the disregard that had caused the western part of Rathan to fall to shambles. A good-sized suburb just north of Philadelphia, Rathan had both its good and bad sections of town.

Adara lived in the nice section, the part of town where the middle-class lived comfortably and longed to join the wealthy in Society Hill.   Unfortunately, layoffs and business closings had contributed to the neglected western half of town, the half that lately had been attracting a very dark element.

She pursed her lips as she drove down her street, a quiet neighborhood of smaller houses catering to singles and newly married couples. Adara left her car and unlocked her front door, bitterly aware that no one awaited her return.

She grabbed the mail that had collected on the ground under her mail slot and shuffled through the bills and advertisements with a huff.

"Nothing," she told her dark haired reflection in the mirror above a small wall table. She tossed the mail on the table, replayed her answering machine and managed a small grin at Maria's message.

"Your article idea seems interesting. Go for it," her editor's voice grumbled. "But let me know if you find anything out there that leads to better orgasms. Quite frankly, I'm getting tired of Herb."

Maria and Herb had been married for over twenty years, and happily so, Adara thought enviously. Yet it was Maria's quirky sense of humor and candid speech that had made her an instant friend. Maria had taken to Adara upon first meeting her and the business they did together blossomed as quickly as their friendship. Maria edited for *Chic Ventures*, a racy woman's magazine that had begun undertaking more serious topics of late.

Maria, however, maintained that as long as *Chic Ventures* continued to talk about sex, sex, and more sex, the magazine would never go out of print.

Adara threw a frozen dinner into the microwave and tossed her satchel on the kitchen counter. As she waited for the meal to cook, she eyed the newspaper article that had sparked the interest for her next story. She read again the news that a fourth woman had turned up missing in the past two weeks, making that now sixteen women in the last four months in the lower southeastern corner of Pennsylvania that had disappeared.

Apparently the few ties the women had were that all of them were quite beautiful, and none of them were particularly well-liked or behaved in life. Several of the lewd women, some prostitutes, drug users and a few alleged criminals had mysteriously vanished, no trace of their bodies ever found. The author of the article had nicknamed the case *The Evils of Beauty*, and the police had no leads on the crimes.

The microwave beeped and Adara grabbed the hot tray with a muttered curse. She ate hungrily, resolving tomorrow not to skip lunch and settled down at the table. She had tossed the idea around in her head several times. Most of these missing women had been speculated to visit the seedier side of life. Since Adara and most of the women she knew rarely ventured into the dark worlds of sex and eroticism, she thought she might generate a bit of interest in the subject with her article.

Good girls weren't supposed to engage in sex without a relationship presumably leading to marriage. Adara smiled grimly to herself. But then, good girls didn't always get Mr. Tall, Dark and Handsome all wrapped up with marriage in a bow. Sometimes Mr. Handsome slept with your best friend. Sometimes his complaints about boring sex with his fiancée sounded because he was too tired from a previous fling with said best friend earlier that day.

Adara swore again just thinking about how blind she'd been. Today she felt more than glad that she'd found out about Marci and James's defection. Her sex life hadn't been all that great with James but she had thought, naively, that with time they would grow closer.

She wondered again about her article. Maybe the 'bad girls' in life had it right. They played by their own rules and didn't get hurt as much, well, with the exception of the missing women. But, she thought wryly, it's not as if she planned on robbing or killing anyone. And who was to say that enjoying one's body was a bad thing anyways? She grabbed her notebook out of her bag off the counter and stared again at the leaflet she'd been handed.

She had a list of several well-known nightclubs but this one, she tapped the red paper, this one had a reputation all its own. Known for its Goth-dressing patrons, vampire hopefuls and no-holds-barred sexual dalliances both in the bar and in the back rooms behind it, Vampland had become the new underground hot spot for singles wanting sizzling, steamy sex and few strings attached.

Adara nodded. Yes. This would definitely be a piece that drove her readers wild. After all, it took a lot of guts and very little fear to enter into a world where anything was allowed.

* * * *

Trey surveyed the moon outside his window and smiled, his teeth bright and white as he grinned in appreciation of the clear October night sky. He didn't grin much lately, his job wearing on his weary mind and soul. He figured the least he could do to lighten his burdens would be to appreciate the beauty of this world.

He sighed and sat back in his office, watching through several monitors the gyrating bodies fleshed out on the dance floor like cattle being led to the slaughter. A knock at the door sounded and he called out for John to enter.

His young manager smiled and nodded towards the large monitor in the wall Trey had been studying.

"Isn't it great, boss? I mean, Trey, this place is jumping with people! Ever since you introduced this new Goth theme, we've been all over the map. In fact," he leaned towards Trey, his blue eyes sparkling with mischief, "We've got several more keys awaiting your interest," John said and threw them down on Trey's desk.

Trey merely sighed and shook his head. "Give them back or keep them, I don't care which." He gestured for John to grab them.

John merely shook his head as he eyed his boss in confusion. At twenty-eight, John considered himself a prime catch. He had an athlete's build, stood over six-two and had a handsome face to match his charm and keen wit. He never suffered for female companionship, but Trey?

Man, he'd never seen a guy get more offers for sex than his boss. And Trey never seemed to accept them.

He knew the guy had to be getting sex from somewhere, but Trey was as mysterious about his sex life as he was about his comings and goings. John covertly studied the man's face as Trey stared into the monitor overlooking his bar.

He looked like he belonged in this place, John thought, a lot more than John did with his boy-next-door good looks. John's last date had said that his boss reminded her of a vampire with his dark hair, black eyes and white skin. But as John studied him, he thought Trey's skin looked more golden than white, his eyes more brown than black.

Trey glanced over at him with a quizzical expression and John flushed, grinning as he grabbed the keys and left. Not only did Trey have a great face that the women loved to watch, but he also had a frame that most guys labored at the gym to build. And John knew Trey didn't work out. He didn't need to. Good genes, he thought with a shrug and rejoined the madness around him.

Trey waited until John had departed down the stairs before he clutched at his head and sunk into the bleak darkness that threatened to overwhelm him did he not heed its call. He searched within himself looking for peace, but found another awaited him. He felt revulsion that he looked forward to the task and berated himself for falling deeper into the blackness that awaited his soul. Trey looked again at the monitor before him, seeing now what he hadn't wanted to see earlier.

A woman in the corner danced with several friends, her long blond hair flying around her as she bounced to the music. Hungrily, he noted her slim body with full breasts bared almost fully through the low dress that she wore. She didn't have too much height and he noticed that though she danced with the others, the black aura that engulfed her didn't drift to anyone else but stayed directly over her head.

The night passed rather swiftly for him as he waited for her to leave. She stayed until the very end and he smiled grimly, glad at least that his club had given her vast entertainment before she had to meet her end.

He locked himself in his office and separated himself from his flesh, moving his spirit through the air on wings of purpose. He hovered over her, attracted to the darkness of her soul. He watched her as she left with one of the men dancing with her. Then Trey moved back with the couple to an apartment to study the blond woman.

Once inside the apartment, she immediately moved in on the man, teasing him with her body, not the least surprised or hurt when he slapped her harshly and pushed her around, looking as he if were taking her by force.

He watched as the man ripped her clothing from her body and plunged into her with haste, his frenzy further exciting the woman. Then he watched as she waited for the right moment.

The minute the man climaxed, she brought a large rock down upon his head with a solid thump. Then she kicked him off of her, running a finger over his bloody head and licking it with a shudder than made Trey hungry to take her now.

The woman moved quickly through the house, grabbing anything she deemed of value, finally stripping the unconscious man of his wallet and watch. She straightened her clothing, put a new shirt on that she slipped out of her bag, and left the house. She walked down the street and caught a cab. Trey followed her to the address, made a note and returned to his body.

Chapter Two

Meg answered the door on the second knock. A man clad in black and looking almost unreal stood there in the darkness, staring at her without words. Amazed at her luck and not questioning the oddness of such a handsome stranger at her door, she grinned and moved back, inviting him inside. He smiled at her and she blinked, thinking he had a tremendously bright smile. He closed and locked the door behind him, staring at her with an absorption that bordered on fanaticism.

"You want me," he said bluntly, his deep voice flowing over her like honey. "Tell me what you want."

Meg cleared her throat, her pale eyes fixed to the burning blackness of his gaze. She had never seen this man before in her life. She could never have forgotten such a face. And yet she answered him.

"I want you to take me hard," she said breathlessly, the words torn from her lips by something she couldn't explain. "I want it rough and I want to feel you ripping through my virginal flesh," she said and watched the stranger staring into her eyes mercilessly.

Meg shook her head. Sure she liked her sex rough, but she'd never really considered doing it anally. Yet she'd just told this large, strong, handsome stranger to ravish her. She wondered if she was dreaming. Nothing about tonight seemed quite real.

She swallowed audibly as he stripped out of his clothes. He looked more than ready for the task at hand. She stared at his body, caught by the dark hair surrounding the large weapon waving at her between his thighs.

He motioned for her to come to him and she moved like a puppet on strings. A tiny bead of avarice reminded her of the quality of his clothing and she vowed that after she'd had sex with this man, she would check his pockets for valuables. Then she moved towards him and all thoughts of theft faded.

He lifted her clothing from her, gently removing the cloth with what must have been a razor in his hands. Though he moved quickly, not a mark or drop of blood touched her. Then he slapped her, not hard, but enough to make her cheek sting, and Meg felt her body instantly respond.

Though she had lain with that playboy a few hours past, he hadn't aroused more than her lust for his money. This man, however, made her seethe with need. He turned her around against the wall with rough hands and tightened his hold on her, pressing into her body, allowing her to feel him large and hard and throbbing behind her.

He gripped her hands above her head and whispered words that had no meaning. He braced her arms and spread her legs further apart, his knee whispering against the wetness between her thighs. Without a word he entered her moist body, his large penis thrusting inside of her without sound and she wondered at the amazing ecstasy flowing through her body.

"Oh, God," she gasped as he pumped inside of her, his body long and hard, almost painful. Then he quickly removed himself and positioned his phallus higher. Meg groaned as he pushed into the tender flesh never before touched by a man. "Please," she cried, shaking her head as her mind tried to distinguish between the exquisite pain her gave her and the raw pleasure that drowned her body.

He grunted slightly as he pushed past her tight walls, pulling out and then slamming harder into her. Meg gasped as the pain-pleasure built. His fingers moved over her, moving into her wet vagina, over her clitoris with ease as he thrust inside of her harder and harder. And then he bent his head and she felt real pain and real fear.

His teeth sank into her neck and she heard him groan, felt his hips thrust faster inside of her until he shuddered and came inside of her. But he wasn't done. His mouth moved over her neck, his touch gentler as he drained her body with a quickness that astounded her.

He inserted his still hard shaft into her wet vagina and again thrust in and out, his hand working the front of her body, teasing the hard nub of desire that grew as Meg flew towards release. Soon the pain and the pleasure mixed until she felt nothing, neither the release of her orgasm as it triggered his second one, nor the black void that consumed her entire body and soul from the light.

Trey breathed heavily as his body pulsed, his desire sated again this night, doubly so as the woman had been darker than the last. She had not only wounded the man she'd robbed earlier, but had killed two others in the course of her thieving over the past month. He tried to relax, to still his beating heart. But the blood that lingered in his mouth tasted so good. He panted and stared down at his now flaccid body, wondering how a man like himself had been so drawn to the darkness.

He shook his head. He didn't like inflicting pain, he thought with a frown, only pleasure. But the woman tonight had begged him to breach her, to cause her pain--a chore that left him with some distaste. And yet, she had asked him for it, and he felt obliged to serve her needs.

He stretched and tried to focus on his success and pleasured body instead of the aching sadness that pushed at him for his crimes. He didn't consider, as the Elders did, that he aided the light. Light didn't feed off of the darkness, didn't strip life from those deemed unworthy by a higher power. Darkness caused death, he thought.

He blinked and his clothes again joined his body. Trey licked at the blood still staining his teeth and sighed at the pleasure that afforded him. He looked inward and saw that he could indeed return home, his task now complete. Then he turned to mist and flew back to his home on wings of emptiness.

* * * *

Adara bit at the pencil in her mouth, surprised that James had the utter gall to approach her at home after all he had done. She opened her door and stared at him blandly, not reacting to the sight of his bruised face and bandaged head.

"What do you want?" she asked coolly.

"Please, Adara, just let me in for a few seconds and then I'll go," he said and winced at the pain in his head.

Adara stared at him and sighed, throwing up her hands and moving back so that he could enter.

"I suppose I should ask what happened to you," she said less than enthusiastically.

"I was robbed," James said, looking pathetic as he blinked at her weakly.

"And I care because...? Shouldn't Marci be tending your wounds?" She couldn't help asking nastily.

"She's at her sister's this week," he offered quietly, and sat down without asking.

"Great," Adara said, her emotional scars throbbing as she

stared at him. "Why are you here?"

"The thief took my watch," he said bitterly. "You know, the one my mother bought for me? The Rolex?" He reminded her. "And I think you might have a copy of the appraisal. I couldn't find it at my place."

Adara stared at him. It had been four months since their split, but Adara kept excellent records. She thought quickly. "Wait here," she ordered, returning moments later with a square envelope. She handed it to him, aware that he was leaving out some interesting details. "So when and where were you robbed?"

"Last night, at my place." He grimaced and stood. "She, I mean, he was pretty rough," he said.

"She?" Adara asked quickly. She could picture it very clearly, as if she'd been there when it had happened. Sometimes the visions struck her like that. "So she screwed you for more than your body, eh, James?"

James stared at her warily but said nothing. "Thanks," he mumbled and walked out the door.

Adara stared at her closed door, wondering at the odd scene she'd envisioned. So James was now into rough sex, hmm? She shook her head and smiled, able to laugh that perhaps justice had been served last night. Now Marci would know what it felt like to be the 'woman wronged'.

Adara moved back into her office and continued working on her computer. Later that night, she dressed with care. She had persuaded a friend of hers, a journalist for the *Rathan Times*, to go clubbing with her as a lark. Sue had a bubbly personality and love of excitement that made her the perfect companion for Adara's venture into the dark side of life, Adara thought.

She had just applied some lipstick when her doorbell rang.

"Come on in," Adara shouted and continued to work on her makeup. She froze as she caught sight of the woman behind her.

Sue Saxton, normally a petite blonde, wore a long black dress showing ample cleavage and a long, fishnet clad leg through a thigh-cut slit. Three-inch killer heels graced her small feet but what really grabbed Adara's attention smiled at her from Sue's face. Sue's blond hair had been spiked, the tips colored black. She'd applied some very white pancake foundation, making her blue eyes look that much more blue surrounded by black liner, black mascara and gray shadow. Her lips, in contrast, were full and pouty, covered in black. Sue wore little jewelry save for a large silver cross around her throat and two silver hoops in her ears.

"How do I look?" the bubbly blonde asked, lowering her voice and sounding like a poor Elvira imitator.

"Like a gothic tramp." Adara shook her head.

"You don't look so bright and shiny yourself, Morticia," Sue joked.

Adara looked at her reflection. She wore black as well, a long dress that covered her from her neck to her feet. The dress clasped at the back of her neck and bared her shoulders and arms while it hugged every curve of her body, flaring slightly around her calves to ease movement. She had decided on red lipstick, not opting for Sue's look, but for a simplicity that would allow her not to feel so odd. The only other makeup she wore consisted of dark eyeliner and a hint of blush. Other than that she wore small gold earrings.

"What about your shoes?"

"Simple black pumps, two-inch heels I'm afraid," Adara said apologetically.

"Great," Sue said dryly. "Well, at least you did a good job with your hair."

Adara had put her dark hair up in a clip, pulling it away from her face and neck so that it gathered fully behind her head, licking at the back of her neck in wisps and small curls. The thick brown mass looked shiny and almost black in the dim bathroom light.

"Well, partner, let's go get 'em," Adara said and grabbed her small clutch.

* * * *

Adara and Sue didn't wait long in line outside of Vampland. Their dresses had them in the door faster than the young vampire groupies and preppy outsiders looking for something different to entertain them.

"Ladies." A large bouncer wearing a thick black cape grinned at them as he took their cover money. Then he waved them inside.

Adara heard Sue gasp and echoed the sentiment as they walked into the crowded club. Adara saw people dressed in all manner of styles, mostly wearing the ever-popular black. She and Sue fit right in, rather nicely, she thought as a woman in a long cape passed by them.

The atmosphere was thick with smoke, not from cigarettes, Adara found with some surprise, but from the fog machine near the DJ. The music was a fast, throbbing techno beat that had people swaying against each other as they overly imbibed.

The large room had been done in dark shades of black and maroon, with large velvet draperies hanging on the walls and along the ceiling to hide the old pipes and construction of earlier years.

Oddly enough, Adara noticed that by and large the men and women in the club were fairly attractive. Most of the patrons fell between twenty-one, per the sign out front, and their mid-thirties, though Adara did note a few older people mingling in the crowd.

After a short time perusing the masses, she and Sue decided on a drink to calm their nerves. They reached the bartender and Sue flirted outrageously, leaning over the bar to successfully capture the bartender's gaze.

"Gee, Sue, at this rate you can be one of my star interviews about raw sex in public. Why don't you just jump him and have your way with him on the bar?" Adara asked under her breath as Sue laughed at something the man said.

Sue smiled at the man and waved as she grabbed Adara's arm and pulled her towards a less crowded section near some tables away from the dance floor.

"Look, we're here to see how 'bad girls' do it, right? Well, tonight I feel like a bad girl," Sue said. "Maybe I *will* be your first interview," she murmured as the bartender approached.

"Hi," he said as he stared at the two of them with an appreciative gaze. "I'm John, the manager." He smiled.

"I'm Sue and this is Adara," Sue said and winked at him. "Great club," she nodded enthusiastically.

"We get a lot of interesting people in here," John said, his gaze wavering between Sue and Adara. Sue leaned closer to him and his eyes again clung to her bountiful breasts.

Adara managed to avoid rolling her eyes as John and Sue made small talk. She heard little of what they said as her eyes scanned the crowd, her interest in the people around her taking over.

"Tour?" John asked and Adara looked up to see Sue and John staring at her.

Adara flushed slightly, caught ogling the masses around them. "Oh, sorry. I was distracted," she said waving her arm at the throng out on the dance floor.

John laughed. "No problem. It's a little overwhelming at first," he said. "So would you like the tour, the complete tour, Madame Author?" he asked with a rakish grin.

Adara glared at Sue who shrugged. "So I told him. It's not as if it's a secret why we're here."

"You don't mind, John? I wouldn't want to take you away from anything," Adara murmured, thoughts of an insider's view intriguing her.

John grinned and looked leisurely over Sue's scantily clad form, making her blush. "It'd be my pleasure. I've got to tell you, we get a lot of beautiful and interesting people in this place. But you two really stand out." He complimented them with a genuine smile.

Sue beamed and Adara smiled her thanks, though she didn't quite understand what he meant. Surprisingly, Adara had been complimented on her looks her entire life. She had never seen anything special in her tall frame and average face. She had dark brown hair and brown eyes, a plain nose and a mouth that had been accused too often of speaking her mind. She couldn't figure out why men seemed to notice her amidst other women. Now Sue, she thought to herself, Sue stood out.

A petite blonde with a surprising amount of curves, Sue had that Nordic blond-haired, blue-eyed sexual bombshell look about her. And her bubbly personality only added to her attractiveness.

But never one to look a gift horse in the mouth, Adara shrugged and moved through the club with Sue and their tour guide.

Chapter Three

Adara noticed that John proved to be an entertaining host. They listened as he explained the bar and its inception.

"Three years ago this place was fairly tame. I mean, we're outside of the city and Rathan, though not small, isn't Philly. This place used to be a billiards pub called Smiley's and it was going downhill fast, like the rest of western Rathan.

"Then Trey happened upon it and suddenly this place turned into an overnight success. We're attracting folks from Philly, Jersey, and even New York when they can get away for a weekend. You guys came at just the right time. Fridays are usually the best nights," John smiled.

"Trey?" Adara asked.

"Trey Blackthorne. He's the owner and the genius behind this place. If he's in, I'll introduce you later." John moved them away from the bar and dance floor towards a stairway leading to a second floor. "Up here is the VIP section," he said and nodded to a large man guarding the stairwell. The man nodded and lifted a velvet rope, allowing them entry.

"We have a number of people who prefer the quiet up here, the dark intimacy and anonymity we can provide away from the dancing lights." John pointed over his shoulder. Adara saw that like the area below, this level was crowded. She noted several curtained booths against the walls.

"Privacy booths," John said with a nod in that direction. "They cost but they're worth it." He looked at Sue and Adara and shrugged. "I know you haven't been here before, but you must know the type of place you've come to tonight. It's an erotic fantasy club," he said bluntly.

"Downstairs is more for the hip, younger crowd. Up here you have a higher clientele," John said and walked with them towards a back stairwell. "This leads us to the backrooms, the whispered 'dark area' of the club. It's all nonsense of course." He shrugged the notion away.

They descended back to the first floor and entered what looked like a posh hotel hallway, nothing seedy or dark around them. Several doors lay on either side of the corridor and Adara could see that the hallway curved further down to admit more rooms.

As they started down the hall, they passed a door through which Adara thought she heard some odd moans.

"We don't endorse drugs, prostitution, or anything illegal or harmful to our patrons," John said evenly as they paused outside of a door. He knocked and then pushed the door open upon hearing a hearty "Come in." Adara noted a group of well-dressed men and women engaged in a rousing game of strip poker. John smiled and closed the door behind them as they left.

"I'll admit we cater to a different crowd. But Vampland is about enjoying your sexuality. You can rent these back rooms for anything you want," he said. "But again, we get wind of prostitution or drugs and you're out. Some rooms are better suited for, shall we say, horizontal entertainments." He grinned and looked at Sue. "Others are fun meeting places for gamers, couples or parties."

"What about orgies?" Adara asked wryly as the moans from the first room sounded louder.

"Interested?" John asked looking surprised. Sue managed to smother a chuckle and he grinned. "Oh, just curious, sure. Well, like I said, we rent the rooms. We don't interfere in our patrons' activities unless we get complaints. All those who enter these back rooms do so of their own consent and their own free will."

"Isn't this all just another way of promoting prostitution and torrid sex?" Adara asked. She couldn't fathom that the law hadn't closed this Trey person down.

John shook his head. "Not at all. Adara, the people who come to Vampland want excitement and adventure, something outside the norm. They don't pay us for sex. They bring their fantasies here and we indulge them. Didn't you see the costumes out front? Now if you want to meet a *real* vampire," he said grinning and led them back towards a door through which they reentered the first floor. "I'll introduce you to my boss."

John escorted them to the far wall away from the dance floor on which rested a wide set of stairs. Adara and Sue stopped at the small landing at the top and waited while John slipped inside. Then he opened the door and motioned for them to follow him.

Adara saw a small room that looked like a seating area. A small couch and several chairs had been carefully arranged around a table. She noticed that the furniture looked surprisingly clean and tasteful, done in dark shades of maroon and navy blue. The molding on the Queen Anne couch was of mahogany, the same as the three chairs and table.

John waited for them by the door on the far wall. He waved them forward and they moved through in file, Adara bringing up the rear. When they entered, she had to adjust her eyes to the low lighting in the room. This room was twice as large as the outer room. It stood in darkness save for the burning lamp over an immaculately organized desk.

John raised a dimmer switch so that the overhead lighting made everyone visible. Sue gasped audibly and Adara caught her breath as they saw the man John had been waiting to introduce.

John grinned. "Sue, Adara, I'd like you to meet the man behind the mystery, Trey Blackthorne."

Blackthorne rose to his feet and moved around the desk to meet them. His eyes, dark and piercing, seemed to absorb their every detail, as if he stared at them from Lucifer's vantage.

He towered over Sue and Adara put him at roughly six-four or five.

"Pleased to meet you," he said in low, courtly tone as he kissed Sue's limp hand. She smiled weakly and stepped back, as if intimidated by the man's larger-than-life presence.

Then he turned to Adara and his body stiffened slightly for perhaps a split second that no one but Adara seemed to notice.

Blackthorne bent over to kiss her hand and Adara felt a burning heat run through her where his soft lips caressed her skin.

"Adara, a lovely name," he said in a deep voice. His eyes blazed with need before he banked the emotion behind a polite façade. John mentioned what Sue and Adara had been doing at the club but Blackthorne's eyes never left Adara's face.

"Interesting," Blackthorne said and spared a warm smile for Sue and John. "I hope you're enjoying yourself?" he asked Sue.

"Perfectly," Sue said and latched onto John's hand. John grinned down at her and Adara saw the amorous glance the two shared. Apparently Sue had decided to try out the bad girl fantasy right away, Adara thought wryly.

Blackthorne must have sensed the same for he smiled and said, "John, why don't you entertain Sue here for a while? Give her the VIP treatment. Everything's on the house," he said. Sue grinned and left Adara without a backwards glance, surprising her friend.

Adara watched her and John go with a bit of unease, aware of being completely alone with a strange man that made her insides burn at his touch. She turned to see that Blackthorne had moved to a small bar against the wall.

"Would you like something to drink?" he asked courteously, his manner perfectly civil.

Adara nodded. "Yes, thank you. Do you have any wine?"

He poured her a subtle blush that seemed to wink at her through the crystal glass he handed her. As he handed her the glass, their fingers touched and Adara couldn't help the gasp that slipped through her.

"Adara?" Blackthorne murmured as he stared at her with an intensity that made her shiver. "Drink your wine," he said in a throaty voice. He poured himself something to drink but his eyes stayed on hers as he swallowed.

Adara felt nervous and uncomfortable under his gaze and blurted out the first thing that came to mind.

"I think Sue really likes John," she said quickly.

Blackthorne smiled, his dark eyes gleaming like burnished onyx as he stared at her face, his eyes tracing her features as if making a memory.

"And John likes her. Right now they're moving along the back hallway towards a nice, quiet room," he said, his voice seductive in its soothing cadence. "Look," he said and lightly grasped her arm to draw her closer to a monitor showing her friend's movements.

Adara watched as John paused with Sue outside of a door and lowered his head to kiss her with abandonment. Adara blushed as she felt Blackthorne's eyes on her.

"Well, I guess they're both adults," she remarked inanely, wondering why she felt so prudish and embarrassed suddenly. She turned her head but Blackthorne's hand cupped her cheek and turned her back to face the screen. Adara's loins quickened at the contact and she had to work to calm her breathing.

"Now do you see what he's doing?" Blackthorne asked softly as he moved directly behind her, staring over her head at the monitor.

Adara nodded breathlessly as she watched John peel Sue's dress apart to reveal her breasts. Then he lowered his mouth to taste her bared skin. Adara watched in amazement as Sue let a complete stranger strip her to her waist in the hallway, a place where anyone could see them. But at the same time, Adara felt a strange flutter in her stomach, a hint of excitement at having the enigmatic man at her back as she watched the sensual scene before her.

She watched with him in silence as John opened the door behind Sue and enclosed them in the room, leaving the rest of their encounter to the imagination.

"Now do you want to know what they're doing?" Blackthorne asked. His breath whispered in her ear, warm and stirring. His hands moved up to caress her hair, releasing the clasp that had held it bound. He sighed as her hair fell over his fingers. "So silky," he said and buried his nose in it. "And so pure."

"How, how do you know what they're doing now?" Adara asked, her body trembling slightly as lust enveloped her. She could feel her heart beating faster, could feel her nipples hard and pressing against the thin fabric of her dress as Blackthorne crowded her.

"My name is Trey," he said as he licked at her ear. Adara gasped and moaned lightly as he ran a large hand over her arm. She looked down at her arm and studied the hand lying there. Long fingered with nails surprisingly well rounded, a smooth palm warm against her skin, his hand looked like a marble work of art. "Say my name," he said and licked at her ear.

"Trey," Adara breathed.

"And though I can't see through a camera what they're doing, I know. Shall I show you?" he asked.

Adara found herself nodding, curious as to how he could know what they did. But she misunderstood his words for he suddenly unsnapped the back collar of her dress.

She whirled to face him, shocked that she had let her unfounded arousal take her this far.

"Shy?" he asked with a small grin. "Don't be," he said and his smile left him. "You have the most beautiful light," he murmured and lowered his mouth to her lips.

Like a dark magician, he brought her body to life with a simple touch. His lips moved over hers sensuously, tasting and yet questioning. She groaned at his heat and his tongue slid over her lips, capturing her mouth. He tasted like wine and something faintly musty, she thought, sighing as his hands moved over her back and down her body.

He stroked her softly with his hands as his mouth stole her breath, her very will. His large hands cupped her smooth bottom, bringing her closer to the large erection pressing into her. Adara could only imagine him to be huge, feeling his body hard and throbbing against her.

"John's a fast worker," he murmured into her ear, his hands moving away from her back to circle around to her front. His hands moved over her stomach and up to cup her breasts. "By now he's got your friend naked and is completely inside of her," he said softly. "But I like to take things slowly," he whispered.

His hands teased her breasts, pinching at her nipples with exquisite care, making her writhe against him, her body seeking release.

"Yes," he whispered, his eyes dark and unfathomable as he stared down at her. "I like to savor things."

He returned to her mouth, licking at every inch of her. She returned the motion, touching his mouth tentatively with her tongue. He moaned softly and she ran her tongue over his teeth, curious when she felt pinpricks of sharpness graze her.

He held her tighter, sucking on her tongue and pressing deeper into her. Then he released her mouth, breathing deeply.

"You make me hunger," he said roughly and stared down at her. He licked at his red lips and lifted her in his arms. Then he sat her on the edge of his desk and moved between her thighs, urging her dress up her knees. "You're soft," he said as he stroked her nylon clad legs, all the while watching her eyes. His fingers inched upwards slowly and he smiled when he touched the lace border of the thigh-high elastic.

Then he bent down on his knees and Adara looked at him in surprise.

"What are you doing?" she asked huskily.

"What you want me to do," he said softly and moved his hands up her legs to her thighs. He pushed her dress up further until he could see her black panties. "Very nice," he said and stroked her through the cloth. He could feel her wetness and smiled hungrily. "Very nice," he repeated and ripped her underwear from her body.

Adara gasped as suddenly her underwear vanished. But

before she could think, he put his mouth where his hand had been and all thoughts fled her mind. He spread her thighs further and parted her soft folds, his mouth settling firmly over her full clitoris. He sucked, groaning softly as he slipped a long finger into her wet and needy body.

Adara's head fell back on her neck and she groaned his name, amazed at what she was doing. "Trey, what are you doing to me?"

But he continued to pleasure her, his hands gripping her thighs hard enough to leave marks, but she felt nothing but his mouth on her. His tongue flickered over her and she gasped with pleasure, her desire building with his every touch.

"So good," she moaned and rocked into him, needing him inside of her right now, right this very minute. Adara Vansant, a woman who'd never done a questionable thing in her life, had suddenly surrendered her body to a complete stranger. But she could not feel anything but the rapture coursing through her as his lips caressed her, as his tongue brought her to completion.

He moved his mouth over her, sucking her more deeply and Adara was helpless to stop her rushing orgasm. She groaned as waves of ecstasy crashed over her again and again, barely aware that she held his head between her legs, her hands clutched in his hair as his tongue continued to lick her.

When at last her body calmed enough that she could focus on Trey, she blinked dreamily at him and watched as he stood and moved his hand to the snap of his dark trousers.

Chapter Four

Trey paused above the snap, staring down at her with an unworldly hunger in his gaze.

"I don't think I can do this," he said softly as he stared at her. Trey had never before experienced anything like what he'd just done, not in his entire life. The familiar hunger had been on him the moment he'd seen her aura, but what an aura to behold.

Unlike the dark blackness of the women whose lives he lived to take, Adara's light shone fiercely, colored as brightly as the woman's passion. A glimmering rainbow of colors pulsed around her, the energy beckoning him to absorb just a touch.

He hadn't realized how she would affect him. He had tasted her mouth, touched her pliant body and been unable to stop himself from licking her essence, the honeyed sweetness flowing between her thighs. And now his body throbbed and pulsed, begging him for release. Yet, he stared down at Adara, entranced by her shimmering beauty.

He couldn't bear to reave her soul from her body. He had never taken a woman without drinking her blood. Then again, he had never felt this raw emotion before. He hungered, yes, but the pounding of his heart, the quiet pulling of his soul, confounded him.

Adara stared at him hungrily, enthralled and still hazily drugged on her own passion.

"You need," she said and nodded, as if aware of the burning hole in his heart. He needed far more than he thought she could give him. But in that he was wrong. As if commanded by something outside of himself, he unsnapped his trousers and freed his engorged penis, offering himself to her.

She watched with fascination as he stroked himself, his fingers gliding along his long shaft and rubbing the moisture beading at the tip. She licked her lips and he groaned, his hand moving over his shaft again and again, imagining her mouth over him.

And then she placed her hand over his, stopping his actions. He stared down at her, his breath coming in heaving gasps.

"What do you want?" she asked him in a husky voice, sounding strangely like himself when he exercised the last moments of life on the women whose lives he was forced to take. Giving himself to her hands, to his fate if indeed his time had come, he closed his eyes and prayed for the strength to endure.

"I want you to kiss me."

She removed her hand and knelt before him, supplicant and worshiping as she kissed the head of his penis with lingering lips.

"I want you to lick me," he rasped and watched as her bright pink tongue ran over his organ, making him shudder with the need to plunge into her violently. He felt his teeth grow and pierce his mouth as he bit down.

"I want you to suck me," he said thickly, his body so poised for completion that he feared he wouldn't last but a minute if she actually followed through.

And then her mouth closed over him and he was lost. She swallowed him, taking him to the back of her throat as her mouth worked him, her tongue stroking him as her lips curled around him, sucking him delicately. Then her mouth tightened around his shaft and her fingers grazed his soft, velvet sack tightening unbearably under her touch.

He panted loudly now, his long fingers gripping his desk hard enough to leave dents. He dared not touch her but couldn't help but thrust his body deeper into her mouth as she suckled him, her warm mouth feeding his lust until he could see naught but the shadow of her rainbow around him.

"Oh yes," he groaned as he thrust. "Yes, yes, Adara, more," he gasped.

And then she sucked harder and his climax burst forth in a myriad of colors. He groaned helplessly as he shuddered into her mouth, his body throbbing and pouring his milky white essence. She swallowed him and continued to caress him with her mouth until he had nothing more to give her. Then she eased off of him and licked him, taking the last drop of his orgasm into her mouth.

She stood and he leaned back against the desk, shaky and confused and utterly sated.

"My God," he said hoarsely as he stared at her. "Who are you?"

Adara smiled and leaned up to kiss him. He shuddered at the taste of himself on her lips, awash in feelings that compounded the throbbing in his heart.

"I guess now I'm a bad girl," she said with a wink and walked out the door.

Trey chuckled lightly and straightened himself in his clothing. He didn't understand why or how it had happened, but he felt as if his humanity had been handed back to him, if only in a little piece.

He marveled that he hadn't needed to feed on her blood to reach fulfillment, but had been thoroughly sated by her honeyed body. He blinked in shock as he tried to absorb what had just occurred in his office.

Never before had he been so thoroughly loved or cared for. And he would wager his soul that Adara had found her orgasm more fulfilling than she'd ever assumed possible, he thought with satisfaction.

But he had to know more about her, he thought in a panic. Then he looked down and saw that she'd left her business card. He breathed deeply, relaxed, and left his office door open to air the room. It smelled like sex, he thought, and wondered when he could next arrange a meeting with the woman who'd started to restore his soul.

After some time spent regaining his control, he moved down the stairs and entered the back rooms, approaching the door where he'd seen John take Sue. He listened and heard groaning. But used to such noises, he opened the door and waited by the entrance for John to finish. John had Sue on her hands and knees on the bed, her breasts swaying as he took her from behind. She moaned and heaved as he thrust into her a final time, his mouth moving sensuously over her neck, a small trickle of crimson sliding down her back.

"Careful John," Trey said softly.

Immediately John eased his hold on her neck and slid out of her body slowly, his eyes closed in pleasure as he felt her body slowly release him.

Trey watched, his eyes darkening as he imagined Adara in such a state. He waited until John had dressed and redressed Sue. Then he reminded John with a small nod to close the wound at Sue's neck. John flushed, apparently still caught up in the aftershocks of feeding, and did so quickly. Then he walked Sue to the door and kissed her good-bye.

"I haven't had such a blast in years," John sighed and flopped back on the bed tiredly. "I'm telling you, Trey, I had her seven ways from Sunday and I still want her."

Trey shook his head. "Keep yourself focused or you'll fall prey to bloodlust. And trust me, John, you don't want to kill her."

John paled and sat up, his mood sobering as he listened to his mentor. "Right." He cleared his throat. "So how did you and Adara get along?"

"Fine." Trey shrugged and could read the disappointment on John's face. He knew the young vampire worried for him, but no one on this earth knew what Trey had been tasked with for the last few years. Trey himself didn't know how much longer he could survive the black void invading his soul. Until Adara, he hadn't seen a flicker of light in anything save the passing of souls into the world beyond.

"Well, I'm sorry things didn't work out." John stood and stretched. "But you can be sure I'll be seeing that little spitfire again. She remembers a bit of what we did, but not all." John grinned, his teeth bright and sharp.

"Well, I think you've had enough play, hmm? Time to get back to work," Trey said with a sigh and waited for John to precede him.

* * * *

Three days later Adara read the paper with a startled gasp. The woman who had robbed James had apparently vanished. She recognized Meg Cabot's picture in the paper from her brief vision of James's robbery.

She frowned as yet another woman went missing. So again some vigilante captured and did God-knew-what with an evil woman bent on thievery and murder. Adara thought James had been lucky that the woman hadn't killed him, as she read the paper describing several of the woman's other victims.

She turned back to her computer and typed the first part of her seven part series. She flushed as she recalled her wanton behavior with Trey Blackthorne. She fumbled over the keyboard and hastily erased the gibberish that appeared on the screen.

She sighed as she recalled his touch. Never before had Adara lusted after a man so completely. And never in her life had she received, not to mention performed, oral sex on a man she'd just met. She flushed, but grinned slightly as she realized she now belonged with the bad girls who wrote in to *Chic Venture* about their 'dirtiest deeds'.

She couldn't imagine James and Marci being so bold, she thought with a huge grin. But at thoughts of James, her mind shifted to Meg Cabot. Her instincts humming, she wondered just why in the past few months so many women had disappeared from this area of the country. Sure, over the past few years there had been instances of women disappearing in record numbers, all apparently beautiful but with surprising secret lives. But things had been rather quiet for the past year.

Adara shook her head. That was a story for Sue, she thought with a grin. Sue had been completely forthcoming about all of her details with John the day following their excursion into Vampland. She made what Adara and Trey had done look like harmless foreplay. Of course, Adara had told Sue that nothing had happened. Sue had believed her. After all, Adara didn't do things like that, never had, and to Sue's mind, never would.

Adara shook her head. At least Sue's story and the tour of Vampland had been great for her first article. She'd gone so far as to use some of Sue's experiences in article one, but didn't want to give it all away and spaced out the more juicy details for the next few articles. She'd changed names and some details, using her imagination to fill in other blanks.

She sighed and sat back, needing a glass of water. Suddenly she felt very thirsty.

Adara moved to the kitchen and guzzled a glass of water,

then quickly grabbed another. Yet still she felt thirsty. She blinked and stumbled when a vision assaulted her. She moaned as she struck the floor, remembering that it had been twenty years since she'd last been hit so hard.

In her mind's eye, she watched as a woman, a svelte brunette in a crotch length skirt and hooker heels, fired into a crowded room. Blood splattered the room and bodies fell over like dominoes. The woman then looked into her purse for a mirror and dropped the gun, putting on her lipstick as the police arrived to take her away.

Adara blinked and was about to get up when another vision hit her, this one darker and more vivid.

She watched as the woman, Brenda something, walked around her cell, pacing like a caged tiger. She tossed her long brown hair, her lewd mouth cracking at the guard serving her dinner. She tossed the plate back at the guard and threw herself onto her cot.

The room darkened to night and the women in the cell next to Brenda fell into sleep. Brenda lay half asleep herself when suddenly a large man covered her. He whispered something Adara couldn't hear and she watched as he pulled the woman to her feet. The woman didn't struggle, merely stood like a weed waving in the breeze.

As if aware of Adara's stare, the man looked over his shoulder and Adara gasped in recognition. Trey Blackthorne blinked remorsefully, as if saddened that he recognized her. But then he turned back to the woman in the cell. With astonishingly long nails that crooked like talons, he rent the top half of the jumper from her body, baring Brenda half-naked, her white skin shining in the darkness.

Trey bent his head and grazed one of her breasts with his mouth, a thin trail of blood seeping down her body when he lifted his head. The woman sighed blissfully and tugged him closer as if she enjoyed his touch. Then he raised his head and stared down at her. He spoke in a soft language Adara could not understand and the woman shook her head slowly.

Then all gentleness left him and he roughly bent her head

to expose her neck, his hand gripping her hair in a tight fist. He bent his head to her neck and Adara watched in astonishment as his teeth lengthened, their bright points impossibly white before they plunged into Brenda's neck. She watched in horrified fascination as he sucked ravenously, soft sounds of need echoing in the dark cell.

Brenda's body seemed to grow blacker, the white of her skin speckled under a shower of darkness as the vampire fed on her. When Brenda stood completely enshrouded in a black glaze, Trey let go of her neck, his teeth fitting neatly back into his mouth. He watched as Brenda sighed, her eyes closed. Her body suddenly shimmered into a dim glow until the blackness that had overtaken her body returned to envelop her. Adara thought she heard a vague shriek as a sudden flash of light popped. And then all was silent.

Chapter Five

Adara blinked and stared at her hardwood floor in confusion. Then her vision came back to her and her eyes widened in fear. She had to get out of here, she thought wildly as she hastily got to her feet. She believed in what she saw, knew the truth in her psychic gift.

"Oh, my God," she said aloud as she hurriedly threw a duffle bag onto her bed and threw clothes into it haphazardly. Trey Blackthorne was a vampire, a blood-sucking sexual creature that had done something decidedly wrong in that prison cell. The woman, Brenda, had completely burned up or vanished, popped out of existence, Adara thought worriedly. And somehow Trey had seen her--Adara--watching it all.

She quickly zipped her bag and stuffed her laptop and folders into her briefcase. Then grabbing everything, she hurried to the front door and threw it open.

"Going somewhere?" Trey asked with a bland

expression, his large frame looming dangerously in her dark doorway. Adara dropped her bags and backed away. But she gasped as he stepped over her door.

"I didn't invite you in," she said. "You're not invited," she repeated firmly, remembering the old vampire myths, her panic growing. "You can't come in!"

"But I'm special," Trey said quietly and closed the door behind him, locking it with an ominous click. "I don't need an invitation."

He stalked her, moving noiselessly over her hard flooring.

"What do you want?" Adara asked, trying to think of a way to stop him. Vampire, he's a vampire, she told herself. She nimbly leapt towards her bedroom, locking the door behind her. Adara raced to her jewelry box even as she heard the doorknob rattle.

Finally, she thought as she clutched the cross in her hands. The door shot open, the lock clearly broken, and Trey stared at her with disappointment.

"I expected better from you, Adara. You're different," he said shaking his head. He moved closer to her when she thrust her crucifix at him.

"Stay back," she said fearfully.

Trey reached out and gently enfolded the crucifix and her fist in his hand. Adara gasped.

"Shouldn't you be smoking or something?" she asked.

Trey's gaze widened, a hint of humor flashing in the serious depths of his eyes. "You watch too much television, Adara. No, love," he said softly, his stare impossibly intense as he watched her. "I'm on His side," he said and held the cross out to her.

She shook her head, her dark brown eyes deepening to black as she studied him, confused. "But I saw you kill a woman tonight." As she heard herself say this, her brain suddenly pieced together the strange mystery of the vanishing women over the last few months. She gasped. "It was you all along." She swallowed audibly. "You murdered all those women."

Trey shook his head. "And I thought those with the Sight were gypsies dressed in long skirts and bangles," he replied, staring down at her curiously. "How did you see me there tonight?" he asked, not commenting on her accusations.

Adara merely watched him, seeking a way to escape. She wondered if any of this was real. Prior images of Trey's raw sexuality and care with her mixed with the violence of this night. She didn't know what to believe.

Trey watched Adara with something akin to compassion. "Adara, please sit down and let me explain what I can," he offered in a quiet voice. Something about this woman called to him and he couldn't let her see him as he did, as a monster. Seeing little choice for herself, Adara quickly sat as far away from him on the bed as she could get.

"I'm a vampire," he began. "This you know. I was born a vampire, but of mortal parents. It's a very odd circumstance." He saw her eyes widen and knew she hung on his every word. "Whether I live to pay back the sins of my ancestors or am destined to make right a wrong I once committed in another life, I cannot know.

"It is an existence I have come to hate. I used to only feel the urges to feed, to survive. But lately the urges are stronger, more intense. The blood is not enough. And the only thing more I can do to quench those urges is to find release in sexual pleasure," he said in a husky voice, his eyes roaming her curvy body, remembering everything about her smell, her taste.

"The hunger is impossible to resist, the darkness a lure that beckons the most stalwart and noble of fools," he said with a bitter curve to his mouth. His eyes stared into hers, his an inky black that seemed to have no ending and no beginning.

"Lately, Adara, things have changed. More and more I see the blackness of those I am sworn to destroy. I can do no other than send them back where they belong."

Adara stared at him and he wondered what moved through her mind. "You see the blackness around them, literally? Like a projection or an aura?"

"Yes."

She paused a moment. "Is my soul black?" she asked

quietly.

"No," he said, his hunger growing as her colors swirled and blazed around her. "Yours is unlike any other I've seen. It's a rainbow of light," he said and stared at her, looking at her fully. Even now his body listened and matched her heartbeat, needing to feel her around him, sheathing him in her warmth.

"So you're not here to kill me?" she asked, her voice wavering. He could tell she tried to appear brave but the violence she'd seen this night had truly shaken her. He wished it could have been otherwise, but perhaps she had needed to see the truth. But could she reconcile that he was the same man who only nights before had taken her to ecstasy?

"No, Adara," he purred, trying to soothe her with his voice. He watched as she shivered under his words, her nipples hardening into small beads of want. His eyes lingered there, needing more from Adara tonight, much more.

"Adara, I need you more than you can know," he admitted, his body hardening and begging him to take her.

"For what?" she asked, licking her lips nervously.

"Adara," he murmured and closed the distance between them. She froze under his touch, but he did no more than stroke her arms, her neck. "You don't understand, love. I don't like what I have to do, what you saw tonight. But I must. For the first time tonight, however, I didn't need to take from the woman sexually."

Adara's eyes blazed and he wondered if she could possibly have felt what he suspected. Jealousy? He shook his head. No, impossible.

"Why not?" she asked, moving slightly. Her breast brushed against his forearm and she gasped.

"Because of you, Adara," Trey said in a low voice. "You sated me the other night, more than I'd ever thought possible." His breath quickened as the memories assaulted him. "You took me in your mouth and sent me as close to heaven as I've ever been," he said huskily. He reached down and unsnapped his trousers, freeing his engorged and throbbing member to her gaze.

"Trey," her voice wavered. "What are you doing?" she asked in confusion. Yet Trey could see she knew exactly what he wanted from her, what he needed. Her own lust warred with her sense of right and wrong, and he knew he wouldn't last until she figured out the truth.

"You want me, Adara," he said as he stared into her eyes. "And you need me. Just as I need you. Your light shimmers and beckons to me, even as my darkness cries out to you." He stroked himself and watched as her breathing quickened. "Touch me, Adara. Touch me the way you want to. Forget about everything but the hunger raging in you," he whispered seductively.

He watched with narrowed eyes as Adara reached out, enthralled by his voice and his close body. She hadn't fought overmuch and Trey felt supreme satisfaction knowing she wanted him almost as much as he desired her.

Her hand wrapped around his erection and he closed his eyes in wonder. He hadn't imagined the pure feeling her touch evoked. Her small hand moved over him, her grip tight and purposeful as she stroked him.

"Ah, Adara," he said with a sigh. "What you do to me." He reached out and opened his eyes, quickly doing away with her clothing and his until nothing stood between them but air.

She continued to work him with her hand and Trey groaned his pleasure. Then he moved forward and kissed her hard on the mouth, bringing their bodies together. She gasped at the contact and Trey stopped her hand, worried at how fast and how close he came to orgasm.

He wanted to savor this night, no matter that he forced her into it. Another mark against his soul, he thought tiredly. And though he knew it was selfish, he couldn't help the utter need that coursed through him at the thought of the fulfillment she would give him and he would most certainly give her.

Trey brought her body down on the bed and leaned over her, his mouth still kissing her ripe lips. His tongue slipped into her moist mouth, touching her teeth and mingling with her tongue. And while he caressed her lightly with his tongue, he slid his body over hers, grazing her hard nipples, his penis rubbing erotically over her dark curls, parting her thighs only to rub between them, tormenting himself even as he brought forth her frustration.

She moved against him. "Trey," she whispered when he finally freed her mouth. "I need you in me." She trembled as he thrust between her thighs, his erection sliding in and out of the warmth there, made even smoother by the wetness of her body that coated him. But still he remained outside of her core, outside of her tight sheath.

"No, Adara," Trey said thickly. "Not tonight. I want to love you in your entirety," he whispered against her ear. "I want to feel your breast in my mouth, your clitoris full and near to bursting when I put my mouth over it. I need to feel all of you warm and wet before you come all over me," he said, his breath heaving as he aroused both of them with his words.

Then he bent his head to her neck, tempting himself with her warm scent. He could see her pulse beating, crying out to him. His fangs lengthened considerably, his body nearing her wet vagina, the tip of his penis dipping in just slightly.

She moaned and urged him forward and Trey moved further inside of her. Then he stopped and forced himself to withdraw, at a great cost to his willpower. She was destroying any control he had, her hunger almost overwhelming his own. Trey swore and trailed his mouth past her pulse down to her breasts.

He pressed his hard length along her thigh, unable to stop himself from stroking against her. And as he did, he drew his mouth down to her breast, to the taut cherry nipple awaiting his caress. With great skill, he suckled at her breast while his hand toyed with the other aroused peak. Adara moaned and arched into his touch, her hands running through his hair making him sigh with need.

"So good," he murmured as his lips left her breast. He blew a soft breath against her nipple, watched it harden even more and groaned. Then he kissed her again, this time his teeth nipping lightly at her, drawing a thin trail of blood. He had given her pleasure in his touch and she felt no pain at the bloodletting, only a further sense of ecstasy as he sucked from her.

Chapter Six

The taste of her sweet blood on his tongue as Adara's naked body pressed into his was almost too much for Trey. He forced himself to let her go and sealed the small pinprick on her nipple. Then he suckled at her other breast, his mouth quickening as his body pushed towards completion.

She continued to arch into him, her lithe body hungry for his own. Trey's lips trailed over her tight stomach, lingering at her navel, wanting desperately to bite into the tender, fruitful flesh but resisting.

"Oh, Trey," Adara moaned. "I want you so," she said and gasped as his mouth blew over her wet arousal. He parted her soft curls and pushed her thighs further apart. And then, memory repeated itself as his mouth moved over her clitoris, teasing the nub into a hard little pebble.

Adara cried out his name as he brought her so close to fulfillment. His mouth and tongue flicked at her, tasting her, and she almost came as his tongue suddenly darted into her moist corridor, but not getting far enough inside. She writhed beneath him, her thighs cradling his head as he groaned, sucking her deeper into his vortex of desire.

"Trey, please," she begged and felt less than relief when his head rose, his blazing eyes meeting hers. A red haze seemed to cover his eyes as he stared at her, his need never more apparent than now.

He rose over her and she looked down to see his thick penis throbbing over her, moisture beading at the tip. She wanted to taste him again, wanted to feel him in her mouth, but Adara knew neither could wait that long. Then he settled over her, nudging her thighs wider with his knee.

He poised above her wet entrance, staring down at her. "Adara, I will take you to places you've never been," he said thickly as he bore down on her. His mouth covered hers and then he thrust deeply inside of her, not slow now but moving like a man possessed. Adara gasped, her breath stolen by the man devouring her. He felt so large inside of her, so big and empowering as he moved deeply towards her womb.

But he wouldn't be still, his body too charged to stop. He withdrew his entire length and returned smoothly back down into her, grinding his body over hers. Adara cried out as he continued to thrust his entire length into her. He consumed her, his large body priming hers as his tongue mated with hers, his penis thrusting over and over again into her wet body, sliding through her honeyed cream with exquisite friction.

"Oh, Trey," Adara said as he released her mouth, his breath coming faster and faster as he moved over her. And then she felt her world come apart as his body rubbed her swollen clitoris roughly once more. Adara screamed and pulsed, her body drawing him in as her contractions of pleasure overwhelmed her.

At her first cry, Trey said something she couldn't understand. Then he buried his face into her neck and plunged his teeth into her skin, the slight pain increasing her pleasure as Adara came again around him.

Trey sucked on her and groaned as his body exploded into light, into feeling, his orgasm bursting forth as he shot his hot seed into her. His mouth continued to move over her as he thrust inside of her, his body shuddering under her wet clenching. And as he continued to suck her blood, Adara felt herself go lightheaded, completely undone from the intense pleasure.

Trey finally stopped moving inside of her and released her neck, licking at the small drops of blood that escaped. He trembled as his tongue met her salty skin and he sank onto her body for a moment, almost crushing her under his weight.

Then he sighed and rolled over, bringing her atop his body.

"Adara," he said hoarsely, his breath still coming fast and furious, his hard member still inside of her. He gently withdrew and Adara moaned his loss. "You give me such pleasure," he said and hugged her to him.

Adara leaned up on her elbows and looked down at him sleepily. She felt more relaxed than she ever had in her life. Something in her mind told her that she ought to protest something, but too tired to do more than rest, she closed her eyes and listened to the steady thrumming of Trey's heart as she succumbed to sleep.

* * * *

Trey lay beneath her for several hours, cursing himself for taking her against her will and yet congratulating himself for finally doing what he had wanted to since he first saw her. He had never imagined that he could feel so good after mating and taking blood from a woman.

Always before he felt dark, sullied by his proximity and need for the darkness hovering over his prey's bodies. But with Adara, it was as if the lightness in her being absolved him of his actions, the pleasure she produced too damn fine to regret.

And yet Trey regretted that he'd had to control her mind in order to control her body. He had told himself he would never do such a thing, not to a woman he genuinely found himself attracted to. But he couldn't help it. Had he not taken her tonight with gentle persuasion, he would have resorted to something uglier. Adara needed time to make up her mind about him. If he could only convince her to come to him of her own free will, that he was not a monster but a dark soul serving the light, then maybe he would have a chance.

Trey sighed. He couldn't get enough of her body to let her make that choice, at least, not yet. He felt sated but needy again. He knew he had taken too much of her blood and so let her rest when he would have taken her again, so soon after their lovemaking. But images of John and what he had done to Sue haunted him and Trey felt an overwhelming lust return. He wanted to take Adara from behind forcefully, to plunge his teeth into her delicate neck just as she came around him.

He groaned at her ability to seduce him with mere memories of her body. How had this happened? A mortal woman had taken control of his desires, like an obsession. And now having had her, having felt her wet body milking him of his passion, Trey would never be able to have another without thinking of her, without seeing or smelling Adara.

He sighed. Perhaps that was for the best then. He didn't like taking more than blood from his victims. It tainted him more than was good for his already dark soul. Adara, however, lightened him. He could feel a goodness seeping through him and knew it was because of her.

She scooted closer to him and her body brushed against his. He held his breath as she turned and mumbled against his neck. He didn't have much time before the sun rose, but knew he had to have her again.

"Adara, waken, love," he said as he nudged her slightly. She smiled in her sleep and curled closer to him. Trey grinned. He hadn't thought of this but it interested him.

He moved out from under her body and tossed back her covers. He stared down at her gloriously naked body, studying her long legs, the delicate curve of her buttocks and her slim back bared as she slept on her stomach. He started caressing her at her ankles, kissing and touching them with reverence as he moved up her body.

She moaned lightly but didn't stir otherwise and he grinned, a full smile that lit his dark face. Then he closed his eyes and savored her body, tasting her honeyed skin against his smooth tongue, fighting the desire to bite her as he rose up her legs. He parted her thighs gently and continued to run his tongue along the inside of her legs.

He could smell his scent on her still and the knowledge turned him as hard as stone. He groaned and kissed her softly, angling to touch her ripe clitoris with his tongue. She moaned louder as he found her and he gently propped her up with his hands under her stomach as he fed on her sultry essence. He inserted a finger inside of her as he licked her, and soon her body began to move of its own accord.

Trey groaned, a rumble of sound that vibrated against her body, wringing a gasp from Adara.

"What are you doing?" she asked sleepily as her breath caught on another moan. Trey hadn't enthralled her this time but had caught her out of sleep. He could only hope she was too caught up in her desire, as he was, as he continued to fondle her.

"Oh, yes," she moaned and shifted her hips. "Don't stop, Trey," she said.

He ripped his mouth from her wet body, his eyes glittering as he watched her aroused face, her eyes closed in ecstasy, her mouth parted slightly, panting for him.

"I have to stop," he said breathing hard and moved to cover her. He propped her up on her knees and pressed solidly against her buttocks, rubbing himself over her as she pressed back against him, groaning. "This will feel so good," he said thickly as his hands moved around to cup her breasts.

His palms grazed her nipples even as his body pressed deeper against her. He needed her desperately, images of what he had fantasized about doing with her dotting his vision.

He quickly rose on his knees and positioned his erection into her honeyed wetness. Then he slowly thrust forward, entering her tight body, her corridor narrower due to this new position. He closed his eyes and groaned his pleasure even as she begged him to move in her.

"You feel so good," he said as he began thrusting in her, his hands clenched on her hips.

"Oh, yes, harder," she moaned and he increased his pace, slamming into her harder and harder as she moaned his name.

"I want you to come all around me," he panted as he continued to thrust. He moved a hand around her hip and gently touched her hard nub, stroking her.

She panted and moved against him, creating an erotic

friction that quickly took them to another plane of desire.

As in his fantasies, Trey waited until Adara neared the precipice of her climax before he leaned down to pierce her soft flesh. The feel of his teeth and his penis embedded deeply in her, his fingers moving magically over her body, sent her into a hard orgasm. Trey could hear it in her cry and could feel it as she drenched him with her spicy scent. His penis slid smoothly in and out of her as he swallowed her lifesblood. And then he removed his mouth, not wanting to hurt her as the force of his climax consumed him.

He thrust inside of her and continued to move, his body pumping as he slid through her silken wetness. He gasped and withdrew but his body hadn't finished, and he placed his penis on her back between her buttocks and watched as his milky white desire flowed over her.

He moaned and gripped her tightly, sliding his sensitive shaft through his seed over her back.

"That was incredible," Adara said breathlessly. She looked over her back as he slid over her, her eyes impossibly dark and watchful as she studied his agonized face, still consumed with his orgasm.

Adara felt another heat wave move through her as she watched him moving on her. How could this be, she wondered? Now that her body had been sated, memories of Trey's actions the night prior invaded her mind. She could smell him on her, could feel the sticky evidence of their actions between her thighs and on her back. And though that made her more aroused and aware of him, it also scared her.

Trey had done something awful last night. He had killed a woman. And then he had overtaken her will and body and given her incredible pleasure even as he came in her body. And his lips, she shuddered, now remembering that he'd plunged his long fangs into her neck and drank her blood, a thought that invoked heated passion rather than the disgust she thought she should feel.

As if aware of her disturbing thoughts, Trey eased off of her body and stood beside her bed. Heedless of his nudity, he stood before her proudly.

"I know you need to think about things," Trey said quietly. "And I shouldn't have forced you last night, but I couldn't help it. I was helpless to deny myself your pleasure. And though it was wrong, I cannot be sorry for it," he said softly.

Adara sat up and watched his face carefully as he confessed to her. Much as her thoughts swirled in confusion, she couldn't deny that he'd given her more pleasure than he could possibly know. He hadn't been selfish but had fulfilled her needs as well. Just thinking about what he'd done made her shiver again with need.

"I'll go now, but you know where you can find me. There are things we should talk about and more we have yet to discover," he said softly and stared at her through narrowed lids, a sated male less dangerous but still a definite threat. "And Adara," Trey said softly, his eyes burning with intensity, "don't make me wait too long."

Chapter Seven

Adara thought long and hard about what to do after Trey left. When the first morning sun shone through her windows, she arose and stepped into her shower to wash away the aftereffects of their passion. She sighed and closed her eyes as she rubbed his still warm seed off of her back, felt it drip down her legs. Traces of Trey lingered and made her forget herself, awash in sensuality as she remembered every exquisite detail of his lovemaking.

Adara washed herself clean, unable to get his scent out of her mind. She had been more intimate with Trey in the past few days than she'd been with anyone in her entire life. And he'd treated her body like a temple, worshipping her with his hands, his eyes, his mouth.

She sighed and continued to stand under the warm water running over her. How could she equate the tempting lover of last night with the demon that killed those women? As she wondered about that, she recalled that the woman Trey had killed had been in a jail cell after killing a room full of people. What had Trey said? Something about the darkness of his 'prey' calling to him?

He'd wrapped his hand gently around her crucifix, not in the slightest afraid of it or what it meant. And he'd mentioned that he worked for 'Him'. Trey implied that he worked to rid the world of evil, that he fought for light. And yet, at what price, Adara wondered?

She turned off her shower and dried off, changing quickly into jeans and a sweater. She thought about Trey throughout the day, wondering about his life and his work.

He owned and operated a very successful nightclub dedicated to serving pleasure to its clientele. She knew he was a very sensuous man, one steeped heavily in the ability to please a woman. And yet, she felt she had had an answering effect on Trey, recalling the stunned look on his face that first day in his office.

She blushed as she remembered it. He said that she had an aura different from those he was used to. She couldn't imagine the hungers that burned through him from day to day. Did he need to feed all the time? Was he really a bad guy, or were all of his victims, like the woman from her vision, evil? Adara had so many questions she wanted to ask him. And yet he had clearly put the next move in her lap.

Adara knew Trey felt bad about taking her will from her last night. But she couldn't hold onto her fear or anger, she thought with a wry grin. Her writer's imagination took over, along with a healthy dose of passionate intrigue.

Trey Blackthorne was a woman's finest fantasy come to life. He had made her body buck and seethe with passion, had given her such pleasure that she thought she would die. And even though he had tasted her blood, Adara felt a curious heat fill her loins, unable to dredge up even a tinge of disgust for the act.

Adara waited all day, needing answers as much as she needed to feel his hands on her body again. She frowned and wondered if perhaps he had marked her somehow, made her an addict for his touch. Thoughts of what he had done to that woman in the prison cell made her slightly jealous. She didn't like the thought of Trey touching another woman intimately. And his admission that his lust had grown, that he could only slake his thirst in a woman's body as well as by drinking her blood angered her further.

"What right do I have over him?" she asked herself. "And do I even want any control over his actions?"

She shook her head, deliberating what to do.

At eleven that evening, she finally gave in to her urges and changed into black jeans and a black pullover. She found herself at the entrance of his club a short time later. One of the bouncers saw her and moved directly to her.

"Mr. Blackthorne is expecting you." He smiled and moved her gently through the doors, refusing to accept any money from her for entering the club. He walked her inside and left her in John's hands.

"Well, welcome back," John said with a broad grin. "I'm so glad to see you again," he said and looked around her.

"Sorry," Adara smiled. "I didn't bring Sue with me. But the last time I talked to her she told me she was looking forward to your next date." Adara had enough sense to note the sexual hunger that flared in his bright blue gaze, oddly enough mirroring Trey's hunger.

Adara stared at John in thoughtful contemplation. Could he also be one of them? But John gave her little time to speculate. Instead, he moved her, not towards Trey's office, but back towards the sophisticated corridor housing private rooms. John guided her around the corridor towards a room at the very end of the hallway.

"Enjoy." He smiled and left her in front of the door.

Adara swallowed audibly and knocked. The door opened immediately before her and she walked in slowly, not able to see much in the black room. The door closed behind her and she jumped.

"Don't be nervous, Adara," she heard Trey murmur to her right before he lit a candle. She stared at his shadowed face with hunger, aware that she couldn't help herself as she touched his face with a soft hand.

He breathed lightly but stepped away from her, lighting the rest of the room in candles on dressers and tables around them.

A large king-sized bed stood along the back wall of the large room and Adara could only stare at it, her body already warming to the idea of sharing it with Trey. She shook her head and sat down in a chair across from Trey, conscious to keep a table separating them.

"I have some questions," she said nervously.

He nodded somberly and sat across from her not speaking.

"I know that you're a vampire. But Trey, do you have to kill to, uh, feed?"

He shook his head. "No. Adara, I only kill those that I am called to kill. I don't like it, but I do it because I have to."

"The black auras," she said and he nodded. "So you see yourself as a messenger, for the light?"

"Yes," he said and sighed. "But since you came into my life, I no longer feel the need for sexual gratification from my victims. I only need drink their blood, those women that must pass the judgment in a higher court. Adara, it's you that satisfies me now."

Adara stared at him, saw the earnest expression lighting his eyes in the flickering candlelight. "I don't understand this," she said. "But I don't think you're evil."

He sighed. "Thank God. Adara, I don't understand this any more than you. For some reason you complete me, your light calls to my darkness. You make me happy," he said quietly. "And it's more than your body, though that thrills me." He grinned.

Adara stared at him, not having seen him smile before. It lit up his entire face, made him seem, lighter, more carefree.

"It's you, Adara. I," he paused. "I know it's too soon and I'm not someone you may ever like, but I love you."

Adara stared at him in shock. "You love me?"

He nodded. "I can't explain it. But I know your soul. It's

pure and good. And you, Adara, you're good. You could have immediately set the police on me, or worse exposed me. Yet you came here first to get my side of the story."

"I needed to know," she said thoughtfully. His words of love made her heart sing. She felt an answering call deep within her but didn't know if she had the strength to see it through. Loving Trey would be entering a whole new world.

"Adara," he said and moved the table out of his way. He knelt in front of her and lifted her hand to his lips. "Know that I can never harm you, not the woman I love. And no matter what you decide to do about me or yourself, whether you expose me or turn me over to your justice, I will always love you."

Adara stared down at his fervent pledge, her hand warming under his touch.

"But if, well, let's say I stay with you," she said. "You would still have to kill people, right?"

Trey nodded sadly. "It's my job, Adara. My true purpose for living. I have to take the guilty away from this world. I'm sorry. I would give you anything I possess to keep you with me, but that is one thing I cannot do."

Adara stroked his hair, soft and silky under her fingertips. "But they really are evil," she said. He nodded. "Trey," she asked. "If you take more of my blood, will that make me like you?"

"No," he said firmly. "That is something that I can do only if you truly desire it. And even then it is a process that does not always take. Adara, my kind has always been likened to evil, but we are a far cry from that. Yes, I live in the darkness. But I don't needlessly seek violence. If you must know the truth, I feared I was getting in too deep with each occurrence. But with you, Adara, my light shines brighter than ever."

Adara smiled down at him, her decision made. "Trey, I love you," she said and watched as his smile lit up his whole face. "I admit this is all new, and I'm still a bit frightened of what you are and what you can do, but I trust you."

Trey lifted her into his arms and stood, hugging her to him and swinging her around. "Oh, Adara, you don't know how I've longed to hear you say that. You won't be sorry," he said. He set her down on her feet and kissed her breathless. "And I have so much to share with you," he said as he stared down into her eyes.

"We have only touched upon the wondrous pleasures of my kind," he said and lowered his mouth to bite at his hand. He released it and Adara watched as two dark dots of blood began to fill. "Adara, if you can accept me, I mean really accept me, I offer you my lifesblood. With this gift, we will be connected, always," he said softly.

Adara stared at him, could almost see his dark aura taking on a shimmer of light as she stared at him. She blinked but the image didn't fade. With her heart in her eyes, she smiled and leaned towards him, kissing the soft trail of blood on his hand.

He sighed in pleasure, more so when her mouth moved over the pinpricks of pain. Adara found to her surprise that his blood called to her, made her desire him immediately.

Adara removed her mouth, a drop of blood on her lips. Trey stared down at her and lowered his mouth to lick the dark red spot. His tongue burned her lip and Adara dragged his mouth to hers, holding him as she ravaged his mouth. She felt a burning hunger to have him, more than she'd ever felt before.

"Adara, come with me." He directed her towards the large bed before she could further arouse him past the point of no return. "I know how much you want this."

Adara looked at him curiously and suddenly found herself staring at his naked body. She gasped only to realize she too stood naked before him.

"I love your body," he said huskily, his hands moving softly over her heaving breasts. "Come," he said and pulled her down on the bed. "There is something you've been fantasizing," he said with a smile.

"You can read my thoughts?" Adara asked in surprise.

"No. But when we are together, your sexual fantasies call out to me. And you broadcast your wants and needs quite loudly." He smiled, his eyes dark and lustful as he stared down at her. "Now let me make you more comfortable," he said smoothly.

Trey lay down on the bed and positioned her on top of him. Adara couldn't think clearly enough to know what fantasy he referred to. She blushed slightly thinking that there had been so many. She knelt over him and bent her head to kiss him when he shook his head mysteriously. She watched in confusion as he nudged her body with his hands to turn around. Then realization dawned on her as she found herself looking down at his throbbing erection.

She closed her eyes in bliss as she felt his warm breath over her clitoris, his hands dragging her loins down to cover his mouth. As his tongue began stroking her, she heard herself groan and watched as his penis twitched, growing before her eyes. Awash in sensation, she nevertheless remembered her first encounter with Trey, recalling how her mouth had almost brought him to his knees.

She smiled and leaned down to absorb his scent. Carefully she licked him, her hands caressing his tight shaft and smooth velvet sack with care. She heard him groan against her, could feel the rumble of pleasure course through her body. She lowered her mouth over him and began to tease him. He lunged up into her mouth even as his tongue and lips intensified on her excited body.

His enthusiasm for her touch showed in his attention to her body and soon Adara was fighting to hold on, not wanting to come until she'd brought him to orgasm. She sucked him further inside of her, tasting and teasing his thick shaft with her tongue until he shuddered and moaned loudly.

And then Adara could take no more. Her climax hit her with stunning force and she sucked harder on his penis, shattering him as well. She heard him groan and tremble as his body exploded, his hot seed spurting in her mouth. Still awash in her own climax, she greedily swallowed him, their bodies pulsing with the same heartbeat as passion reluctantly released them.

Trey exhaled deeply and turned her around, bringing her head down to his chest. "Oh, Adara," he groaned and hugged her tightly. "With you I feel so much lightness. You are truly my heart," he said and kissed her tenderly on the head.

Adara sighed in pleasure and tilted her head to meet his eyes. "As you are mine, Trey," she said and smiled. "It's funny but now that you've mentioned it, I can see a light shining around you, a kind of rainbow that isn't going away."

He smiled, his heart in his eyes as he caressed her cheek with a long finger. "You have saved me, Adara," he said. "And I will never take you for granted, ever."

A few moments of silence filled the room as they lingered in the haze of ecstasy still throbbing through them.

"Trey?" Adara said hesitantly. Now that she'd finally accepted and admitted her love for him, she could never let him go. Just trying to imagine a life without him made her soul cry out in pain. "I want you to make me like you."

Trey stiffened beneath her and Adara sat up to watch his features. "Are you sure, Adara? Once the conversion begins, there is no turning back. And even then, it may not take."

"What does that mean?" she asked.

"Well, if I try to convert you to my kind and it works, you will know immediately. But if it doesn't, you will be more than you were, but not vampire. And if that is the case, know that I will end my life when yours ends," he said simply. Adara stared at him and felt tears burn her eyes. He spoke of forever with her so easily, in his lifetime or that of a normal human's.

"I want to try," Adara said and touched his chest above his heart. "I'm yours forever, Trey."

Chapter Eight

Trey perused the November issue of *Chic Ventures* with a large grin. The photographer had captured a wonderful picture of John and Sue dressed as vampires during the club's Halloween Bash and the accompanying article made him more than proud.

He stared at the new Mrs. Blackthorne as she typed furiously at her computer. It had only been two weeks but he couldn't have asked for two better weeks in his life. Perhaps the Elders had seen that his soul was in jeopardy, for he couldn't believe Adara to be anything other than an angel heaven-sent to save his soul.

He wondered at the pulsing light that always enveloped her, though now it burned with a touch of darkness that proclaimed her one of his kind. Adara on the other hand, loved the rainbow of colors that now coursed around him, even if his aura was a few shades darker than her pulsing brightness.

"I can feel you staring at me," she said as she continued to type, a smile on her mouth. He watched her lips purse and a sudden image of her in the bedroom overwhelmed him.

Adara suddenly stopped typing and looked up at him, her eyes dark as she smiled sexily at him. Her conversion to his kind had been surprisingly simple. It had taken only one deep exchange of blood, draining her body and refilling it with his essence. Even John had been harder to convert and Trey had done so at the Elders' request.

Adara clearly saw what Trey envisioned and she smiled. Adara's psychic gift had been enhanced by her new abilities as a vampire. And she liked to tease him by sending him projections of what they would do whenever he could grab a moment of peace with her.

She moved seductively towards the bedroom and he growled as she laughed and ran into the room. She had moved in with him in his house, where they could be assured of safety during the day. Adara's article had been an instant hit and apparently her agent wanted her to do a full-length book on being the 'bad girl'. Success and happiness abounded in their lives.

He found her lying naked in bed, a velvet scarf hiding her

breasts and loins from his view. As he stood there looking down at her, he thanked God for blessing him with such happiness. He still took those needing justice into the afterlife, but no longer did he hunger for anyone save Adara.

"So when are we going to make a little vampire?" Adara asked with a grin.

"Oh, you won't be fertile until your body has been pleasured beyond thought," Trey said and smiled at the intrigued look on her face. "And it will be more than my duty to ready your luscious body." He grinned as he stripped out of his clothing. "It will be my utmost pleasure."

The End

THE DARK ONE

Goldie McBride

Chapter One

The tour guide had touted it as one of the most haunted places in western Europe. Samantha Lancaster felt a delightful shiver skate down her spine as she studied the ancient chateaux. Her mother would've loved it.

A wave of loss washed over her at the thought. Resolutely, she dismissed it. The two of them had planned the trip together. She was determined she was going to enjoy it to the fullest for both of them. She knew in her heart that her mother would've wanted it that way. Her mother had spent most of her adult life yearning to visit Europe, to track down family roots, if possible, but more importantly, to visit every reputedly haunted site on the continent.

The Chateaux du Beauchamp had topped her list.

A sense of excitement replaced her melancholy as she studied the stone building in the fading light almost with a sense of awe. It never failed to amaze her that people had managed to build such masterpieces of architecture centuries ago with the most primitive of tools.

The closing of a door drew her attention from her study of the gargoyles that guarded the chateaux's roof top. She turned to look toward the front door of the chateaux. A young man, dressed in what looked to be authentic late medieval clothing, was striding rapidly toward her. He stopped beside the car and Samantha rolled her window down, looking up at him questioningly as he said something to her and gestured toward the side of the building. She hadn't a clue of what he'd said, but the language and accent sent a thrill of pleasure through her. She hadn't been in France a full day and she still wasn't used to finding herself in a world where no one spoke her language. She'd found she didn't particularly care, though. She loved the French tongue. They could say shit and it still sounded beautiful.

"I'm sorry," she said apologetically. "I don't speak French." She'd studied French in high school, but that had been almost ten years ago. She hadn't used it since she graduated and she didn't remember enough to do her much good.

"American?"

She nodded.

He pointed to the narrow driveway that wound around toward the back of the chateaux. "You must leave the automobile in back. I will take your luggage, if you like."

Samantha smiled at him gratefully and got out so that he could reach the luggage she'd piled in the back seat. He grunted as he unloaded it, straining much as she had when she'd loaded the suitcases in.

Packing light wasn't her forte`. She hadn't been tempted to change her ways when she was traveling all the way to Europe.

Finally, he had all of the bags out and stacked. "I see you brought everything," he commented.

She supposed she should have been insulted, but she couldn't help but laugh. "Believe it or not, I probably missed a few things."

Climbing back into the rental car, she started it up again and pulled around to the back of the chateaux. A gravel parking area had been added just beyond the cobble stone courtyard that stretched from the back of the chateaux to what must have once been the stables. She pulled the tiny car into a space between a sports car and another compact like the one she was driving and got out.

The chateaux was almost as beautiful from the back as it was from the front, she decided appreciatively. Glancing around at the outbuildings, she saw with a twinge of disappointment that it was going to be too late by the time she registered and settled in her room to do any exploring until the following day.

Heaving a sigh, she crossed the cobblestone courtyard and climbed a set of stone steps that led up onto a verandah. Several French doors let out onto the verandah where tables were scattered here and there for outdoor dining. The glass-paned doors undoubtedly led into the dining room, she decided, and turned toward the only wooden paneled door, more than half expecting to find it locked. It opened easily, however, onto a dim hallway lit only by a couple of wall sconces.

She ran smack into the man just inside the dim interior, a gentle collision that nevertheless plastered her full length against a hard, muscular body. Embarrassed, she took a step back. "Excuse me," she muttered, barely glancing at the man as she rushed past him.

To her relief, she found that the corridor led to the front desk.

The man at the desk looked at her in surprise as she appeared out of the darkened corridor. "Sorry. I guess I was supposed to go around to the front?"

His brows rose. "Are you checking in, madam?"

Samantha blushed again, this time with a pique of annoyance. She wasn't married, wasn't wearing a ring, and she wasn't even twenty eight yet. Surely she deserved a 'mademoiselle'?

On the other hand, she'd had a mature look about her her entire life. She supposed it was her narrow face and the high cheek bones. If she'd had rounded cheeks, people might've thought she was younger.

She forced a smile. "Yes. .. uh … Oui. I'm Samantha Lancaster. I was supposed to be here earlier today, but the flight was delayed and then I had trouble getting the rental car...."

She allowed her voice to drift off, looking around at the room she found herself in as he nodded and began thumbing through a file on the desk. Undoubtedly, the area had originally been part of the great room that seemed typical of most castles. Now, it was a guest lounge and office.

The walls were wainscotted in a dark, rich looking wood. Above the panels, the walls had been covered in what looked like silk, but was probably just wallpaper made to look like silk. She wondered if it was anything like the original or if they'd opted for the pale blue watered silk to lighten the area.

She jumped when she saw the man staring at her from across the room. Dressed in clothing somewhat similar to the 'bellhop' who'd first greeted her and taken her luggage, she assumed he must be staff, but if he was, he was brazen.

He was propped against a wooden column that doubled as a newel post for the stairs that wound upwards from the great room to the balcony above. His expression was a mixture of boredom and annoyance.

Dark and brooding, her mind supplied descriptively.

Despite his unwelcoming demeanor, the man had a 'pant' factor of ten on a scale of one to ten. His hair was black and undoubtedly long, swept back from his face and tied behind his head. His complexion was swarthy, his features almost classically refined, but there was something about him that made her think of gypsies. Maybe the devil may care attitude?

He was tall, lean and well shaped. She had a feeling he was tautly muscular, lean rather than merely slender, but she wasn't certain why ... until it occurred to her that it was the same man she'd run into as she was coming inside.

Smiling at him a little uncertainly, she returned her attention to the concierge as he called her name for the second time, blushing when she realized that neither man could be in any doubt that she'd gone into zen meditation when she caught sight of the hunk lounging against the wall and burning holes in her with his gaze.

"I have found you," the concierge announced, smiling faintly. "We were not certain that you would come when you did not arrive this morning, but we are slow now. We still have your room."

An uncomfortable jolt of panic and irritation went through Samantha at that calm pronouncement. It hadn't occurred to her, before, that she might've lost her reservation, but there didn't seem much point in dwelling on the fact that, if they'd given her room to someone else, she might've had to drive miles and miles to find somewhere to stay--it wasn't like the chateaux was close to a major city. She supposed it didn't matter now, but it was unpleasant to think she'd had such a close call through no fault of her own. "I did say that I might be delayed," she pointed out.

"No harm." He struck the bell on his desk. "I will have Antoine take your bags up for you and show you to your room."

Antoine, it transpired, was the young man who'd greeted her upon her arrival. He didn't look terribly enthusiastic about lugging her bags up, but hefted two of the three and started toward the stairs. Samantha did her best to ignore the dark man--whom she saw was still giving her that enigmatic examination--as they approached him where he stood by the stairs. Despite her determination, she found she simply couldn't resist glancing up at him as she came abreast of him.

He was taller than she'd realized. Something about his build had suggested that he was probably no more than medium in height. She saw now, though, that he must be at least six one or two. She was short and she was used to looking up at people, but even so, she noticed when she was around anyone taller than average.

She couldn't have failed to notice the man in any case, even if he hadn't shown so much interest in her. There was something about him that went beyond his physical appearance that was purely magnetic.

He was, she discovered, looking directly at her when she glanced up. Their eyes met for what might've been a half a dozen heartbeats if Samantha's hadn't paused painfully in her chest, forcing the air from her lungs as if some unseen arm was squeezing her chest. His eyes were an eerie, pale blue that sent a jolt through her like an electric current.

With an effort, she looked away, stumbling slightly as she misjudged the height of the first stair. Fortunately, she'd gripped the banister and caught herself. Ignoring both men now, her heart beating unpleasantly fast, Samantha concentrated on each step as she carefully made her way up to the second floor. She paused at the top, waiting for Antoine to take the lead and show her the way to her room.

The room he led her to made up for the disconcerting beginning she'd had. As she moved to the middle of the room and stared up at the ceiling, a sense of wonder filled her. The painting--a depiction of some mythological tale--had deteriorated over the years, but it was still beautiful. Plaster moldings of intricate design framed the ceiling painting. The upper portion of the walls were covered in the same blue, watered silk as the great room below. The paneling below that and the molding had all been painted a creamy white, giving the room the intricate charm of a fancy gift box.

The stone mantel piece that surrounded the fireplace, supported by a pair of snarling griffins, was the crowning touch.

The room's furnishings, lavishly carved and made of some gleaming, well polished, dark wood, were almost certainly reproductions. Though they looked to be antiques from several different periods, she could hardly credit it.

On the other hand, antiques in Europe, because of their long history, weren't quite the same as American antiques. To them, the room might be furnished with nothing more than second hand castoffs.

The clatter of her suitcases hitting the floor drew her attention away from her study at last and Samantha looked around in surprise to discover that she'd been so enthralled Antoine had already made the trip downstairs and back with the rest of her luggage. Digging in her purse, she produced a tip and thanked him.

Obviously pleased with the offering, he glanced around the room. "The Chateaux was occupied during the war, first by the Germans and later by the Allied forces. It survived the war with only minor damage. It was restored in the early 1900's and some modernization was added, but it remains today much as it did during the life time of the Count du Beauchamp, who was reputed to be a very powerful witch."

"Warlock?"

Antoine's brows rose, but he nodded.

"He died before the revolution, didn't he?"

"Oui et non. The count was defeated in a duel between himself and another powerful warlock. He was cursed, madam, and never seen again. The portrait in the corridor is believed to be a likeness of him.

"Many believe the Chateaux itself was enchanted, for it has survived much turmoil since his time and remained virtually unscathed, even by time. It has been vandalized and looted many times, but somehow the original furnishings always seem to find their way back to the chateaux."

Samantha thanked him again for the brief history lesson and smiled dismissively. Shrugging, he pointed out the room's amenities and left, closing the door behind him.

She'd read most of what he'd told her in the guide book, which was why her and her mother had chosen the Chateaux to begin with, but she was curious to know how much of it was 'invented' history, and how much was actually true. Dismissing it finally, she lugged a suitcase onto the bed, extracted her toiletries and a change of clothes and went into the tiny 'modern' bath that had been added…she supposed when the chateaux had been renovated into a bed and breakfast landmark--or maybe not.

Either they'd gone out of their way to find antique fixtures for the bath to make it as unobtrusive as possible, or the bath had been added at least a hundred years earlier.

It worked reasonably well, though, and that was all that really mattered. She'd rented the room for the atmosphere, and the thin hope she might actually encounter the ghost. If opulent accommodations had been the object, she could've stayed at one of the modern luxury hotels.

When she'd freshened up, she left the room, locking the door behind her. Instead of heading down to the dining room immediately, though, she went in search of the portrait Antoine had mentioned. She found it about halfway down the corridor. There was no missing it, for it was very nearly big enough to be a life sized portrait, and framed in an ornate picture frame that looked as if it must weigh every bit of a hundred pounds.

The corridor was dim and the portrait dark, but she noticed at once that the clothing the man wore was very similar to that adopted by the staff. He was seated in a chair of the Louis XV variety, as ornately carved and gilded as the picture frame, his posture casual rather than formal, one knee bent, the other leg sprawled casually. His arms were resting on the arms of the chair, but in one hand he held a cane topped by large crystal.

The lights in the room below brightened as she peered at the painting, illuminating the portrait, and she stepped back so that her shadow was no longer blocking her view.

Her heart skipped a beat as she raised her eyes at last to study the face.

He looked uncannily like the man she'd seen downstairs when she checked in.

Samantha frowned, wondering if it was merely her imagination running wild, or if it was no more than a trick of the light--or perhaps a strong strain of genetics? People had never really moved around a lot, historically speaking, and after generations of people in a particular area had intermarried, family traits had a tendency to show up.

Of course, he'd been an aristocrat and they never married beneath them, but from what she knew that had never stopped them from sleeping with the lower classes, and breeding with them. Maybe the man she'd seen below was the great, great grandson or something like that?--from the other side of the blanket, most likely. The French had pretty well disposed of their aristocrats during the revolution--all of them that hadn't had the good sense to run, and most of them had apparently been too arrogant to flee in time to save their necks from the guillotine.

Despite her preoccupation, Samantha sensed that someone had come up as she stood examining the portrait. When several moments passed and the newcomer neither turned away nor passed by her, she glanced absently toward him.

A jolt went through her. It was the same man she'd seen earlier. This time, however, he spoke when she looked at him. His voice, deep and resonant, washed over her like a caress. Goosebumps rose on her flesh. She gaped at him incomprehensibly when he stopped speaking. "Uh… I don't speak French."

One dark brow arched, the other descended as if he wasn't at all pleased with the fact that she was a foreigner. "You are English?"

Samantha bit her lip, but couldn't help but chuckle. "American by birth, southern by the grace of God. You're probably the only person in Europe who'd mistake my accent for English. I can't even understand the English accent half the time … or vice versa."

She gestured toward the portrait. "It looks like it could be you."

A gleam of amusement entered his eyes as he followed her gesture. "I, myself, think it is a poor likeness."

Samantha shrugged. "I suspect it didn't do him justice. I think a lot of the artists way back then were more into developing a particular style than actually capturing the person's likeness. I mean--either half of Europe was related and looked like it--or they just painted everybody to look that way. Except for the clothes, they all had bug eyes and thin lips."

"Back then?"

Samantha shrugged. "I've never been much for history, except where it has to do with reputed hauntings, that is, but even so I have a hard time with dates. The count lived way back before the revolution--at least three centuries ago, I think–more or less. You probably know a lot more about it than I do. You work here?"

"Non. I live here--in a manner of speaking."

Samantha glanced toward him in surprise.

"You don't work here, but you live here?" she persisted, frowning.

A thin smile curled the corners of his mouth. "I am Gerard, Count du Beauchamp."

Samantha felt her jaw go slack with surprise, but that was as nothing compared to the jolt that went through her when he abruptly vanished.

Chapter Two

Samantha looked around in disbelief, but the man was no where in sight. She'd been staring straight at him.

She thought she had.

Maybe she'd glanced back toward the portrait, though? Even if she had, would that have been enough time for him to disappear so completely? She couldn't believe that it would've been.

But maybe he'd strode away while she was looking in the other direction? He moved quietly. The carpet on the floor was thick and would have muffled his footsteps regardless, but she'd only sensed his presence when he'd come up beside her to start with. She hadn't heard his approach.

The fine hairs on the back of her neck prickled, but she shook it off. It had to be a practical joke--or maybe it was something like a play the chateaux put on to entertain their guests? Or perpetuate the ghostly rumors?

He'd all but said he was a ghost, but the plain fact of the matter was, there'd been nothing at all ghostly about him. He'd appeared as substantial as she was herself. Of all the tales she'd heard over the years, or read about, she couldn't recall a single incident where a ghost had been described as appearing as solid and substantial as a living person. Mostly, their presence was only sensed, generally as a wave of frigid air.

And that was another thing. If she discounted the frantic signals of animal attraction she felt just being next to him, there wasn't a single thing to indicate otherworldly manifestation. She hadn't felt 'odd', 'chilled', or otherwise unnerved--not until he'd disappeared, that is.

She shook it off. She was trying too hard, that was all. When she and her mother had planned the trip the year before, they'd convinced each other that they would at last experience the ghostly encounter their hearts desired. The car crash on the way to the airport had ended those plans when it had taken her mother's life, but, quite possibly, it was *because* her mother had implanted the idea so firmly in her mind, or because she so desperately wanted to experience what her mother had hoped to, she was allowing her mind to fantasize that it was actually happening, when it wasn't.

Moving back down the corridor, she gripped the handrail firmly and descended with care. The stairs and the mezzanine had almost certainly been added long after the chateaux was originally constructed, but they were still old for all that and not built to the standards required by American safety standards. The stairs were too wide and the risers too deep, particularly for anyone as short legged as she was.

Reaching the foot of the stairs without mishap, she followed her nose to the dining area. There were several couples already seated at the small round tables. Feeling uncomfortably like a fifth wheel, she stopped a waiter and asked if it was permissible that she take a table on the terrace.

Nodding, he led the way. Throwing a pair of French doors wide, he pulled out a chair for her at a table nearby and produced a lighter to light the candle set in the center. Relaxing fractionally, Samantha breathed deeply and appreciatively of the evening air. The scents of burgeoning life assailed her, but the early spring air carried a hint of a chill still, which wasn't nearly as pleasant.

The menu, she discovered with some relief, was in both French and English--not that that was particularly helpful since she wasn't familiar with French cuisine. She wasn't a wine drinker either. The waiter looked at her as if she was mad when she ordered water as her beverage, but finally shrugged and went off again.

While she waited, Samantha gazed off at the darkened landscape beyond the terrace and allowed her mind to wander. She was to be given a tour of the chateaux the following day and the day after that a walking tour of the estate. Beyond that, she had no particular plans.

When she and her mother had been discussing the trip, they'd known that they would have each other for company and had not considered doing anything beyond exploring the chateaux exhaustively and hoping they would be lucky enough to bump into the ghost. She hadn't really thought it through, she supposed, but lazing around the chateaux for five days, by herself, didn't have nearly as much appeal. She was accustomed to being busy.

She glanced back toward the dining room where the other guests were dining. As she did so, something near the end of the terrace caught her eye and held it. Despite the gloom, she knew it was the man again, the one who'd called himself Gerard. He pushed away from the stone railing surrounding the terrace and sauntered toward her. Without a word, he sprawled in the chair opposite her, studying her.

He was hardly an unwelcome intruder, and yet it sent a twinge of annoyance through her that he assumed a welcome.

"You intrigue me."

Samantha cocked her head to one side, studying him in return. "Should I be flattered?" she asked neutrally.

His sensual mouth tipped up at one corner. He ignored the comment. "How do I appear to you?"

Samantha lifted her brows. "Are you fishing for compliments, too?"

The faint smile widened. "You feel it, as well, then? It has been so long I wondered if I had imagined it."

Samantha was a little taken aback. "Feel what?"

The smile vanished. He frowned. "I prefer your frankness of before. I've no patience with coyness."

She felt her own annoyance surface. "Really? Well then you won't mind my bluntness in pointing out that I didn't invite you to share my table; I have not been 'coming on' to you; and I would not welcome a little 'interlude' to chase away the boredom of traveling alone."

He stared at her a long moment and finally chuckled. "You remind me, very much, of someone I knew once-- long ago."

Samantha wasn't certain how to take that remark, but it was so obviously intended as a compliment--or sorts--that she felt her irritation wane.

He frowned. "You have misunderstood me. I can not offer an interlude, as you put it, as much as I would like to. "

She eyed him skeptically, but refused to be baited into questioning why he was unable to offer something she had just denied any interest in. "What did you mean, then, when you asked how you appeared to me?"

"Precisely that. You see me?"

Samantha gave him a look. "Of course I see you. There's nothing wrong with my eye sight."

He studied her thoughtfully for some moments. "You are aware that no one else does?"

Samantha was about to ask him what he meant by that, but at that moment the waiter arrived with her dinner. The tray he was carrying, balanced on one arm, shifted in the direction of Gerard's head. Before she could do more than gasp at the impending collision, however, the tray passed through Gerard as if he were no more substantial than mist.

"Will that be all, madam?"

It was several moments before Samantha could find her voice. "How did you do that?"

"Do what, madam?" the waiter asked curiously.

"He will think you mad if you ask him about me," Gerard said, his tone almost bored.

"Why?"

"Why, what, madam?"

"Because no one else can see, hear-- and they most certainly can not feel, my presence."

"You're saying you're a ghost?"

"I do not believe that I did," Gerard responded.

Samantha's eyes narrowed on the waiter. "This is a show for the tourist, right? You pretend he isn't there and I'm supposed to be convinced that I've been chatting with a ghost."

The waiter jumped, looked sharply around. "He is here?"

"Of course he's here. He's sitting right there in front of you."

The waiter turned an unfocused gaze in the direction of Gerard, glanced down at the chair, and took a step back. A shiver went through him.

He was a very good actor. Samantha had to give him that. "Excuse me, madam," he threw over his shoulder as he whirled and trotted briskly back inside. Watching his departure with a mixture of irritation and uneasiness, Samantha turned at last to confront Gerard with his deception only to discover that he'd once more vanished.

"Cute!" she muttered out loud, peering through the darkness surrounding her, but not really surprised when she saw no sign of the illusive 'ghost', Gerard.

The food was far richer than she was accustomed to, but delicious. Finding with a little surprise that she was really hungry, Samantha concentrated on her meal. When she'd finished, she sat staring at the stars for a while and finally rose and headed back inside when the waiter didn't reappear.

She couldn't help but notice that the concierge stared at her rather hard as she left the dining room, but she decided that she wasn't going to worry about the meal. They were certain to add it to her bill and she could settle when she was ready to leave.

As tired as she was from traveling all day, she didn't head directly to her room. Instead, she stopped to study the portrait once more. If she'd hoped another look would convince her that she'd been mistaken before about the similarity between the man in the picture and the mysterious Gerard, she was disappointed. The situation was quite the opposite. The more she studied the painting, the stronger the resemblance.

Dismissing it finally, she fished her key from her pocket and headed toward her room. Unlocking the door, she felt around inside for the switch and finally found it. A lamp across the room came on, casting more shadows than it chased away.

Stepping inside, she closed the door firmly behind her and locked it, then tossed her handbag onto the bed and headed for the bathroom to prepare for bed. She'd already undressed when she realized she hadn't taken her night gown out. Shrugging, she gathered her clothes and left the bathroom. Flipping open the suitcase that still lay on her bed, she dropped her clothes inside and unearthed a night gown. As she turned to put it on, she discovered that Gerard was leaning against the fireplace mantel.

Her gown, forgotten, fell from suddenly nerveless fingers. A scream clawed its way up from her chest and lodged in her throat.

"You are more beautiful even than I imagined, cher."

She wasn't even aware that he'd moved until he was standing directly before her. Tentatively, almost reverently, he lifted a hand. She shivered as she felt it skate over her bare shoulder.

A strange look settled over his features. "I can feel the warmth and texture of your flesh. It feels like warm silk," he murmured thickly. "I can smell the fragrance of your hair. What witchery is this?"

Samantha gulped, managed to dislodge the lump of fright as something far more powerful seized her muscles and grounded her feet to the floor, a weightless weakness that made her knees tremble with the effort of holding her upright. "How….?" She managed.

He sifted his fingers through her dark, shoulder length hair, crushed it in his hand and lifted the strands to his nose, breathing deeply. "Are you a witch?" he murmured, releasing her hair and stroking a hand down one arm to grasp her fingers. "No one has breached the barrier … even I have not managed it in all these years. How is this possible?"

Samantha watched, bemused, as he lifted her hand, examined each finger and finally sucked one into his mouth. Her belly tightened on a spasm of pleasure as she felt his tongue curl around the digit, felt the hot, moist suction of his mouth. "How did you get in here?" she murmured faintly.

Slowly, he pulled her finger from his mouth. "I no longer exist in the physical world. I have not in many years, not since … Babette ensorceled me many years ago. I have hungered for this so long that I thought I would go mad. Perhaps I have? Perhaps you exist only in my mind?"

Samantha's heart skipped a beat. For several moments she felt herself teetering between unfulfilled desire and fear of this intoxicating stranger. Fear won out at last and she took a step back.

"You *are* mad. We live in the same world. How did you get into my room? The door was locked. I know it was. You have a key, don't you?"

He stepped toward her, closing the small space she'd put between them. "It is you who have breached the doorway, not I … you who hold the key. You can free me from this prison of existence that has tormented me so long, to be and to know without truly living."

"I don't know what you're talking about."

"You must."

Samantha took another step back. "I don't."

His face darkened with anger. "He has sent you to torment me," he ground out. "Has he not? To give me a taste of what I have lost so that he can destroy the last thing I hold dear, my mind."

Samantha's eyes widened. "Nobody sent me! I came because this place is haunted. I wanted to see the ghost myself. That's all."

"I am no ghost."

Samantha glanced around a little wildly, but he was standing so near her that she couldn't see any chance of escape. She shivered, reaching blindly behind her for something she might use as a weapon. Her hand touched something cold and solid on the bed behind her--her blow dryer. She ran her fingers along it a little frantically, found the handle and wrapped her fingers firmly around it. "No. You're not a ghost. You're an intruder," she said tightly, and swung the blow dryer at his head with all her strength.

He didn't move. He didn't so much as blink. The blow dryer passed through his head as if it were as unsubstantial as mist. The force of her swing almost sent her sprawling. She gaped at him as he gripped her waist tightly and pulled her roughly against him.

"I cannot feel pain," he muttered through clenched teeth. "I cannot feel anything .. . except you."

Catching a fistful of hair at the base of her skull, he wrapped his other arm around her waist and dipped his head toward hers. Samantha gaped at him, still stunned, still unable to grasp that she could feel him, as real and solid as any man, and yet the blow dryer had touched nothing but thin air.

His mouth was hot as it covered hers, his lips hard, punishing. She bucked against him, struggled to evade his grip and when she could not, made a small whimpering sound as he ground his mouth against hers, abrading the tender flesh of her inner lips with her own teeth. He stiffened at the sound, withdrew slightly, his mouth poised above hers so closely her lips tingled from his nearness. His harsh, panting breaths infused her with his essence, clouding her mind with the drugging sweetness of carnal need.

More tenderly then, but with a hunger that spawned an answering clamor within her, he covered her mouth once more. His tongue flicked out, skated lightly over the wounded surfaces, sending tingles of heat flooding through her. Another whimper caught in her throat, though this one spoke of desire, not fear or pain, as his tongue stroked along hers in a restless, intimate caress. Like strong wine, his taste, the feel of his tongue, the heat and strength of his body pressed so tightly against her, made her senses riot, closed her world to all but the sensations flooding through her.

Her fingers clenched in the fabric of his jacket and she realized with a touch of surprise that she'd lifted her hand to hold herself more closely to him. Seeking more of him to fill her senses with the pleasure he'd already given her, she slipped her hand along his shoulder to his neck, threaded her fingers through the long, black hair that hung loosely from the ribbon tie at the base of his skull. His arms tightened around her. His mouth and tongue caressed hers more fiercely. The hand he'd threaded through the hair at the base of her skull clenched more tightly still for several moments. Then his grip loosened and he skated the hand down her back along her spine. Cupping one buttock in his hand, he clenched the tender flesh tightly as he thrust his hips against hers, pressing the engorged flesh of his erection into her belly.

Self-restraint yielded to irresistible temptation, and Samantha felt the last shreds of her defenses crumble as heat and moisture flooded through her nether regions. Her belly tightening with need, she kissed him back, skated her hands over him in her own exploration, arched to meet the thrust of his hips.

He tore his mouth from hers abruptly, lowered his open mouth to her neck and sucked the flesh there into his mouth. A shudder went through him, and then a quaking seemed to seize his muscles as he pulled slowly away with an effort, staring down at her with an expression of baffled fury.

"Is this a ruse--designed only to bring me more torment, I wonder?"

Disoriented with lust, Samantha could only stare at him blankly. "A ruse?"

Releasing her, he stepped back, squeezing his eyes closed for a moment as if in pain. After a moment, he opened his eyes once more, stared at her enigmatically an finally turned, striding away.

Her jaw sagging with disbelief, Samantha stared after him blankly as he stepped through the wall of her bedroom and disappeared from sight.

Chapter Three

The morning light spilling through the window was almost painful as it touched her clenched eyelids. Groaning, Samantha rolled over and pulled her pillow over her head. She'd still been tense when she'd finally drifted to sleep, tense with frustrated desire, fearful that he would come back--and that he wouldn't, and she would never see him again--all at the same time. The tension had translated into stiff, achy muscles overnight. The lack of restful sleep had manifested itself into an aftereffect similar to a hangover.

For a short while, she drifted, half awake and half asleep. It occurred to her after a few minutes, however, that she'd planned to take part in the morning tour of the chateaux and she cracked an eye and peered toward her alarm clock.

It was a quarter till ten and the tour was supposed to start at ten.

Galvanized, she leapt from the bed and dashed into the bathroom for a quick shower. When she emerged, she dressed hastily, shoved her feet into a pair of sandals, grabbed her purse and dashed out of the room. She'd nearly reached the stairs when she remembered she hadn't locked her door.

Not that it would keep Gerard out--or that she had anything of any great value with her, but she turned and went back to lock the door.

A half a dozen people were assembled in the great room when she arrived, breathless from her rush. Several of them glanced her way, but almost immediately returned their attention to the staff member who was gesturing around the room, pointing out first one thing and then another, and describing it--in French.

She was about to ask him to repeat it for her benefit in English, when her gaze fell upon Gerard.

As he had been the day before, he was lounging negligently against the column at the foot of the stairs, his arms crossed, his eyes narrowed as he studied the group of tourists wandering about the great room, gaping up at the architectural features the guide was pointing out. As if sensing her gaze, he turned his head slightly and stared at her for a long moment. Finally, he pushed himself away from the post. Samantha was still trying to decide whether to run or stay when he strode up to her.

His gaze flickered over her face searchingly for several moments, but some of the tense anger vanished from his features. He turned to study the tourists enigmatically for several moments. "My home is filled with intruders-- gaping like morons, giggling and pointing--as if they are strolling about a fair."

Samantha studied his profile, trying to imagine what it must feel like to exist as a shadow within one's own home, aware of the real world, but unable to touch it.

"Should I entertain my 'guests', I wonder?"

Samantha knew he was speaking more to himself than to her. She might have commented anyway except that, before she could decide what to say, he'd strode toward the group. Plowing through them, he swept the contents of an occasional table to the floor, then turned and knocked the guide's wig askew.

Two of the three women present let out squeaks of surprise. The third clapped a hand to her mouth, staring around wide eyed. The youngest of the three women, who looked to be in her early twenties, giggled nervously. Almost at once, the group began to exclaim and comment on the manifestation. The guide, white faced, straightened his wig and ushered his group quickly from the room.

Samantha bit her lip. Really, it wasn't funny--the man had a dangerous temper. On the other hand, she supposed she might be a little dangerous herself if she'd been trapped for several lifetimes….

She broke the thought off abruptly. Was she really accepting his wild claims as fact?

Could she do anything else?

If she hadn't seen, with her own eyes, that he had passed through, not between, the people standing on the other side of the room …. She would've liked to put it all down to some sort of scam the bed and breakfast had manufactured to entice guests, but she simply couldn't explain away some of the things Gerard had done, particularly the most recent exhibition. To consider it a trick, she would have to accept that the guests weren't actually there, that they were some sort of projection.

It didn't fit. The room was too bright even for some sort of sophisticated equipment to work convincingly.

She couldn't put it down to persuasive acting, either. The 'guests' could have been plants and pretended they hadn't seen or heard him, but they couldn't pretend he'd walked through them.

Some sort of hypnotism?

She couldn't rule it out, but she'd never been a true believer of hypnotism. She could believe he was a ghost about as easily.

Without having once actually looked at her, Gerard vanished when the guests departed. She was vaguely surprised, and disappointed that he'd ignored her, but then memories of the night before drifted through her thoughts, suffusing her with warmth. What had he said? He could feel nothing of the physical world--except her.

He seriously thought she was some kind of witch? That she'd come here with the sole purpose of making his life more miserable than it was already?

Frowning, she turned a little absently to catch up with the tour, wondering what was different about her that had seemed to reach him when no one else, apparently, ever had.

She was a paranormal buff, which a lot of people considered 'different', to say the least, but she'd never actually dabbled in the occult. It wasn't that she didn't believe in any of it. Some aspects of the occult were hard to explain away. She'd never considered that she had any sort of talent in that direction, however, and had been disinclined to try her hand at something she expected to fail in.

She shook her head at the direction of her thoughts. She couldn't have some sort of paranormal power she was completely unaware of. She was twenty seven years old. Surely, if she had, she would have noticed it by now?

Maybe it wasn't her at all, regardless of what he seemed to think? He'd indicated that some sort of curse, or enchantment, had been laid upon him. Maybe this was all about the curse, not her? Maybe it was wearing off at long last? Maybe it had never been intended to hold him forever, but only for so long that the world he'd known had vanished forever?

She realized it was rather pointless speculation. If she knew what the actual curse was, she might be able to figure it out--might. It seemed very unlikely that she'd stumble upon the answer otherwise.

She caught up with the tour group once more in the yellow salon. He was just finishing his spiel when she arrived. "What do you know about the Count himself?"

Everyone turned to stare at her. The guide shrugged. "Not much is actually known, Miss….?"

"Samantha Lancaster," she supplied.

He nodded. "There are many tales, but there is much … confliction in the stories. The only thing that is certain is that the count was a man much speculated about. If you'd joined the tour on time ….."

"I did. But since I don't understand French, I didn't catch the story."

He looked more annoyed than apologetic. "Pardone, madam. The story is that he was married very young and fell madly in love with his young bride. She died little more than a year later, however, in child bed, and his heir died with her. He was inconsolable over his loss, but it was his duty to produce and heir and he married again several years later. That wife died, as well, only about a year after they were wed and people began to speculate that he had only wed to gain money and power and then disposed of his wives.

"Many years passed before he again wed. It is believed that he was in his early thirties when he wed for the third and final time. He had been dabbling very much in the black arts since the death of his first wife and was considered one of the most powerful witches in Europe.

"There are tales that the Countessa de Moyer, a young and very beautiful widow, who also happened to be a powerful witch, was to be his third wife, but there were also rumors that she was barren. He jilted her to wed a young heiress and the two became rivals and enemies.

"On the night of the gathering, the Countessa not only defeated him, proving that she was the most powerful witch of all and becoming high witch, but she placed a curse upon him because he had spurned her love for another."

It was a rather sordid tale, but what had she expected? He was supposed to have been an evil man who had finally gotten his just deserts. "The Countessa loved him, but she placed a curse on him?"

The guide nodded, then smiled rather condescendingly. "It is said hell hath no fury …."

Samantha gave him a look. As if a man scorned hadn't been known to do some really nasty things! "What was the curse?"

He frowned. "That is not known. Naturally, there were none at the gathering except the witches and their minions. But everyone is quite certain that it had to do with his cold heart."

The guide resumed the tour then. Samantha followed, but paid very little heed. As beautiful as the chateaux was, she was too preoccupied for much to filter through to her.

The story he'd told wasn't exactly a revelation. The gist of it had appeared in the pamphlet about the chateaux. She had to wonder how much of it was true, or if there was even a grain of truth in it. She supposed, after a few moments, that his marriages must be a matter of record, probably the deaths of his wives and his child, as well-- although not necessarily.

There were European newspapers that predated the French revolution and had survived the intervening years. She'd read the account of the execution of King Louis in the London Times. On the other hand, the Count du Beauchamp had lived, and died--or been cursed to exist only in another plane--a good many years before the revolution. The British had been far more preoccupied with keeping records, as far as she knew, than anyone else, and, despite his reputation, she was fairly certain the Count hadn't been large as a historical figure. It seemed unlikely she would find any actual records of events, and even if she did, how much faith could be placed in them?

The fact was, no one really knew except Gerard himself, and he didn't seem the type to confide in anyone.

It was luncheon when the tour wound to a close and everyone, including Samantha gravitated in the direction of the dining room where a buffet of fruits, vegetables and cold cuts had been laid out. Samantha took her meal on the terrace once more. She supposed she should make a push to acquaint herself with some of the other guests since she would be staying for several days, but she didn't feel comfortable intruding on the others when they'd arrived in pairs and she had the distinct feeling that some of them, at least, were honeymooning.

On the one hand, it seemed an odd sort of place to choose for a honeymoon, but it was quiet, out of the way, very much off the beaten track of the typical tourist. Moreover, if one considered the possibility that they were as 'in' to hauntings as she was, it was certainly no more absurd as a destination than some of the strange weddings and honeymoons Americans often concocted.

She didn't know whether to be disappointed or relieved when Gerard did not 'join' her for lunch. She'd more than half hoped he would, but the story the guide had told had made her uncomfortable. Even though it hadn't come as much of a surprise, she'd formed a preconceived notion that the Count du Beauchamp was a tragic figure. The cold calculation that the guide had attributed to him seemed uncomfortably nearer the mark of the man she'd met than her own speculations.

He'd tried to seduce her. She'd wanted him to, been so caught up in the sensations he evoked in her that she'd been terribly disappointed when he'd abruptly left. Now she wondered if he'd used his powers against her to get what he wanted. He was dangerously attractive to her. She doubted he would have to resort to anything so underhanded as using magic to seduce her, but she wasn't certain he hadn't and she didn't like the idea that he might.

Then, too, if ever there was a relationship doomed to fail, one with a ghost, or whatever, certainly was. She was still vulnerable from the tragedy that had befallen her only the year before when her mother had been killed in a car accident on the way to the airport--to take this very trip. Finding herself suddenly alone in the world, she'd fallen for a con artist out to reap the rewards of her mother's life insurance--their insurance salesman, no less. It wasn't until she'd set her sights on completing the trip she'd planned with her mother that she'd finally realized that Kirby Higginbottom's only interest was in her money, not herself. He'd been outraged that she would even consider 'throwing away' money on such an absurd jaunt.

She'd refused to be swayed, however, which had led to the discovery that he'd 'invested' most of her money and lost it. He didn't want her throwing away the last of it when he already had plans to invest in something sure to regain all that had been lost and more besides.

If she'd really been in love with him, she supposed it would've been a crushing blow to discover that he was in love with her money. As it was, it had merely turned her stomach. She was furious about being used, but not hurt.

She hadn't even particularly cared about the money because the truth was it felt like blood money, and she would never have been able to enjoy spending it under the circumstances anyway.

Finishing her lunch, she rose and left the terrace, deciding to take a long walk to try to throw off the morbid turn of her thoughts. It helped, but eventually her thoughts came full circle and she found herself speculating on the count once more.

What would happen, she wondered, if the curse were lifted? He claimed that he had not died, but had merely been trapped here, but the fact was, with or without the curse he would have been long dead. If there was even a way to lift the curse, it seemed it could only result in freeing his spirit of this place.

The thought saddened her in an indescribable way, but amused her too. The owners of the chateaux weren't going to be happy if it was no longer 'haunted'.

She frowned. Whatever he had done in his life, she didn't believe he deserved to be tormented for eternity--unless, of course, he actually *had* killed his wives so that he could enjoy their wealth without having to put up with them.

But then, who was she to make such a judgment? If there actually was a way to break the curse, and she was the only one who had a chance of doing so, wasn't she obligated by some higher order to try?

It was late afternoon by the time she finally headed back to the chateaux and climbed the stairs to her room. She sensed Gerard's presence the moment she entered the room.

Chapter Four

"A quaint tale, wouldn't you agree?" Gerard murmured near her ear.

Samantha's heart thudded with a combination of fear and ... though she hardly acknowledged it, excitement.

Slowly, she turned to face him. He was standing so near, she could feel the heat of his body. How could he not be real? She wondered. "I suppose by that comment that you mean it was entirely made up?"

His gaze flickered over her face assessingly. After a moment, he moved toward the window and stood looking down at the formal garden beneath her window. "So ... you believed it?" he countered.

Samantha studied his rigid back for several moments. "The statistics would be easy enough to check, even now, I suppose."

He glanced at her over his shoulder, one dark brow lifted questioningly.

"The marriages."

Frowning, he returned his attention to the view. "I was eighteen when I wed Juliette. She was just turned fourteen when she bore a stillborn son and died."

The words were spoken with detachment, but Samantha sensed, whether true or not, that the detachment was an effort to distance himself from pain rather than a reflection of a lack of emotion. She moved toward him. "So young?"

He didn't glance at her that time. "It was not so unusual in my time. She was not yet ... a woman full grown when we were wed. I was urged to wait to consummate our marriage until such time as she was--which I did. Her mother urged me to wait longer still--which I did not--because I was young, thoughtless, enamored with my Juliette and I could not contain myself. Did I kill her? Yes."

"You loved her?"

He seemed to think it over for some time. "I believed that I did. Now, I am not so certain. So many years have passed. I wanted to feel nothing--no guilt, no remorse, no pain for my loss, and, eventually, I felt nothing. I have felt nothing for so long that I can not recall what feeling something was like."

She might not have understood that so completely if she hadn't been wrestling with guilt, and remorse, and loss herself. She could certainly empathize with feeling responsible for the death of a loved one, however. If she'd been a better driver ….

She shook the thought off. There'd been times when she'd wished she felt nothing at all. Feeling too much seemed so close to hell that she'd begun to think living *was* hell and death was heaven, because it was the only time a person found peace from suffering … Except Gerard obviously had not found it.

"A second marriage was arranged for me when I was twenty five. I killed her, as well, and in much the same manner. She was kind enough to produce the much sought after heir, but he was weak and sickly and did not live to see his first birthday.

"I refused to wed again, but after the deaths of my parents I came to realize that it was my duty to produce an heir and wed for the third time. My third wife produced my heir and lived to the ripe old age of sixty. No doubt she would have followed my first two wives if I had not been … ah … constrained from doing her in."

"It wasn't really unusual for women to die in childbirth back then, though, was it? From what I've read, it was pretty common well into the 1900's."

He turned slightly, his brows rising. "What is the year?"

Samantha was a little taken aback by the direction of his thoughts. "It's 2004."

He stared at her in disbelief for several moments. "Could it be that so much time has passed?" he murmured, more to himself than to her.

"The part about the curse, was that true?"

For several moments, she thought he wouldn't answer. Finally, however, he seemed to emerge from his dark thoughts. A wry smile tipped the corners of his lips. "Behold me. Trapped for near an eternity. Does this seem to be a blessing to you?"

Samantha's lips tightened. "You wouldn't be the first spirit trapped long after your death in a hell of your own making."

A wave of fury abruptly washed over his features. "Then I am justly served, am I not?" he ground out, seizing her waist and jerking her full length against him.

Before Samantha could protest, he caught a fistful of the hair at the nape of her neck and kissed her brutally, his mouth hard, punishing. Despite that, or perhaps because she knew it was pain, not true anger, that inspired his roughness, Samantha felt herself responding. Lifting her arms, she laced her fingers together behind his head, pushing against him, soothing the rape of his tongue with a caress of her own. A shudder went through him. He lightened the pressure of his mouth over hers, lessened his bruising grip, but there remained the savagery of a deep hunger for all that that poured through Samantha's veins like a drug, making her dizzy, bringing heat and moisture to her sex.

She might have many doubts about Gerard, and in fact did, but she was in no doubt at all that she wanted him deeply inside of her as she had never wanted any other man. Restless to feel more intimate contact, to feel his bare flesh against her own, his body striving toward fulfillment, she moved against him, mindlessly, silently, urging him to claim her completely.

It was Gerard who broke kiss, as abruptly as he had claimed her. Through narrowed eyes, he studied her, breathing heavily. "You do not protest?"

Disappointment flooded her, but a touch of amusement, as well. "Should I?"

"A lady who would not, would most certainly have a motive."

Samantha's lips tightened. "If you're so damned certain I only came to add to your torment, why even come to me? Why start something you're not going to finish!"

Briefly, a look of surprise crossed his features. "Because I can not help myself."

He looked chagrined that he'd admitted that much, and then angry because he no doubt felt she'd somehow forced him to say it. "I am not a witch. I couldn't put a spell on you if I tried!"

"Release me, then," he said tightly.

Samantha pushed away from him. "I just told you, I'm not a witch. I can't release you. The curse, if it is a curse, isn't of my making and I can't break it."

"You lie," he said through gritted teeth. Turning, he strode across the room. Fully expecting him to simply disappear as he had before, Samantha was surprised when he turned to look at her once more. "You alone of all who have come have breached the barrier that imprisons me from life. You could not do that unless you were a powerful witch. You could break the spell that binds me if it was your wish. I can only conclude that it is not and that your only purpose in being here is to add to my torment."

"Then tell me what the curse is!" Samantha demanded. "I can't help you if I don't know what it is!"

His eyes narrowed suddenly. "You do know it. It was you who placed the curse upon me."

"Me?" Samantha gasped, stunned, indignant. "You think I'm … the reincarnation of the countessa?" she added with sudden insight.

"I do not think … I know who you are … Juliette."

He vanished. Some moments passed before Samantha realized that her jaw was hanging at half mast. Juliette? That didn't make any sense at all.

Frowning, Samantha turned to study the gardens as Gerard had before, her mind elsewhere.

It was completely absurd to try to make any sense of a situation that made no sense, that had no foundation in logic, or the real world. Yet, it would have made a strange sort of sense if he'd accused her of being the reincarnation of the Countessa, the woman who had purportedly cursed him to begin with.

She rubbed her aching temples. She didn't believe in reincarnation. She never had. It would have been a great comfort to her if she'd been able to. Since she didn't, though, it made it very difficult to try to unravel the possibilities.

It occurred to her, briefly, to wonder how much personal reluctance was currently influencing her reasoning. She couldn't deny that she'd felt resentment at the suggestion that she was not a unique person, that she was nothing more than a newer version of someone who'd lived before. It was worse, even, than being told you were 'just like so-and-so' or reminded someone of someone else. She didn't think she would've liked it if anyone had suggested such a thing, but it had genuinely hurt coming from Gerard.

Deciding she had no desire to probe those thoughts or emotions further, she resolutely dismissed it from her mind and concentrated on Gerard's revelations, such as they were.

She wondered if he'd been suggesting that Juliette had been a witch.

Now that she thought on it, it seemed plausible. He'd begun to dabble in the black arts, according to the stories, after her death. What might have turned him in that direction if his young wife had not practiced the arts? It wasn't something, as far as she knew, that men and women of the aristocracy had seemed inclined to dabble in. Maybe Juliette *had* introduced him to the craft?

Even if she had, though, he'd lived many years after her death. If it had been Juliette who'd cursed him, he, surely, would have vanished after her death, not married twice more and met his end at the age of thirty six, or there about.

What, she wondered, was actually known about his first wife? She had been so young when she died that it was hard to believe that she might have lived long enough to have accomplished anything more noteworthy to history than her marriage.

After a while, she left the room again and headed downstairs to ask the concierge the directions to the family cemetery the guidebook had talked about. She was supposed to join a tour the following day, and the cemetery would be a point of interest on that trip, but she felt an odd sort of urgency to see it now.

The concierge suggested she wait for the tour, but finally shrugged and gave her directions. It was considered to be within walking distance of the chateaux, but it was nearing dusk by the time Samantha reached it.

A low, wrought iron fence surrounded the small plot. In the center stood a mausoleum, which took up most of the small cemetery. Around the mausoleum, there were several other, newer graves with headstones, but Samantha focused her attention upon the mausoleum.

Dredging up her rusty French--which she'd learned to read and write better than to speak--she studied the writing carved into the front of the mausoleum on either side of the door. The name 'Juliette du Beauchamp' practically jumped out at her. Despite the intervening years since it had been carved into the stone, the letters had obviously been cut deep and were still easily read. Below her name was a male name--Gerard. Her heart skipped several anxious beats, but it occurred to her after a moment that it was the infant, the child that she'd born.

A wave of terrible sadness washed over her. How devastating it must have been for poor Juliette, to carry that child for months beneath her heart, to feel the life inside of her, and then labor to bring him into the world, only to discover that he had died even before he had had the chance to live. Juliette had not been much more than a child herself--not in modern terms, anyway--but in her own time she would've been considered a woman full grown, would've thought of herself in that light. She would have suffered, no doubt, both the emotions of a child and a woman.

It occurred to her that Gerard had professed a great love for Juliette. He had not said that Juliette loved him as he had her. An oversight? Or had he been nothing more to Juliette than her duty?

She finally decided that that was unlikely to have been the case. Juliette would've had to have felt strong emotions toward Gerard to consider cursing him, wouldn't she?

But then, everything, including the circumstances of Gerard's disappearance, pointed to the fact that the Countessa had placed the curse upon Gerard.

The conclusion she finally arrived at wasn't very palatable.

Gerard had loved Juliette beyond reason. He had had no interest in marrying again after her death. He must have meant, rhetorically speaking, that Juliette had cursed him because she had deprived him of his joyeux de vie. He had not found love again, only heartache--which was a curse in itself and required no magic beyond a deep emotional attachment.

She couldn't help but wonder how she reminded him of Juliette. It seemed doubtful that it was her appearance. Surely, if it had been that, he would have pointed it out?

Realizing that it was growing late, Samantha shook the thoughts and turned her attention to examining the mausoleum while she still had enough light to see. On the opposite side of the door, she found two more inscriptions. Both of the names were women's names--his second and third wives, undoubtedly.

It struck her as a little odd that his last wife, who had outlived him by many years, had taken her place in the mausoleum with the others, but, perhaps, it was only because it was her place and had nothing to do with an emotional attachment to the man she lived with so briefly?

Sighing, she left the small cemetery and headed back toward the chateaux. She'd only arranged to stay at the chateaux a few days. Truthfully, she really couldn't afford to stay longer, even if she decided against going to the other places she'd had it in mind to visit. Considering the way they'd done her about arriving late, it seemed doubtful that she could convince the management to allow her to stay longer anyway.

She wasn't certain she wanted to.

She'd achieved what she'd set out to do--met the spirit that inhabited the chateaux. She would never have thought in her wildest dreams that she might get caught up in trying to solve a several hundred year old mystery.

She certainly hadn't expected to be drawn in emotionally.

She realized with a great deal of dismay that she had, though. It was the very fact that she was reluctant to leave that made her all the more certain that she needed to go. If she'd had any sense, she would've packed her bags and left already.

By the time she'd reached the chateaux once more she'd decided that she would leave. She would stay and take the grounds tour the following day, do a little sightseeing in the nearest town, and then she would hit the road and put as much distance between the Chateaux du Beauchamp as she possibly could and put it, and Gerard du Beauchamp, out of her mind.

Chapter Five

Although she didn't realize, at first, what it was, the sensation of being watched woke Samantha. Confused, she opened her eyes slowly. As her vision focused, she discovered that Gerard was seated in the chair at the desk near her bed.

He stood up. In an almost leisurely fashion, he began to disrobe, tossing each article of clothing to one side without glancing to see where they landed.

Samantha's heart skidded to a halt, then leapt into a frantic pace. Her mouth went dry at the purposefulness of his expression. It never occurred to her to protest. A sense of glad anticipation filled her as he advanced toward her. Her flesh tingled. Her nipples rose, hardened, throbbed. Her belly tightened, flooding her feminine passage with hot lubrication as he placed a knee upon the edge of the bed and flipped the covers away from her.

She stared up at him as he paused, mesmerized by the sheer beauty of his form as moonlight, streaming through her window glinted off of the play of muscles with every breath he took, every slightest movement.

Capturing her wrists, he tugged her upright.

Samantha stared into the gleaming eyes of a predator and still could not find voice to protest.

"I may be twice damned," he muttered, "but I cannot stay away."

It delighted her. Resolutely, she closed her mind to the little voice in her head that pointed out that he yearned for life itself, had been deprived of it for centuries. His desire might have all to do with that and nothing to do with her. With an effort, she pushed the warnings from her mind, and the hopelessness of the situation, even if his feelings were indeed for her alone.

His words sent a thrill of need through her and Samantha leaned toward him, tilting her head upward. A faint cleft creased his chin. She traced the indentation with her tongue and lightly nibbled the edge of his chin with her teeth.

He caught her face between his palms, covering her mouth with ravenous urgency that made the muscles in her belly jump and clench. Samantha ran her palms along his biceps and then downward along his sides. His flesh was warm, silky smooth, the underlying muscles taut and hard-- his body was lithe like the body of a dancer--or swordsman, as he had no doubt been in his time.

Like duelers, their tongues danced one along the other, entwined, stroked. His breath came hard and fast. Her own struggled from her chest and their breaths mingled as they kissed, each sharing their essence with the other, feeling their desire reeling out of control.

He broke the kiss, skating his hands down her throat and over her shoulders, following with his mouth. Samantha dug her fingers into him as a rush of heat washed over her skin, making it hypersensitive to the touch, as if she was flushed with fever.

It had become a fever. She ached. His touch soothed the needs of her flesh and at the same time made her body demand more. Lowering her head, she nipped and then sucked at his shoulder as he caught the spaghetti strap of her night gown with his teeth and tugged it down her shoulder. Abruptly, he caught her shoulders in his hands and pushed her back against the pillows, following her down. Capturing her hands when she reached for him, he clamped them to the pillows on either side of her head and, dipping his head, tugged the neck of her gown down with his teeth, nuzzling the cleft between her breasts. Then he traced a path along the upper slope of her breasts with his tongue and lips, pausing to suck a string of love bites.

Moaning, Samantha arched her back, thrusting her breasts upward, urging him to caress her more thoroughly. Restlessly, she twisted beneath him, grinding her hips against his thigh as he insinuated first one of his thighs and then the other between her own.

Opening his mouth, he covered one nipple where it thrust against the sheer fabric of her gown. The heat and moisture of his mouth sent a shudder of pleasure through her. His tongue teased her, sending sharp currents of delight sizzling along her nerve endings that nevertheless left her wanting.

She began struggling to free her arms. She wanted to feel nothing between them. His hands tightened, imprisoning her. Panting from her struggles as well as the desire that stifled the air in her chest, she went limp abruptly. "Gerard?"

He caught her lips beneath his once more, kissed her, silencing her, making her heart race with an element of uneasiness as well as need. Despite that, or perhaps because of it, she felt herself falling deeper under his spell, felt all consciousness spiral away as her senses narrowed in upon the sensations he created inside of her.

She wasn't even aware that he'd released his almost bruising grip on her wrists until she felt the tug on her nightgown, heard the snap of breaking thread and felt the coolness of night air on her bare breasts. His hand covered one breast, massaging. Capturing the distended nipple between two fingers, he pinched it lightly, rolled it between his fingers, sending delightful shocks through her. Abruptly, he broke the kiss and covered the nipple he'd been toying with with his mouth, sucking hard as he cupped her other breast with one hand and teased the nipple as he had the first.

Finding her hands free, Samantha lifted them, threading her fingers through his long, silky hair, holding him to her. She'd become desperate for more, however, felt the need rising inside of her to feel him stroking the walls of her sex, filling her.

Slipping her hands along his back, she caressed him, urging him to fulfill her.

He ignored her urgings, moving to her other breast and stimulating her to mindlessness. Moving restlessly beneath him, she caressed every part of him that she could reach and finally began to work her hand between them. He lifted slightly away from her as she struggled to curl her fingers around his erection. Grasping him at last, Samantha stroked him as he reached between their bodies and slipped a finger into her cleft, rubbing tiny circles against her clit.

Samantha jerked, moaned and released her grip on his cock, clutching the sheets as she arched upward to meet his teasing finger, feeling the muscles of her passage clenching and relaxing in an ever increasing rhythm as her body surged toward culmination. Leaning forward, he caught one throbbing nipple in his mouth once more, teasing it in concert with her clit until, abruptly, her climax seized her, making her cry out with pleasure too intense to contain.

Even as the quakes began receding, however, he grasped his distended flesh and thrust inside of her. The walls of her passage, quaking with the echoes of her climax, clutched at him, impeding his possession. He struggled, gritting his teeth as he pulled away slightly and thrust again. Samantha lifted her hips and met him. Her heart felt as it if would explode with joyful thunder as his flesh melded with her own, as she felt him sink to her depths.

Lifting her arms, she locked them around his shoulders, gasping as she met him thrust for thrust. Her body, only just fulfilled, responded to the feel of him inside her with renewed need, climbing again toward completion.

His thrusts, hard, demanding, shifted her upwards on the bed. She dug her heels into the mattress, opening her body fully to him, feeling a rising ache with the abrasion of his hard flesh against the inner walls of her body.

A thin sheen of sweat broke from her pores, bathing them both in the scent of her desire. His body began to shudder and jerk as he neared his release, feeding her own desire until she felt herself on the verge of coming and then felt release explode inside her so powerfully she felt as if she would faint. Her gasping moans sent him over the edge. He groaned, a low, animalistic sound of pain and joy and release, shuddered, lost the rhythm of his thrusts as his body moved beyond his control.

The strength fled their muscles. Weak, trembling, they collapsed together, struggling for breath. With an effort, Samantha lifted her hands, stroking his back soothingly, brushing the damp hair from his forehead. He went perfectly still for several moments and then, abruptly, he vanished.

A coldness washed over Samantha. Stunned, disbelieving, she hardly breathed for a handful of seconds. Finally, slowly, her heart still hammering in her chest, she sat up and looked around the room.

There was no sign of Gerard--no sign that he'd ever been with her. The clothing he'd discarded--that she'd thought he had discarded on the floor, was gone. She glanced down at herself and saw that her gown was intact.

Lifting a shaking hand, she pushed her hair from her face, taking in a deep, shuddering breath. As she did so, ever so faintly, she smelled him on her skin.

Hurt surged through her and behind that, anger. "You take, but you can't give. Is that why she cursed you, Gerard? Because your heart was stone cold dead already?"

There was no answer. She hadn't really expected one.

She lay down again, staring at the ceiling.

She hadn't imagined it. She could still feel the heat and pressure of his body. Her sex still throbbed from his possession. She could taste him on her lips.

A knot of misery gathered in her throat. Resolutely, she pushed it from her mind and turned over, punching her pillow. Despite her misery, her sated body begged for rest and eventually sleep claimed her.

When she rose a sense of purpose filled her. She would join the tour as she'd planned, and visit the nearby town and then, the following day, she would cut her trip short and return home. She'd looked upon the trip as a getaway to escape the sense of loss that still lingered from her mother's death. She'd hoped that she would become engrossed enough in the search for restless spirits to banish her own ghosts so that she could look forward once more to a future. Instead, she'd taken on more baggage and the only way to escape that was to leave as soon as possible.

After showering, she dressed in comfortable clothing and walking shoes and went downstairs for brunch. She didn't know whether to be glad or sorry that she saw no sign of Gerard, but she finally decided that she was glad. She hoped she wouldn't see him again. Perhaps, since he appeared to be so convinced that she was only here to cause more trouble for him, he would avoid her.

The tour began promptly at eleven on the terrace. Only two couples had opted to take the walking tour around the estate. Since one of the couples were from the UK, the guide was kind enough to conduct this tour in English.

The buildings directly behind the chateaux had originally been built as a stable and carriage house, as she'd thought. They strolled past empty stalls while he expounded on the fine horses the Count du Beauchamp had reputedly owned. The estate carriage, to her surprise, not only remained, but had been carefully restored to its original glory. Like the chateaux, it was not only a work of art, but appeared to be surprisingly comfortable, as well.

Not far from the stables and carriage house were other buildings. One was a winery--apparently the estate had once produced its own brand of wine--and next to that was an ice house. Built similarly to the old ice house she'd seen on an old American plantation she'd visited--or maybe, she amended mentally, it had been the other way around--it was little more than a pit dug deeply into the earth. In the winter, ice was cut from the nearest lake and stored away layer by layer with straw packed between each to act as insulation. The straw and the earth and the building above it preserved the ice through the warm months.

It was easy to see, just from the way the guide talked at length about it, that this was a rare facility in France and Samantha decided she might have mistaken the matter when she'd assumed the American ingenuity was actually an adaptation from European craftsmanship.

They spent a few minutes examined the smoke house and storage buildings and then made their way toward the family cemetery she'd visited the day before. Once there, the guide gave them a list of those of any interest buried in the family plot and then moved around to what Samantha had assumed was the rear of the mausoleum. It was, in point of fact, the front. On either side of the door a list of the earlier Counts and Countessa's of Beauchamp had been carved.

"What about the one that haunts the chateaux?" the English woman asked.

"Ah," the guide exclaimed, smiling as he held one finger in the air and then pointed to an inscription above the door. "The Countessa, his last wife, had an inscription carved above the door here in his memory."

Samantha felt as if someone had punched her in the stomach. She scarcely listened as he translated the inscription for them.

"He's buried …ah … entombed here?" she asked faintly.

"But non! His body was never recovered. According to legend, he simply disappeared and was never seen or heard from again. It is for this reason, we believe, that the legends arose that he had been cursed, or bested, by his rival and banished from this world."

"Wait a minute," Samantha said when he turned away and motioned for them to follow him. "Are you saying there's more than one story about how he disappeared?" she asked, falling into step beside the guide.

"Oui, there are several. The only fact that we know with any certainty is that there is no record of his death, only his disappearance. There is also some documentation to indicate that he dabbled in the black arts. He was accused of it in any case, and since his disappearance coincided with a recorded event of a gathering of witches, the disappearance is assumed to have the connection with the event. It is possible he took part in a black mass and was sacrificed, and his body hidden. This is one explanation that is also believed by many. Some also believed that he simply left his wife for another woman and never returned, but not many have placed credence in this. It seems unlikely he would have abandoned all that he owned."

"To say nothing of his wife and child," Samantha added dryly.

He shrugged.

Samantha walked in thoughtful silence for a while. "So nobody really knows whether or not he was cursed?"

The guide smiled thinly. "The Countessa de Moyer wrote of him in her memoirs. This is where the story of the black magic originates. She claimed that the gathering was called to determine whom would be the grand witch and that she defeated the Count du Beauchamp, her nearest rival. She had written long passages professing her love for him, however. Alas, he wed another and her love for him became hatred. This is where the other story originated, as well. Some argued that, rather than having defeated him with her black magic, she had him killed."

He wrinkled his brow as if struggling to remember. "I can not recall exactly what it was that she had written, but the gist of it was that his heart and soul had long since gone to the grave and that he should be deprived forever of the warmth of life that he had chosen to close himself off from."

"Sounds something like 'a woman scorned' to me," the English man commented.

His wife frowned at him disapprovingly.

Samantha felt a coldness wash over her as she recalled what she'd shouted at Gerard the night before. Had it been purely coincidence that the words had popped into her mind? Perhaps even a natural inclination to say such a thing, given the circumstances? Or was there some truth to what Gerard had accused? That she was reincarnated, not of Juliette, but the Countessa who'd cursed him?

"She cursed him to live forever, but be forever denied the warmth of life," she murmured.

The guide glanced sharply at him. "But oui, madam! I believe that is it."

"She gave him no hope of escaping the fate she cursed him with?"

The guide shrugged. "It is only legend, madam--stories made up to fool the credulous." He seemed to dismiss it, but after a few moments, he frowned again. "He had spurned the love offered to him. One must suppose he was not capable of loving another and it was that which condemned him to begin with."

Samantha found she really had no interest in the remainder of the tour. She was tempted to return to the chateaux when they'd finished exploring the estate, but the thought of running in to Gerard was enough to spur her to continue with the tour of the village. It was several miles away and they returned to the chateaux where a tour bus awaited them.

Gerard was standing on the terrace, near the door where she'd bumped into him that first day. Looking away quickly, she followed the others as they climbed into the bus and resolutely studied the carriage house as the bus pulled away.

The little town was quaint in an old world way, too far off the beaten path, and too poor to have changed a great deal with time. A couple of buildings still stood that bore the scars of wars that had ravaged the countryside. When they'd finished the tour, they stayed to dine at a local outdoor café.

The tour guide was kind enough to share a table with her since she was alone.

"You have seen the ghost, madam?"

Samantha smiled faintly at the understatement. "Would you think I was a crazy American if I said yes?"

He shrugged. "I, myself, have never seen him, but there are many who say that they have. And, I must admit, strange things have happened at the chateaux that I find difficult to explain."

"Like the incident the other day during the tour of the chateaux?"

He nodded. "And others."

Samantha considered whether or not to pursue the subject and finally shrugged mentally. What difference did it make what they might think of her? She was leaving anyway. "He was angry … partly with me, I think. But also because he feels the guests are intruders in his home."

The man's eyes narrowed shrewdly. "In a very real sense, I suppose we are intruders in his home, but under the circumstances …. Why do you suppose that he is angry with you?"

Samantha smiled wryly. In for a penny, in for a pound. "He believes I am the reincarnation of Juliette."

The man's busy brows rose almost to his hairline. "And you, madam? What do you believe?"

Samantha was almost relieved when the waiter interrupted them at that moment to deliver their food. She discovered that she was wrong, however, in thinking his question merely idle curiosity.

"Do you believe you are his Juliette?"

"Before I came here, I didn't believe in reincarnation at all. I'm still not sure that I do."

He nodded. "It is like faith. One feels it in one's heart … or not."

"I suppose," Samantha said a little doubtfully. She sighed. "I think that if I believed I was reincarnated, I'd be more likely to believe it was the Countessa de Moyer."

The man studied her for a long moment. "The Countessa believed that she was Juliette. The Count du Beaumont did not believe her. He was infuriated that she would claim such a thing. In his mind, it was a desecration of his beloved Juliette, I think. A great hatred arose between them, according to the countessa's memoirs."

Chapter Six

The concierge was at the desk when Samantha returned. Samantha stared at him for several moments, torn, but she knew her decision, however, emotional, was still a sound one. She needed to go.

Dragging in a deep breath, as if she were about to dive into a pool of cold water, Samantha marched across the foyer and stopped before the desk. "Something's come up. I'll be leaving tomorrow," she said before she could change her mind.

His brows rose. "There is a problem with the hotel, madam?"

Samantha shook her head. "I've enjoyed my stay. It's just … I have to get back now."

"But … you are paid for two more days."

And obviously, he was reluctant to refund the difference. Samantha resisted the urge to grind her teeth and forced a thin smile. "And since I reserved the room and I'm sure you won't be able to rent it out, I don't expect to get a refund, but I do have to go."

She turned then and headed for the stairs. Gerard was propped against the post and she hesitated mid-step, then continued as if she hadn't seen him, passing him and climbing the stairs. Her heart was pounding unpleasantly, but she did her best to ignore that, as well.

He was standing by the window in her room when she opened the door and she stopped abruptly on the threshold. She'd hoped she wouldn't see him again. She'd hoped she would be able to simply leave without another confrontation between them.

Entering the room, she closed the door and moved to her suitcase. She'd been walking most of the day and felt the need to freshen up. Moving to her suitcase, she dropped the parcel she was carrying. She'd purchased a few small souvenirs while she was strolling about town. She had no idea why. It wasn't likely that she would ever forget her trip to Europe, but she supposed it was force of habit. She'd always had the habit of buying something where ever she went to commemorate her trip.

"You are going?"

"Yes. It's time I went back." She didn't look at him. Instead, she riffled through her suitcase in search of a change of clothing. It was too early in the evening to dress for bed.

Time hung on her hands. She wasn't certain what to do with herself until it was time for bed, but she supposed she might explore the chateaux a bit and then sit in the great room and entertain herself by watching the other guests.

"This was not your plan."

Samantha's lips tightened. "The thing about a vacation is that one really doesn't make hard and fast plans. I came to relax and enjoy myself." She sighed. "And to come to terms with the loss of my mother. Coming here was something she desperately wanted. I suppose I had it in my mind that I was doing it for her, that, maybe somehow, she'd know and …. I realize now that it was just one of those crazy, completely irrational things grieving people do to appease the spirits that haunt them."

She looked up at him. "The harsh truth is death is the end of all we know. Whether there's an afterlife, or reincarnation, doesn't really matter to the living. You've lost them. You can't get them back and you have to learn to live with it."

His face hardened. "Stay."

Samantha studied him a long moment, trying to sort the chaotic emotions that swept through her. She swallowed with an effort against the knot that formed in her throat. "I wouldn't if I could. You're dead. The living belong with the living. Why do you linger here? Go to your beloved Juliette."

Something flickered in his eyes and then his face twisted. "I stay because I have no choice. I can not reach the world I was banished from, but I am not a ghost, not a spirit. I am living flesh. I can not go the way of those released from their flesh."

Samantha stared at him, almost wishing it was true, but she knew better. "You died, Gerard, long ago. You just don't realize it. It's your belief that you're still alive that ties you here. The Countessa de Moyer killed you."

Rage suffused his features. "What do you know of the Countessa?"

"Very little," Samantha admitted. "Only what the tour guide told me that he recalled from her memoirs. But it was enough to give me some idea of what must have happened."

He stunned her. One moment, he was standing near the window, the next he was directly in front of her, gripping her forearms tightly. "You know nothing," he ground out. "She practiced the black arts."

Samantha stared at him blankly. "Didn't you?"

"I did NOT! I practiced wiccen, the white arts. There is a vast difference between the two, mon cher. She had chosen me as her consort. I declined." He released her abruptly and paced the room.

"She summoned Juliette's spirit. Twisted it to her purpose and used her against me."

Samantha turned it over it her mind, but it was useless. She simply couldn't not grasp it. "I don't understand. How did she use Juliette against you? What did she do?"

He rubbed a hand over his face. "If I knew how, I could've broken the spell."

"Then it's just as possible that she slew you, or had you slain, and you simply didn't understand or realize it, isn't it? That is what traps a spirit in a place, the emotion that tied them there remains and they can't move on."

"If she had killed me, I would feel nothing now," he ground out. "You are the key, cher. I felt it the moment I saw you. If you leave, you condemn me to this half-life forever."

Anger surged through her. "You accused me of coming here to torment you further. Why would you trust me now?"

He stared at her a long moment. "I … need you."

Samantha shook her head, as much to shake the lure of those words as to deny them. "I can't help you. I don't know how. I couldn't stay even if I wanted to--and--I don't want to." She turned abruptly and went into the bathroom to take a shower. More than half expecting him to follow her, she was vastly relieved when he didn't. He was gone when she returned to the room.

Exploring the chateaux had little appeal. Restlessness consumed her, however, and after a little thought, she decided she might as well prepare for departure. She would leave as soon as she woke in the morning. After selecting a change of clothes for traveling, she repacked all of her suitcases except for her overnight bag, hefted one and started downstairs with it. The bellhop, Antoine, met her halfway down the stairs and offered to help, but she declined. She needed something to do or she would've decided to take her bags to the car the night before her departure. When she'd tossed it into the car, she went back up to the room and grabbed the other large suitcase and carried that down, as well. After locking the rental car, she strolled around the grounds for a little while, wondering if she'd be able to change her departure date on her plane reservation, or if she'd be forced to stay until the end of the week as she'd originally planned.

What, she wondered, would she do if they wouldn't change it?

Deciding she'd face that hurtle when, and if, she came to it, she went back inside. She didn't want to chance running into Gerard again, but she couldn't very well pace the grounds until bedtime. In any case, there was no way to stop him if he was determined to confront her again unless she wanted to sleep in the car, beyond his reach. And she had no intention of sleeping in the car.

She wandered aimlessly through the public areas of the chateaux for a while and finally climbed the stairs once more. It was still earlier than she liked to go to bed, but if she could sleep--and she felt emotionally and physically weary by now--then she would wake early, as well, the sooner to be off.

She paused when she reached the upper landing, however, glancing toward the portrait of Gerard down the corridor. Finally, unable to resist, she moved toward it. Oddly enough, now that she'd come to know him, it seemed to her the portrait had more life than she'd noticed before, more energy, more personality. A faint smile played about his lips and she wondered why she hadn't noticed that before. Antoine had said that the portrait had been painted shortly before his disappearance and she couldn't help but wonder what he'd been smiling about. What thoughts had gone through his mind to produce just that expression?

It almost seemed to beckon her and, without quite realizing it, she moved closer. Lifting one hand, she touched the painting curiously.

It felt warm, as if ….

The hand she touched turned, clasping hers. Startled, she glanced up at the face, but it was no longer flat and one dimensional. The smile on his face was grim, purposeful. His hand tightened on hers and tugged.

Samantha gasped, felt herself falling forward and threw out her free hand to catch herself. She touched nothing but air.

Her cheek collided with something hard and solid--not the wall or portrait, but living flesh. She struggled for balance and looked up in stunned surprise.

"I can not allow you to leave, mon cher."

Samantha gaped at him. "You can't stop me!"

He shook his head slightly. "But I have, cher. If you will not free me, then you will join me."

Catching the hair at the base of her skull, he tilted her head back and opened his mouth over the pulse in her neck. Heat surged through her blood stream. Dizziness followed. She clutched his shoulders for purchase. "Don't," she said shakily.

He lifted his head, stared at her for a long moment. "You want me," he said harshly.

She did, desperately, but she feared she would be consumed by him and never be the same again.

Moistening her lips, she swallowed with an effort against her dry throat. "No," she lied.

Releasing her arm, he placed his palm above her pounding heart. One dark brow rose. "Non?"

Samantha bit her lip. "In my heart, no."

He paled slightly and she felt the jolt of shock that ran through him. Abruptly, his face hardened. "I've no need of you heart, cher. Only your body," he said harshly, dipping his head and covering her mouth with his own. The hunger of his mouth was consuming, pulling forth sensations she was reluctant to feel, that she tried her best to suppress. It was useless. The battle was lost the moment she felt the heat of his mouth upon hers, the rake of his tongue along her own in an intimate caress that plundered her depths.

Her fingers clenched, dug into his arms as her body seemed to grow weightless and heavy at the same time. Her flesh became hypersensitive almost with his first touch. Each slightest brush of his body against her own as their breaths mingled and their breathing became labored with need created ripples of exquisite sensation that was drugging in its lure. Moisture gathered in her sex, pooled, dampened her panties as her body, regardless of her will, readied itself to receive him.

She struggled to close her mind to the temptation to yield to him. She couldn't be only a warm body to him, couldn't bear to think it meant no more to him than that. Regret filled her with the realization that she could not simply enjoy their joining as pure animal lust.

He released her so abruptly that she stumbled back. To her surprise, she encountered the yielding surface of a mattress. Disoriented to find herself in her own room, weak from his kiss, she felt backward onto the mattress, staring at Gerard in surprise.

His face a grim mask of both anger and barely suppressed passion, he discarded his jacket and loosened the ties of his shirt. Jerking the tail of the shirt from his breeches, he pulled it over his head and tossed it aside.

Recovering her presence of mind, Samantha rolled onto her stomach. Before she could either push herself away from the bed or climb across it, he caught her. One hand like a manacle across the back of her neck, he held her against the bed and reached beneath her to unfasten her jeans. Samantha slapped at him, but she could do little, pinned on her stomach to the bed. Despite her efforts, he jerked her jeans and panties down.

She went still as she felt his palm skate over her buttocks. His fingers found her cleft, traced it until he discovered the heart of her pleasure. She moaned as he massaged it, uncertain of whether she most wanted to evade his touch or move toward him. He leaned over her, teasing her clit, delving a finger inside of her and discovering the creamy moisture that beckoned his possession. Gasping, Samantha squeezed her eyes tightly shut, feeling her body succumb to his persuasion despite her will.

When he ceased to torment her and reached to unfasten the closure of his breeches, she began to struggle to free herself once more. Something hard and rounded parted her buttocks, slipped along her cleft and pressed into her. Samantha bit her lip, holding onto the moan of pleasure that threatened to escape. Panting, she lay perfectly still, fighting the urge to push back against him, closing her mind to the building desperation to feel him forcing his turgid flesh deeply inside her.

Need won out. She parted her thighs wider, pushed back against him, moaning as she felt his cock stretching her.

The heat and weight of his body settled over her as he leaned forward. Slipping one arm around her waist, he slid a palm over her mound, parted her flesh and rubbed her clit. Her belly clenched with need. A moan scraped past her throat as it jolted her.

Panting, he pressed more deeply inside her, stretching her to her limits. She shuddered in intense gratification as he filled her completely and withdrew slowly until only the head of his cock remained inside of her. When he thrust again, he slipped more smoothly through the juices her body had produced for him. Grinding his hips against her, he pulled away once more.

She stretched up on her tiptoes and he pressed inside of her again, aching, needing to feel him deeper, deeper. Her body began to hum with electric shocks of intense pleasure.

Abruptly, he withdrew completely. Scooping her up, he tossed her fully upon the mattress and followed her, burying his face against her lower belly. Catching the edges of her pants, he tugged both jeans and panties down her legs and off her feet and then tossed them aside. Catching her ankles, he pushed them up the bed until her knees were bent, her feet flat on the bed. He dug his fingers in the curls of her pubic mound, his eyes gleaming as he smoothed the hair away and studied her clit, teasing it. "Mine," he murmured with satisfaction, then glanced up at her. "You are mine."

Samantha swallowed convulsively. Before she could decide whether she would or would not dispute his claim, he leaned forward, covering her mound with his mouth. His tongue teased her as his finger had, but far more devastatingly. Samantha gripped the sheets, her back arching, her hips lifting to meet him. Struggling for breath, she lost it as he sucked her clit. Her heart seemed to jolt to a halt. It began to pound frantically as the pleasure intensified with each stroke of his tongue, the suction of his mouth.

He lifted his head, sucked the tender flesh at the top of each thigh and then moved up her belly, sucking a string of love bites across her quivering flesh.

Samantha reached for him, desperate to feel him inside of her once more. Instead, he moved up her belly, shoving her shirt upwards until he'd uncovered her bra. Pushing the thin fabric aside, he scooped a breast into each hand, suckled first one nipple and then the other.

Samantha arched met him, digging her head into the pillows, crying out.

She could stand no more. She reached for him, slipped her hands beneath his clothing and cupped his buttocks. He ignored the silent plea, teasing her nipples until she was writhing, until the pain of need wrestled with the pleasure that continued to build and build inside of her. She slipped a hand between them, grasping his cock, massaging it. Gritting her teeth against the exquisite pain/pleasure of it, she rubbed the head of his cock back and forth against her clit.

He gasped, let out a sound that was part growl, part groan of sweet agony. Brushing her fingers aside, he grasped his turgid flesh and guided it into her once more. Lifting her hips, she thrust, gasping as she felt him filling her, slipping deeply inside her with agonizing slowness.

"Gerard," she gasped. "Please."

Slipping a hand beneath her hips, he drove deeply inside of her. She raked her nails lightly down his back and gripped his buttocks, demanding. A shudder ran through him and then he began moving, thrusting hard, deep, almost painfully so. She welcomed it, urged him with counter thrusts, licking and biting his shoulder and neck and throat.

Release caught her unaware, explosively. She felt her body convulsing around his, clutching his cock like a massaging fist, milking him of his seed. His cock bucked, tugging against the mouth of her passage, jerking as her body brought his own culmination upon him.

The effort sapped every ounce of strength and will from her. Her arms and legs, too heavy to move, went limp even before the last echoes of pleasure dissipated. She lay still, struggling to catch her breath. Gerard, sated, lay limply on top of her. The urge to caress her lover was nearly overpowering.

Samantha ignored it.

He wanted her body, not her love, and only that because it was a handy vessel. He'd made that clear enough.

Moments passed. Finally, he gathered himself and rolled off of her. Samantha lay as she was for some moments and finally turned on her side, giving him her back. From no where, the urge to cry welled inside her. Ignoring it, she focused on the room, wondering now that her mind had begun to clear of the haze of lust, how she'd come to be here.

It wasn't her room, she realized.

Sitting up abruptly, she looked around. "Where am I?"

"In my own private hell."

Samantha glanced toward Gerard. She saw that he had rolled onto his side and was watching her, his head propped in one palm. His breeches were around his hips, his sated cock wresting against one thigh.

It seemed obscene, suddenly. She glanced away, faintly embarrassed by his half dressed state and her own. Lust wasn't so pretty in aftermath. With no tender emotion to tie them together, and no passion to blind one, it became nothing more than a sordid tryst between two strangers.

"I don't feel like playing riddles," she said tightly, scooting off the bed and searching for her discarded clothing. The stickiness from their lovemaking felt suddenly repellent. She glanced around, feeling the need to shower. "Where's the bathroom?"

He gestured toward a door near the head of the bed. Samantha moved toward it but discovered, to her surprise, that she couldn't grasp the knob. She stared it, stared at her hand in disbelief. She turned to look at him, wide eyes with dismay, her heart beating fearfully in her chest. "I don't understand."

His lips tightened. "Don't you?"

Samantha frowned, trying to remember how she'd come to be in the room with Gerard. She shook her head.

"I am not without power."

"What is this place?" Samantha demanded, fighting a sense of panic.

Gerard shrugged. Rising from the bed, he adjusted his breeches. "A dimension between two worlds?" he hazarded. "You are as I am, neither living, nor dead."

"That's … that's not possible."

"Unfortunately, mon cher, it is."

Samantha stomped her foot. "Stop calling me that! I am NOT your dear! Why would you do this to me?"

He frowned. "I have needs."

Samantha stared at him. "So my own needs … my wishes, are of no importance?"

He crossed the room, catching her chin in his hand. "I gave you pleasure, mon cher. You may lie if you wish, but your body betrays you. You want me as much as I want you."

Chapter Seven

A cold finger crept along Samantha's spine, sending a shiver through her. Slowly, she shook her head. "You can't give me what I want. You don't have it to give."

Something flickered in his eyes. "I am a cold blooded monster, oui? I could almost believe you truly were Elise, Contessa de Moyer, incarnate."

Anger suffused her, chasing the chill away. "I am Samantha Lancaster! No one else. Don't seek her in me. You won't find her. You won't find your beloved Juliette either!"

"Then I will just have to make do with Samantha Lancaster," he said coolly.

Hurt surged through her at the callus remark. She slapped his hand away. "I won't stay."

His eyes narrowed. "If you are neither Juliette, nor Elise, then you have no choice, for you have not the power to deny me."

Turning abruptly, he strode from the room--passing through the wall as he always had. Samantha frowned. "It made sense that he could do that in my plane of existence, but if this was the plane where he exists, then how could he do it here?" she muttered, confused.

"The house does not exist here. Nothing exists here, save me … and now you."

Samantha looked around, but she couldn't see him. She glared at the ceiling. "The bed exists."

He chuckled. "Only because I willed it."

If that was true, and he wasn't simply playing some sort of mind game with her, then she should be able to pass through the walls too. Taking a deep breath, she walked toward the door. At the last moment, her nerve deserted her. She closed her eyes and took another step. When she opened her eyes once more, she saw that she was in the corridor.

She turned slowly, looking around. The bellhop Antoine was striding toward her. He passed through her and continued down the corridor. Samantha gasped, pressing a hand to her pounding heart.

It was true then.

A deep melancholia filled her. She hadn't realized how much life meant to her until now. If he had cared for her, she thought she would have stayed gladly, but he didn't. He couldn't.

She wandered aimlessly around the chateaux for a while and finally, drawn by the sunlight she could see flooding the terrace, she went outside, lifting her face to feel the sun's heat.

She felt nothing … not the warmth of the sun, not the breeze she could see ruffling the leaves of the trees and shrubs. She found she could not move beyond the terrace.

Time had no meaning. She didn't feel its passing. As she watched the light dimmed and stars took the place of the sun in the sky and then it was morning once more. Fascinated, she watched the cycles again and again, saw flowers bloom and die.

Days passed. Weeks? Finally, she turned and entered the chateaux once more. Without quite knowing where she was going, she returned to the room where Gerard had made love to her--had given her passion, she corrected herself, looking around.

Gerard, she saw, was propped against the wall near the window, studying her, his expression unreadable. She moved toward him, stopping when they were toe to toe.

He swallowed convulsively, his gaze skating over her face. "Don't look at me like that," he said harshly.

"How?" she asked quietly.

He shook his head. "I can not bear the sorrow in your eyes."

"Why would it matter to you?"

His face twisted with anguish. "Leave me! Go!"

"I can't."

"You can," he said angrily. "I release you! Go!" Grasping her arm, he thrust her away from him.

A wave of blackness washed over her. Samantha clutched her head in her hands, fighting to keep her balance. When she opened her eyes, she found that she was standing in the corridor before the painting. Simulation pounded at her from every direction, it seemed, at once, sound, light, the caress of air. She shivered, so confused that it was many moments before she realized that she felt … her own world.

He truly had released her, thrust her back into her world. Why? The question pounded against her temples in time to her pounding heart. She turned to look up at his portrait. "Gerard," she whispered. Lifting a hand, she touched the cool canvas with shaking fingers. "I love you. Take me with you."

Beneath her fingers, she felt the warm clasp of his hand. She stepped closer, needing to feel the warmth and closeness of his body.

"I love you far too much, cher, to live with your unhappiness."

She shook her head, leaning into the warmth of his embrace. "That's all that I wanted, all I need."

"Pardone, Messiure, Madam. You are guests?"

Irritated by the untimely intrusion, Samantha glanced toward the man who'd spoken. To her surprise, she saw that it was Antoine.

Surprise etched itself on his face, as well. "Madam Lancaster? But .. this is incredible! You have disappeared, leaving all behind, and now you come back?"

Samantha stared at him. Slowly, she pulled away from Gerard. "But I didn't …" She remembered then that she'd seen the days passing. "How long was I gone?"

He frowned and finally shrugged. "Many weeks. Will you and the gentleman be staying with us?"

Samantha glanced at Gerard as Antoine's words slowly sank in. Gerard, she saw, was white faced. Cautiously, he lifted his hand and slid it across the wall behind him. A look of wonder crossed his features, but was followed quickly by confusion. "I don't understand."

Samantha felt faint with the excitement coursing through her. "The spell, Gerard!"

She glanced at Antoine, who was looking at them as if he suspected they'd lost their minds. "We're not staying. I just …. Brought my friend to see the chateaux."

Taking Gerard's hand, she tugged him behind her as she headed for the stairs. He pulled her to a stop when she reached the door and dragged him outside. "I do not understand, cher. You broke the spell?"

Samantha laughed. "You broke the spell! We broke the spell! I don't know. I don't understand and I don't care." She practically danced down the steps and onto the walkway. After a moment's hesitation, Gerard followed her.

"It is true then."

Samantha threw her arms around his waist, hugging him tightly. "Tell me again."

He pushed her a little away and captured her chin in his hand. "I love you, cher."

She smiled up at him. "I love you. Let's go home."

His brows rose a look of doubt surfaced. "Home?"

She tilted her head to one side. "You want to stay here?"

He shuddered. "I will be happy if I never see this place again."

"Good. My place it is. I have to warn you, it's not nearly as grand as this."

"You are not worried, cher, that I am a fish out of water? I do not know this world of yours."

She snapped her fingers. "You're a warlock. I think you'll handle it just fine."

The End

Printed in the United States
46581LVS00001B/40-42